DESERT FOUNTAINHEAD

DESERT FOUNTAINHEAD

A Tale about the Borderlands

MAREK FRIEDL

RESOURCE *Publications* · Eugene, Oregon

DESERT FOUNTAINHEAD
A Tale about the Borderlands

Resource Publications
An Imprint of Wipf and Stock Publishers
199 W. 8th Ave., Suite 3
Eugene, OR 97401

www.wipfandstock.com

PAPERBACK ISBN: 978-1-7252-8910-9
HARDCOVER ISBN: 978-1-7252-8911-6
EBOOK ISBN: 978-1-7252-8912-3

01/25/21

Preface

MANY HAVE ASSISTED ME immeasurably by reading early drafts and sketches of this work. I have benefitted from the advice I have received about various topics which figure in the story: forestry, law enforcement, agriculture, irrigation and water law, etc. Mistakes in these areas are my sole responsibility.

The reader may have an understandable interest in identifying the geographical setting of the story and the identity of its various characters. The story takes place in the Southwest borderlands. However, most place names that occur in the narrative are fictitious. When an existing geographical feature is named such as Verde, Arena, or Gila, it is only suggestive. The characters in the story are entirely fictitious

I am especially grateful to the wonderful people I have been privileged to know over a twenty-year period of my own residency and visits to the borderlands. This novel would never have emerged without them.

I am especially indebted to those who have reviewed this book in its many stages. First was Art Colby, now deceased, who struggled through the original draft and suggested that it needed to be cut in two. Then I must mention Caryn Rivadeneira, whose editing revealed many faults which I hadn't noticed. Finally my wife, Mary, read successive drafts and always came up with valuable suggestions. Mary Schwaderer provided the sketch of Arena Valley.

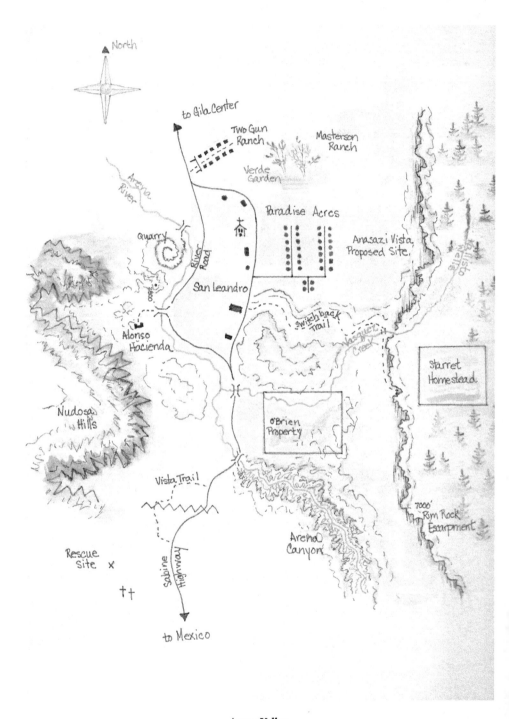

North

to Gila Center

Two Gun Ranch

Masterson Ranch

Verde Garden

Arena River

Paradise Acres

Quarry

Anasazi Vista Proposed Site

River Road

San Leandro

Alonso Hacienda

switchback Trail

Vasquez Creek

Starret Homestead

Nudosa Hills

O'Brien Property

Vista Trail

7000' Rim Rock Escarpment

Rescue Site ✗

Arena Canyon

††

Sabine Highway

to Mexico

Arena Valley

I

AUGUST 2015

1

WHOAP, WHOAP, WHOAP, WHOAP! The three migrants heard the approaching staccato of helicopter rotors. Terrified, they searched the horizon.

"*¿Adonde?*" Marcelino cried out.

"*Del oeste.*" Ernesto pointed toward the west where a ridgeline still hid the chopper from view. It was coming on fast. They had no time to waste.

"*Escondite!*" Jorge scurried about, but there was no place to hide.

"*Pronto! Pronto! Las mantas!*" Marcelino shouted, resorting to the last, desperate means of concealment.

They had rehearsed the drill repeatedly and had learned to do it in less than a minute. Jorge and Ernesto untied their blanket rolls before assuming fetal positions with their backpacks on top. Marcelino spread their blankets over them, and they tucked in the edges. Then he curled himself into a ball between them in the same way and stretched this own blanket over himself while his companions reached out to secure its edges beneath him. The gray blankets blended with the desert landscape and gave the appearance of an outcropping of weathered rocks.

The chopper's noise rose to a roar. Blasts of air from the rotors pressed down, and Marcelino tightened his fingers around the edges of his blanket. The moment of danger was soon over, after the helicopter had passed over at two hundred feet.

Willis Carr piloted the chopper. He had earned his wings in the military forty years earlier and never lost his zest for flying. His once-a-week stint with Border Watch, a privately funded vigilante group, was only one of his clients. It mattered little who hired him, as long as he received prompt payment. He sported a leather jacket that carried the insignia of his earlier military life, wrap-around shades, a holstered Ruger .44, and a fire-red kerchief knotted around his throat.

He held tight to the controls as the chopper skimmed low over desert scrub, just high enough to stay clear of saguaros, yet low enough to read the desert floor.

Stanley Unruh, burly and intense, rode shotgun and hunched forward, as he peered intently down to search for any trace of migrants.

"Seen any tracks yet?" asked Willis. The chopper offered maximum visibility, a feature prized by Carr's customers: nature photographers, wild-life monitors, Forest Service personnel, and immigration vigilantes. The cockpit was enclosed by tough plastic that afforded visibility all around. This was perfect for a vigilante like Unruh, a "tracker" who zealously intercepted the trails of cross-border traffickers and migrants.

Their flight path followed a predetermined grid pattern parallel to the border in order to "cut sign," namely to spot any trace of movement heading to the north. When "sign" was spotted, the location was reported to im-migration enforcement officers so Border Watch volunteers were shielded from any personal confrontation, a protection that Unruh valued because at an earlier disastrous encounter with smugglers, he had lost an eye.

"Nope, I haven't spotted a damn thing," Unruh replied. "But the ground surface here is too hard to take footprints well." He leaned forward, straining against his shoulder harness, to scan the ground directly below.

"On the way back we'll be a mile further to the north where it's sandier," said Unruh. "There tracks will show up better."

Unruh's regular job as a deputy with the San Ysidro County Sheriff's Office left him with a day off every week to devote to Border Watch. A vengeful passion motivated him, rooted in his fracas last year with a gang of smugglers. He single-handedly intercepted a van loaded with drugs along a dirt road in the desert. The smugglers got the better of the fight and left him with an eye patch and an unceasing resentment.

WHEN THE SOUND OF the chopper receded, Marcelino peered out from un-der his blanket. He sat up, surveyed the desert to the north, and detected an arroyo that promised cover. He urged his companions onward, "*Vamanos, hermanos!*"

They drank as much of their remaining water as they could and left their half-empty plastic jugs behind so that, unencumbered, they could move faster. They packed up without a moment to spare. The chopper would soon be back.

There were six miles to go by nightfall to where a cache of water and food would be secreted at the head of a canyon, where their coyote had promised to leave it. If they arrived before dark a lineup of the plastic bags, made to appear caught in the bushes, would lead them to their life saving provisions.

Ernesto and Jorge rolled up the blankets and attached them to their backpacks. Marcelino rushed ahead and cut a desert broom bush to drag behind him to cover their footprints. They headed north in single file with Marcelino in the rear dragging the bush. They tried to steer clear of the spines of prickly pear and the thorns of acacias.

THE BORDER WATCH CHOPPER returned. Unruh leaned forward and pointed, "There! See those water bottles!"

Willis banked sharply to the left and circled around at only a hundred feet.

"Let's land."

Willis maneuvered to a level patch of open ground and gently set the machine down. Stan ripped his shoulder restraints free and leapt down to the desert floor.

"Look at those water jugs," Unruh said. "They heard us coming and ran." Unruh scanned the tracks from the south, but lost the trail to the north. He returned to the chopper as Willis was verifying their coordinates.

"Do you want to report the location to ICE?"

"Of course," Unruh said, "but they've already moved on." He waved his arm in the general direction.

While Willis reported the location, Unruh grabbed the half empty jugs and spewed their contents onto a creosote bush. "It's wrong to let water go to waste out here," he said. Then he drop kicked the empties against a prickly pear.

Willis stood by until Unruh had calmed down. "You ready to go?"

"Yeah, I guess there's nothing more to do here," Unruh muttered.

MARCELINO'S COYOTE RECOMMENDED A remote desert route, a trek more hidden though far more challenging, suitable only for vigorous young men. They tramped along arroyo bottoms where mesquites and palo verdes offered some cover and even a little shade, but this also meant an exhausting slog through soft sand. The first leg covered twelve miles and ended where the coyote had promised a cache of food and water. Then there was another ten miles to a remote two track, where a car would meet them.

When the arroyo dropped down into a canyon, they searched for the plastic bags that would signal where their cache would be hidden. Desperate for food and water they beat the bushes in every direction. But the coyote had also noticed the chopper and had taken no chances. He took cover and left nothing. Deprived of water, Marcelino consulted a crude map and decided to alter their route about ten miles toward the mouth of an intermittent stream, the nearest place where they had hope of finding water. They were on their own.

AFTER LANDING AT THE Ysidro County airstrip, Willis noticed Unruh's disappointment and tried to put a positive spin on their efforts. "It's not been your best day, but you did spot a set of tracks and those water jugs."

Unruh shrugged off any sense of achievement. "I'm afraid they slipped away this time. Another dozen miles and they will probably meet a coyote and be free." Then he continued in a brighter tone. "But maybe not. I think I know where their route will take them, and I'm going to try to catch them the day after tomorrow."

Willis tied down the chopper and entered their trip into the log. "I do this mostly to keep up my flying skills, so the outcome of these trips doesn't matter that much to me. I think that more is needed than you guys can accomplish, if you really want to solve the border problem."

"People say a tall border fence would help." Unruh said; then he added with spite, "But that would be a monumental construction job, and it would only result in a big market for ladders a half foot taller."

Willis chuckled. "There are only two things that will do any good if you ask me: more jobs down there and fewer druggies up here."

Unruh raised his hand to touch his eye patch and added bitterly. "That's for sure. You know what the law says about being an accessory to crime. I wonder if there are any drug users who admit that they are accessories to all the mayhem and murder that their habit causes. It's the reason I'm missing an eye."

Willis looked up and nodded. "Being an accessory to crime depends on what the crime is and who's doing it."

"Yeah, I know. But suppose my loss of peripheral vision prevents me from seeing a crime scene clearly, and I make a mistake because of it. Who's at fault for that? Me or the users who keep the smugglers in business?"

Willis had no reply. "Want to join me for lunch? How about meeting me at the Pancake House? The mouthy waitress there is always fun."

"Okay, give me a half hour."

DIANA FLORES WAS BALANCING servings of hotcakes for a group of three just as Willis Carr pushed through the door. She motioned with her head towards a free table. Unburdened, she brought him coffee.

"How's the best waitress in desert country?" Willis flirted.

"Flying too high has addled your brain," she replied.

Willis loved the teasing. "Actually, this morning we were flying really low. I may have nicked a few saguaros."

"Out with Border Watch again, were you? Does that mean that black beard will join you?"

"Unruh should be here any minute," Willis said.

"Should I wait till he gets here, or do you want some toast to munch on?"

Just then, Unruh arrived. She motioned him over to the table. "With the both of you guys here, I expect there's gonna be trouble."

"Not if you've been on your best behavior," Unruh retorted.

"It's not me that would cause a ruckus. I'll put in your orders before you get rowdy. I presume you want hotcakes like always."

Unruh merely waved his hand.

After they had devoured their breakfast, Willis presented his statement. "Here's the voucher for you to initial," Willis said. "Two hours in the air. The rate is going up to $225. I need to cover higher maintenance and insurance. You know how it is."

"Okay, Border Watch is good for it." Unruh said as he initialed the paper. "Do you get into this part of the county much?"

"I do some flying around here. Bill Starret asked for aerial photos when he was planning his development, Paradise Acres. I'm sure you know who he is."

"Of course, everybody knows Bill. He still owns his granddad's old place. There used to be a sawmill up there and I guess there's still a shallow well. Who else do you fly for?"

"The Verde Forest is a regular customer. When they add property they want a view from above. I also get calls for an emergency rescue every so often. When that happens, I have to move fast.

"Sometimes a rancher wants help. Tony Friedson was having trouble watering his herd and he has asked me to take a look at a remote part of the ranch to see whether he can enlarge an earthen tank."

"You guys still palaverin'?" Diana asked. "You know the longer you stay, the bigger the tip is supposed to be."

"Being welcome here is priceless," Willis replied with a wink. "We'll be on our way before we wear out our welcome."

"Be sure to come back and tell your friends . . . both of them." Diana waved them off.

2

Two days after Unruh's foray into the desert, Chris O'Brien, a northerner and a recluse, turned off the Arena highway and drove into the desert on a seldom-used two track that the locals called Vista Trail. It followed a ridgeline overlooking a broad valley toward the west and wound along a succession of undulating hills covered with sporadic junipers, mesquites, chollas, prickly pears, creosotes, and an occasional palo verde. Chris maneuvered his battered old Jeep around serpentine curves and carefully avoided outcroppings of rock that threatened his undercarriage.

The hot sun baked the earth, and the tattered canvas of his Jeep offered little protection. Yet Chris found an uncommon comfort in this parched and desolate landscape, as if its very desolation sucked out and displaced the aridity of his own existence.

Still in his twenties, Chris had recently moved from Montana, more as a retreat from disappointment than in search for new opportunity. He had finished college at a small liberal arts school, where a standard curriculum still included required courses in literature, history, foreign language, and philosophy—an old-fashioned and restrictive program in which he thrived. His enthusiasm moved from one field of study to the next, as one professor after another challenged his receptive mind. Even after he had completed his first two years and should have concentrated on a major field, he continued to indulge his varied interests and the offerings of his favorite profs. Ultimately he graduated with a major in general studies.

Chris's unfocused college record did not help in finding a decent job, so he transferred to a graduate program in mechanical engineering, where he also received a license in surveying. Here he found the love of his life, Angela, a vivacious, fun-loving undergraduate math student who became his love and his anchor. Married shortly thereafter, they indulged in the delights of mutual discovery and intimacy on an extended road trip to as many national parks of the west as they could cover in a two-month safari.

When Chris and Angela were driving back to Montana from Yosemite, an oncoming van swerved into his lane. He turned sharply to the left to elude the impact, but only enough to cause its force to crush the passenger side of the car. Angela died instantly. Chris escaped serious injury, but his spirit died beside her. He embraced her bloodied body and wailed with inconsolable grief.

Why didn't I react in time! I should have veered to the right. I drove too fast. I didn't deserve her love. I'm not worth it.

He wandered aimlessly for months and took one meaningless job after another. His appearance matched his mood—slovenly, unkempt, and wayward. His latest trek brought him to the Southwest.

With the remainders of his insurance settlement he bought two hundred barren acres in the desert. The price was reasonable, and he especially prized it because it was far from the nearest neighbors. With an abandoned trailer and a half-finished cabin, Chris pronounced the place adequate for his needs. He adopted a hermit's lifestyle, but without the inner grit that such a life demands. Inevitably economic necessity forced him to seek a part-time position at San Ysidro Community College, where he taught English to foreign-language speakers. Chris lived so simply that this meager income sufficed. He bought a vintage Jeep from a local dealer and somehow managed to keep it running.

Chris followed Vista Trail for a couple of miles in the direction of the lowering sun. The road, if one could call it that, veered to the north where eventually it merged with a paved secondary road that led back to the Sabine Highway a few miles beyond the point where Chris had turned off from it. Chris stopped as the trail curved and brought into view an austere, low-lying panorama that stretched from the Mexican border northward into the haze of the horizon. In other climates the shape of the basin would have resulted in a perennially flowing river down its middle, but here only a dry, sandy wash appeared that seemed even more barren than the slopes that led down to it. He stopped where a wide spot in the trail offered a turn-around under the meager shade of a juniper.

His arrival disturbed a jackrabbit that hopped lazily into the brush of a dead mesquite. Chris watched it hide and reflected on its carefree survival in such a spare environment.

Regretting that he had forgotten to bring a book, he gazed instead toward the desert sun slowly lowering onto a ridgeline in the west. Leaning back he lowered the brim of his hat to his eyes and allowed his mind to slip into unfocused daydreams. A welcome breeze tempered the early evening heat, and the faint sound of the far-off evening bells of the San Leandro church roused him from the edge of sleep.

He sat up and was fishing for his keys when he spied movement in the distance. It might have escaped his notice had it not been blue, a color out of place in the endless browns of the desert. His curiosity aroused, he retrieved his binoculars and leaned against a palo verde to steady his view. He could make out a pickup with the markings of the sheriff's office on its door. The officer, who leaned on the pickup's open door, scanned the distance with a pair of binoculars.

How absurd is this, he thought, *for me to be watching a watcher?* He noticed that the distant figure had a coal-black beard and an eye patch and realized to his amazement that he was looking at Stanley Unruh, the sheriff's deputy.

Unruh was surveying the desert to the south, so Chris trained his glasses in that direction too, hoping to spot what the deputy was trying to see. In spite of his efforts, nothing unusual came into view.

Suddenly Unruh put down his binoculars, started up his pickup, and slowly bushwhacked his way to the south. Chris followed his progress. When Unruh stopped and stepped out of his pickup, Chris saw that he had also uncased his shotgun and pumped a load. Gun at hip level, he moved slowly forward. Still Chris could not make out what attracted the cop's attention. His steps slowed and then stopped as he lowered the gun barrel toward the ground and pushed forward with it, as if he were using a shovel. Now Chris could discern the object of Unruh's efforts: a corpse. He could make out a second corpse when Unruh turned it over in the same way. Chris drew the obvious conclusion: Unruh had found the bodies of migrants who had succumbed to the hazards of desert migration.

Unruh put the gun aside and bent down, evidently to check for identification. Not yet satisfied, he walked some distance in every direction, at times bending low and kicking whatever was underfoot. Finally contented, Unruh made his way back to his pickup. After he opened its door, he stopped abruptly and turned to look to his left. He brought his gun up again, hesitated, raised his hand to shelter his eyes from the sun, and then—step by step—approached the object of his renewed interest. After about a hundred feet, he stopped and leaned forward, keeping his gun ready.

Chris watched intently and adjusted his binoculars to maximize the focus. An intervening mesquite obscured what had captured the deputy's interest. Chris wondered whether this could be still another corpse.

Unruh had clearly reached whatever had aroused his curiosity. He lingered for a while and bent down; his posture indicated that whatever he was looking for was just at his feet. Then he backed away with his gun still leveled. Again he stopped, hesitated, and finally got into his pickup, while still holding his shotgun. Chris wondered about the reason for his indecision.

Unruh started the pickup and slowly backed away. Chris watched him turn around and drive north, where he would regain the pavement and continue on toward Sabine Highway.

When Chris felt certain that the deputy would not return, he continued down the two track following Unruh's tracks. He approached the two bodies and confirmed that they were dead. He always kept a small tarp and a jug or two of water whenever he ventured into the desert, careful never to drive beyond the distance from where he could walk out with only these supplies. He covered the two bodies with his tarp.

Then he walked in the direction where Unruh had lingered a few minutes earlier. Here he discovered a young man lying on his back under a small juniper. When Chris leaned down towards him, he detected some movement. The young fellow was still alive. Chris retrieved a jug of water from the Jeep, propped up the migrant's head, and wet his lips. He tried whatever he could think of to cool him down. Finally his efforts were rewarded. The migrant slowly regained consciousness and began to take a few gulps of water.

Chris ventured a few words. "*Sono un amigo.*" Then switched to English. "I'm a friend. Here's some water. Do you hear me?"

He received no reply. Chris improvised some shade with his shirt and continued to help him cool down by keeping his head wet with a soaked handkerchief. After a quarter hour Chris called upon his rusty high school Spanish, "*¿Como te llamas?*" His efforts were rewarded with a weak response.

"*Ern . . . esto. M'llamo Ern . . . esto.*" And the young man lapsed back into unconsciousness.

Chris had already used up most of his ready Spanish and switched to English. "Can you get up?"

Again there was no reply. Chris took his wrist and detected a rapid heartbeat and noticed that his eyes seemed to focus at times. Chris retrieved his second jug of water and tried again and again to get him to drink. Slowly Ernesto became more responsive. He looked straight at Chris, "*Usted no es un migra!*" Chris could barely hear what he said and did not grasp the meaning.

Chris spoke to him in soothing tones, even though he didn't really think that Ernesto would understand his English. "I want to help you. I will take you to my Jeep. Do you think you can walk?"

After a while he stopped this monologue. When he did, Ernesto unexpectedly raised his hand and pointed at the Jeep. He spoke in clear, though heavily accented, English. "Take me with you. Help me."

Chris helped him into the passenger seat of the Jeep and strapped him in. He drove slowly along the two track to Sabine Highway and then to his friend, Claudia Gomez, who ran the ready-care clinic at the San Leandro satellite campus of San Ysidro Community College. He rang the emergency bell, unstrapped Ernesto, and helped him to the entrance.

Claudia, capable and efficient, emerged at the entrance, attractive in her nurse's blue. "Who's this?"

"His name is Ernesto. I found him in the desert off Vista Trail. He was unconscious. I gave him some water, but he needs more help than I can give him."

"Okay, let's get him on a gurney."

Claudia noticed her patient's nervousness, so she spoke in Spanish to reassure him. She asked him his name and explained everything that she was doing for him. She asked how long he had been in the desert, whether he felt any pain, when he had last had anything to eat and drink. She explained the purpose of the intravenous hydration that she prepared and warned him of the poke in his arm.

She treated his bloody blisters and infected cactus spines, after removing his shoes and trousers.

She told Chris, "Check his legs for more cactus stickers and thorns. You can't always see them; you have to feel them. Here's a set of tweezers. If you find a huge bunch try using sticky tape." She demonstrated how to apply the tape.

Claudia did his vitals. "He's actually doing pretty well. I'm going to defrost some soup for him.

Soon Ernesto was in a gown, sitting up and spooning his soup. He spoke in rapid Spanish as soon as he discovered Claudia's fluency and came to believe that she could be trusted.

After a lull in the conversation she turned to Chris. "I want him to stay here for a while just in case there's something I'm missing. I think he's going to be okay. When he's recovered, can he stay at your place temporarily?"

"Sure. I had already planned on that."

"One more thing, before you go. Visit the Vincent de Paul thrift store and get him some clothes."

She wrote a voucher for three outfits and handed it to Chris.

On his way back to the clinic Chris stopped to call the sheriff's office from a pay phone. When the dispatcher answered he left a brief message. "There are two corpses in the desert. Take Vista Trail off Arena Highway; go about two miles, then follow tracks to the left."

He hung up without identifying himself.

Late that afternoon, Deputy Unruh received a call from the sheriff's dispatcher. "We have a report of corpses in the desert; I'm calling the medical examiner. Deputy Smith will go with you."

Unruh had intended to go the next morning to pick up three corpses; he felt certain that the third person was at the point of death and would not have survived no matter what he did for him. That a report about the bodies had come in so soon surprised him.

"Okay, we'll be in for directions," Unruh said. But he knew where they would be going.

Smith arrived at the station first. The dispatcher waved him over, "Here's the information I've got: About four miles south on Sabine Highway, then west on Vista Trail about two miles. Watch for tire tracks leading off to the left. The call reported two corpses. Here's a sketch with directions. One more thing—that call was anonymous, so it could be a hoax."

She handed him a note and a map.

When Unruh arrived, Smith handed him the note. "We'd better get going. It's getting late."

Unruh took a look at the note and realized with a jolt that it mentioned only two corpses. "Just t—" He caught himself just in time. "Just tell me where will we meet the examiner?"

"Wait for her on the Arena about four miles south at Vista Trail," the dispatcher said. "She'll be waiting for you. Take two body bags."

Unruh grabbed an extra one . . .

Clara Studer, the medical examiner, had arrived and knew the officers well. "It's going to be another sad one."

"One too many," Smith agreed. "Want to ride with us? We're going to need the pickup to bring out the bodies. There's room for three of us in the cab."

"Okay. You guys know the trails as well as I do."

"I'll take the wheel," Unruh moved in. "You be the navigator; since you've got the directions."

While Unruh was driving, Arthur watched for tracks. After about two miles he spotted them. "Here it is. Go slow. You look to the left; I'll take the right."

"Right there, up ahead," Clara pointed. "Somebody covered them with a tarp."

Unruh's jaw dropped. *A tarp! Someone's been here . . . after I left!*

Smith saw no need to hesitate. He removed the tarp. Clara did the routine checks and found no sign of life. She commented in routine fashion. "Probably heat stroke. The pathologist will establish the cause officially."

Whoever left the tarp must also have been the one who made the call to the police station, Unruh figured.

"Let's check for ID before we put them in the bags," Clara said.

Unruh's mind was elsewhere.

"This pocket has been turned inside out." Smith nudged Unruh to get his attention.

"Yeah, I see."

"Here's something. They're from Sinaloa," Smith said.

"Good." Clara said. "When we hand over the bodies, they always try to ID them. Any place name helps."

Clara looked at the cops. "I'm done here. You can finish up."

Meanwhile Unruh had slipped away to check on the place where he had found the third migrant. Dumbfounded, he discovered that there was no third corpse. *I was sure he couldn't have lived long.* The ground under the juniper was wet. *The water! It's got to mean someone helped him! Maybe he survived after all.*

"Give me a hand with this bag," Smith yelled as he struggled with the heavier of the two bodies.

But I was sure he couldn't have survived.

"Hey, over here," Smith insisted. "Give me a hand."

"Coming. I'll be right there."

They loaded both body bags onto the bed of the pickup.

There sure was someone out here after I left. These two bodies weren't removed, Unruh thought, just *covered. He removed the third one, so that's probably because he survived.*

Smith noticed a third bag. "Why did you bring the third bag?"

Unruh didn't reply.

I left here about four o'clock. The call to the dispatcher came maybe about 5:30. That's really close. Whatever took place, it happened within an hour and a half.

The temperature dropped after sunset; nevertheless, Unruh was perspiring profusely. He looked off into the distance as if that would unravel the puzzle. *Did anyone see me? If so, could he identify me? Could there have been even a third person who arrived before the tarp person and did the rescue?*

The three drove back to Arena Highway where Clara had left her car. Amid the small talk Unruh asked Clara, "Were there any other calls to pick up a body recently?"

"There always are. We get about two hundred every year. There was one two days ago. Too long gone to be ID'd."

This helped solve the riddle. *No other corpse today.*

Got to figure this out. There's the tarp, the water, the call to the dispatcher. Are they all the same person? Most likely. Got to trace the phone call!

When they got back Unruh asked the dispatcher whether the call could be traced.

"Sure. It won't take long."

The next morning Unruh picked up a note from the dispatcher. The call came in at 5:30 from the public phone near the clinic. Unruh slipped away to figure things out. *Whoever found the third migrant took him to the clinic where Claudia most likely treated him. That means he survived. Therefore, at least three people know about the third migrant: the rescuer, the rescued, and Claudia. But asking her about it can't be done.*

Unruh worried. *What else did they know? What did they see? Who are they?*

Unruh returned after hours the next day and undertook a sort of crime scene investigation. He made molds of the tire tracks and the footprints. To his chagrin, they yielded no useful evidence. The tires were mostly bald and the footprints were those of a common hiking shoe. Much to his dismay, he could not exclude the possibility that he had been seen by someone. The critical question remained: *Could this person identify him? Who is this person?*

3

WHEN CHRIS AWOKE IN the morning, he realized that he would be sharing his shack, and so he saw it with new eyes. He noticed that various remnants of abandoned projects were scattered here and there. He gathered the tools strewn about after his efforts to install insulation between the exposed studs in the space serving as his bedroom. The shack had just one presentable room, a ten-by-twelve space at the front door, but even this was hardly finished, for the rough plywood subfloor was covered only with a carpet remnant that did not reach the walls. A cast-off couch faced the front door, and two straight-backed chairs lined a side wall. An assortment of books, the cherished reminders of his former life, were piled on the floor and on shelving devised with bricks and boards. A small desk held a lamp with an unshaded bulb, whose extension cord snaked from the bathroom. This completed the furnishings.

A SUCCESSION OF OWNERS had lived in the shack before Chris, and each of them had made some changes. It began as a hunting cabin built by one of the foremen of the Alonso Ranch, when the village site of San Leandro was no more than a corral and a water tank.

A craftsman who produced leather belts and saddles came next. The shack still reeked of tanned leather. This owner installed a toilet, shower, and sink along with a septic tank and leach field. Beyond these improvements, it remained unfinished without any interior walls and doors.

He also made a significant improvement by drilling a shallow well. This provided only a small flow because it did not reach the underlying aquifer but only seepage from Vasquez Creek, a perennial stream that flowed down from the rim rocks above. Drinking water had to be obtained separately.

The next owner added a trailer, now parked at the rear door. But his financial circumstances led to foreclosure, so the property became a listing of San Leandro's only realtor, Carmen Montez, who sold it to Chris when he arrived from Montana.

CHRIS MADE FITFUL ATTEMPTS at improvements, like his recent efforts to insulate the interior walls. After he had begun to add blanket insulation between the studs, Raimondo, an amateur electrician, whom he had run into at the Pancake House, pointed out that wiring had to be roughed in before insulation could be installed. Raimondo promised to do the wiring, but his job at Lightner's sawmill allowed time to freelance only on weekends and an occasional evening. Besides, Raimondo had other wiring jobs to finish, so Chris's work on the shack had come to a halt.

He had grabbed a broom to dislodge the sand that had settled in the cracks between his floorboards when he noticed a dust cloud on the road. He stood at the window and watched as a car rounded the last curve and then disappeared as it splashed across Vasquez Creek. When it reappeared, he recognized Claudia's SUV with Ernesto in the passenger seat.

The Chevy had a full load. Claudia knew Chris had no accommodations for a permanent guest, so she brought a cot along with sheets and blankets, a supply of groceries, a card table, and an assortment of Spanish-language books. She also handed over instructions in English and Spanish about Ernesto's care during his recovery. Finally she brought a used bicycle, so Ernesto could travel the eight miles to the village and to her clinic at the college.

Ernesto emerged from the Chevy with surprising energy. Chris, by contrast, held back. He had acted spontaneously and instinctively when facing someone at death's door, but he was more reserved welcoming a total stranger to his home. Ernesto embraced Chris and nearly knocked him off the front steps.

Claudia said, "Ernesto knows quite a bit of English and he is eager to practice it."

Ernesto nodded. "Thank you. You saved me. Your help I needed."

Unsure of what else to do, Chris accepted Ernesto's embrace.

Claudia clicked open the SUV and everyone helped to unload it. They made up the cot, stowed the groceries, and found space for Ernesto's newly acquired clothes.

She grabbed Chris's hand to command his attention. "He's told me a lot about why he made the trip from Mexico. He's interested in desert agriculture, so the horticulture program on our campus is just what he needs.

Fortunately most of the courses are taught here, because Verde Gardens is nearby. If he needs to get to the main campus in Gila Center, we have a twice-a-day shuttle. I'll make sure that he can sit in on any of the workshops we offer here."

"Wonderful," Chris said. "I always knew you were the one to make things happen."

She warded off the compliment with a shrug of her shoulders but added insistently, "You have to deal with his need for legal residency."

Chris brightened at this important role. "Sure, I'll get the paperwork started."

This new sense of purpose gradually eased Chris's dissolute spirit and awakened the enthusiasm which Angela had once found so appealing.

Addressing Ernesto in Spanish while pointing to her written instructions, Claudia ordered him to take food, drink, and medicine as directed. Then she added with some emphasis, "Stay out of sight as much as you can . . . just in case."

Thus began Ernesto's rapid transition to life in the States over the next months. He could not have found a better place to make a start. Claudia became his mentor and provided access to the resources of San Ysidro Community College, including a class in English that Chris was teaching. Life in Chris's shack became crowded, but Ernesto soon added an interior wall to give him some private space.

The college had scheduled a workshop on residential wiring, which both Chris and Ernesto attended. They wired the shack and then installed insulation and wallboard; it became much more comfortable. Ernesto's English improved rapidly so that he was able to mingle easily among the many other Latinos who lived in the area.

ERNESTO AND HIS TWO companions had left from the same village, San Jorge in Sinaloa, whose population had been much diminished by emigration. Many young men had crossed the border in search of work and sent remittances back to support their families. However, the main cause of the migration to the north was the chaos caused by gangs competing for the drug trade. Marcelino's father had been one of the *federales* responsible for the maintenance of public order and had lost his life during a gunfight with members of a cartel. Marcelino did not escape the turmoil. He received an unmistakable warning to leave the village, so he took the earliest opportunity to head north. No hope remained for any future outside the clutches of the cartel.

When Marcelino and Jorge set out, Ernesto joined them. Not looking for work, as his companions were, he sought to further his education in agriculture, which local circumstances could not provide. Now Chris's acres became his laboratory and the college his educational resource.

"Here's something from the college for you," Claudia said. She fished a letter out of her jacket pocket. "I stopped at the mail room before leaving."

Chris tore it open and whooped with delight.

"Do I owe this to you?" he asked.

"I wouldn't know until you tell me what it's about."

"Starting next term I've got a full time job here," Chris said. "It's not just ESL, but also regular English classes."

Claudia hugged him. "I didn't have anything to do with it; but I would have. So what are you going to do with your newfound wealth? Are we going to see the last of your shack?"

Chris looked heavenward as if for inspiration. "I think I should get rid of my old Jeep and get some new wheels."

"I should have known," Claudia said. "Guys buy cars, not homes."

"Ernesto can have the old Jeep."

Chris drove up, grinning broadly. He celebrated the occasion by blowing the horn to announce his used pickup. "How do you like it? It's an F-150."

Ernesto's response didn't match the joy that Chris felt the moment demanded. Instead he had a request to put the new vehicle to use. "Please take me out to the place where you found me in the desert," Ernesto said. "I want to mark my rescue with jugs of water."

"Great! Let's go get Claudia and take her along. I want to show her where I found you."

When Claudia saw the jugs in the bed of the pickup, she asked, "What made you want to do this?"

Ernesto replied soulfully, "It's a holy place for me, as if I died and rose again. Maybe I can make the miracle happen for someone else."

When they arrived, no sign of what had once transpired remained. Only Chris recognized a subtle sign of where Marcelino and Jorge had once lain. He didn't speak but only pointed to the spot where he had covered the two bodies with a tattered tarp. Ernesto bowed his head and crossed himself. Claudia joined him and took his hand. He did not resist his tears. Together they recited the traditional prayer for the dead in Spanish.

Ernesto cleared a small perimeter of desert debris with the soles of his shoes. He picked up a dead ocotillo and sharpened one end to fix it into the ground; then he fastened a second piece with a vine to make a cross.

"This is where we will leave two jugs of water, one for Marcelino, the other for Jorge."

Chris led them to the juniper where he found Ernesto. He pointed. "Under this little tree is where I found you."

Ernesto knelt down on the ground. Claudia and Chris joined him on either side and extended their arms around his shoulders while he recited prayers. Finally he got up and cleared a spot at the base of the juniper, much as he had done before.

Chris brought the third jug of water. Ernesto placed his hand on it. "It is Marcelino who saved my life. He gave me his share of water after the coyote failed to leave us any."

He turned to Claudia. "Let's come back here every week and keep it full."

II

MAY 2016

4

CHRIS MET CARMEN MONTEZ every Tuesday for breakfast at the Pancake House. He did not think of her as a soul mate, or even admit to the concept, but that's what she had become. The weekly breakfast with her had become the highlight of his week.

Diana Flores, a tall, sprightly waitress, had presided at the eatery for a dozen years and had acquired a loyal following of regulars, including Willis Carr and Chris O'Brien. She was equally adept at serving steaming plates of hotcakes and well-aimed wisecracks.

Chris met Carmen soon after he came to San Leandro from the north, and they became fast friends soon after. Meeting her at the Pancake House had become the bright spot in Chris's humdrum routine.

Chris was looking for a permanent place to live, and she found some high desert land for him. She was the only realtor in the village, and she did it only part time; her main income came from a quarry in the Nudoso Hills, which provided the area with gravel, crushed rock, and the rental of heavy equipment. In her role as a realtor, she found a remote, desert site that suited his needs.

While waiting for Carmen, Chris scanned the community messages mounted on a corkboard under a roofed lean-to. Chris made it his business to organize the postings by date: items for sale, help wanted, public notices, day laborers for hire, etc.

When he sat down Diana appeared with coffee and asked, "What makes you think that this table hasn't been reserved?" She held the coffee to her side as if to withhold service.

"When have you guys ever had a waiting list?"

"We're trying to upgrade the caliber of our customers, and we thought we might have to restrict you to the lean-to. Of course, we wouldn't want to banish Carmen, so I'll let you stay here as long as she still consents to eat with you."

"Just keep the coffee coming." Chris dismissed her taunts. He gulped his first cup before it began to cool.

About five minutes later Carmen strode in with confidence and nonchalance. She was someone who would always attract attention by her easygoing manner and infectious smile. Diana noticed her and immediately quipped, "Your mate just got here. Careful, he's already given me a hard time."

"Nah, you just have to humor him; he's really harmless." She greeted Chris with a friendly shoulder jab. "How's life in the desert?"

"Not as lonely as it used to be now that Ernesto has joined me. He always comes up with something new. Just when I think we've settled in, he has another project in mind. "

"I'd say that's just what you needed. You know that I've always admired you, in spite of your futile effort to be invisible. You've never been cut out for the life of a hermit, and Ernesto's arrival has been a blessing, whether you admit it or not."

"You're probably right, though when I first got here it wasn't small town life that attracted me. If it hadn't been for me," he added mischievously, "you would never have found a buyer for that desolate patch of scrub that you sold me."

"You're belittling my unique insight as a realtor. I knew just the place for a recluse like you."

Diana reappeared with more coffee. "Do you need a menu?" She held them at arm's length. "I wouldn't think so; you always order the same thing."

Chris watched as she refilled his cup. "The stuff we order here is always so good; it's your fault that we get into a rut and order the same thing over and over again."

"I'll let the cook know about your problem. I'm sure he can fix it"

Carmen laughed and then put an end to the repartee. "I'll have a short stack with maple syrup and a half melon. Chris always orders an egg over well, dry whole wheat, and bacon. Isn't that right, Chris?"

Chris couldn't think of a smart reply. He just waved his hand, as if the choice was of no concern to him.

Waiting for their orders, Carmen uncovered her knife and fork, noticed a sticky syrup smudge, and rubbed it off with her paper napkin. Meanwhile, Chris struggled to refold the Gila Center Observer he had been reading.

Diana brought their plates. Another party of four had arrived so she simply said, "Enjoy," and hurried to take their orders.

"Ernesto has big plans for a market garden," Chris said. "He says he's going to make the desert green."

"Yeah, Claudia mentioned that when I stopped at the clinic to have her look at this scrape." She extended her arm to reveal a nasty contusion.

Chris took her hand. "How did that happen?"

"Just a rusty nut. It wouldn't turn; I used an extender and then it slipped off the socket."

"You should have a mechanic do that kind of stuff."

"You gonna apply for the job?"

Chris laughed, "I don't think I've got the necessary experience. Besides I'm suddenly getting busy at my place, and I've also got some great news."

"What's that? Are you running to be the local muckraker?"

"Naw, that's far too challenging. I just got hired full time at the college. I'll be teaching regular students, not just non-native speakers. In case you didn't notice on your way in, I just got a pickup to replace that old Jeep."

"Does that mean that you won't want to spend time with me anymore, now that you're one of those filthy plutocrats?"

Chris suddenly allowed unfeigned tenderness to show. "I'd never give up my time with you."

This caught Carmen off guard; she was secretly delighted but hurriedly changed the subject. "Tell me, what's the latest with your new roommate?"

"Like I said, Ernesto is going to make the desert green. It's all about water, and he's already making use of the little creek that comes down from Kallisto Wells. There isn't much rain around here, but he thinks there's enough to make his garden project work out. He's a firm believer in subsistence agriculture, and I've let him take over half of my two hundred acres. After all, I haven't been able to find any way to make the land productive."

Carmen ignored the implied criticism. "You know I have earth moving equipment you can rent, and I'll even cut you a good deal. I'm sure that Ernesto will eventually need to do some serious landscaping."

"I don't think he's ready for that. Right now he's engrossed in how much water he can harvest. If he can catch enough runoff to make the desert bloom, he will design water storage, canals, growing beds, and everything else. But all this is still in the future."

"That sounds like lots of planning. Are you going to help him with the surveying? I'm sure he will need to shoot elevations before bringing in a front-end loader."

"Sure. I can help him with that. It isn't often I get to make use of that part of my training."

"Yeah, I keep forgetting about your checkered college days."

"I don't regret any of it. I think I learned a bit about values and how to live them out. It's just that those things don't seem to make any difference on a resume."

Diana arrived with the check. "It's my turn," said Carmen, snatching the slip from Chris.

"Next week, same time, same place?"

"Wouldn't miss it."

5

THE FIRST STARRET TO settle above the Arena Valley was Josiah, who built a log cabin, dug a well, and started a sawmill in the 1880s. From this site behind the rim rocks, he supplied the rough sawn boards for the corrals of the Alonso Ranch in the valley below.

Bill Starret, Josiah's grandson, tall, muscular, and resolute, roamed about his ancestor's homestead and sat down on a rotted beam—the remnant of the original log cabin. Hardly sentimental in his outlook, Bill nevertheless felt ancestral devotion as he surveyed the remains of the old sawmill, the well, and the stately second-growth ponderosa forest all around. His developer's eye appraised the site, as he stood upon the heights and looked down onto the valley far below. Turning around toward the east, he viewed the distant purple of the majestic Vermilion Mountains.

He had just finished the final build-out of Paradise Acres, a housing development just upslope from the village of San Leandro, a venture that had made him rich and had taught him the secrets of construction and real estate. Bill had the instinct of a builder, so when that final house in Paradise Acres was done, his life seemed empty. His wife, Emily, noticed his discontent and suggested that he find purpose in his appointment as chair of the church's finance committee. But he found no satisfaction in altruism; rather, he deemed such concerns unworthy of his efforts.

In the early spring, by chance, he had met a seasonal visitor from Salt Lake, who was staying for a week at a rental to escape the last of the winter. Bill pointed to the rim rocks high above, where his grandfather had settled, and proudly told his visitor about his family's history in the valley.

"Build a winter home up there for me," his guest proposed while handing him his business card. Bill laughed it off at the time; now that chance remark had created an epiphany. Walking along the rim, he imagined it transformed by a magnificent development. Recalling a trip to canyon lands in Utah, he pictured the rim with winter homes fashioned after the cliff dwellings of pre-Columbian Americans. Bill had his inspiration and the rough outlines of his next construction project—one that would challenge the future of the village.

6

Willis Carr buckled into his usual chopper and set the rotors in motion.

Riding with him was a photographer who would take pictures of the eastern rim of the Arena Valley and record its elevation for a client named Bill Starret.

Willis flew to the extreme southern end of the valley, where the Arena River began its course by plunging down the thousand-foot Arena Canyon. Seen from above, the valley was shaped like an arrowhead pointing to the south. The canyon was at its extreme south end

From there the chopper flew north, hugging the eastern side of the valley just below its rocky escarpment at nearly seven thousand feet. They passed over Chris's two hundred acre plot of high desert, so near to the Arena Canyon that he could hear its roar after a heavy rain. Just above the rim and behind a jumble of boulders was the site of Josiah Starret's sawmill and his shallow well that was still usable. From here the old Switchback Trail meandered down to the valley floor, a two track that was still used by high clearance vehicles. Next to the Starret homestead lay over a mile of Verde Forest land, where the waters of Kallisto Wells oozed out of rock formations just above the rim.

Below the Kallisto as the slope lessened were Verde Gardens, Masterson Ranch, and the village of San Leandro, all blessed by the Kallisto's waters. The rim gradually lessened and split into a series of ridges that became the contours of Two Gun Ranch.

The western side of the valley was a barren wasteland of hogback ridges called Nudoso Hills, too desolate even for open range. Its vacant hills were interrupted in the west by the layered formations created by the evaporation ponds of a thriving copper mine.

The Arena River, never totally dry, flowed along the edge of the Nudoso Hills opposite the village of San Leandro. A gravel roadway splashed across the river and gave access to Yolanda Alonso's old ranch house set in a box canyon near the Arena River. Nearby was the entrance to Carmen Montez's rock quarry and beyond it the San Leandro cemetery.

Bill was delighted with the aerial photos and elevations that Willis gave him. His enthusiasm for a new challenge propelled him onward. He set out to search for funding even before he had done the detailed planning that such a complicated project required.

He met with an investment banker in Gila Center to present the outlines of his new development, which he named Anasazi Vistas. The banker's reaction left him crestfallen; even Bill's assurance that he already had a well-heeled buyer from Salt Lake, who assured him that there would be no end of additional customers, didn't arouse the banker's enthusiasm.

"We can't proceed until you give us a detailed business plan with a timetable and a schedule of funding requirements," the banker insisted.

Bill protested, "Obviously I'm not going to spend money I don't have. You would only be asked to provide some bridge funding when my expenditures would be temporarily greater than my receipts."

The banker ignored this explanation with a wave of the hand. "You will need to complete an environmental impact statement as well." He followed up with forbearance, "You can get these forms at the Commerce Department."

Bill subsided into reluctant silence. The banker continued almost apologetically. "You'll also need to provide assurance of a hundred years' supply of water. I expect that you're already aware of that."

Bill had not even brought up another complication; the project would be built on land that belonged to the Verde National Forest, and he needed to acquire ownership of it. The only way to do so would be by making a land swap with the Forest.

His premature visit with the banker had been futile, but it was not in Bill's nature to allow this reversal to fester. He would no longer seek funding from financial institutions, with all their complicated paperwork, but would pursue local investors. In San Leandro there were only two individuals who had the means.

7

ERNESTO DIDN'T WASTE ANY time making a new life for himself. In addition to English language classes at the college he made improvements on the plot of land that Chris made available for him. He fashioned a small kitchen garden along the banks of Vasquez Creek, the southernmost flow from the Kallisto. He built a small earthen tank to catch runoff from occasional summer rainstorms and harvested a crop of tomatoes, peppers, carrots, and assorted greens. Meanwhile he delved into the mysteries of desert agriculture, water harvesting, soil enhancement, and the best choices among crop varieties and cultivars for desert conditions.

He made a visit to the Gila Center weather station to obtain reliable statistics on rainfall.

"Here are our fifty-year records," a helpful green-shirted meteorologist said as she handed over a weather summary for Gila Center.

"You'll see that there are some consistent patterns. Desert rains come in two seasons: localized, and often violent, thunderstorms during the summer monsoons and widely spread gentle rains in the winter, associated with low pressure systems riding a jet stream southward and moving inland over Baja California." She called attention to a bar graph to illustrate the trends.

"What about dry periods?" Ernesto inquired.

"There certainly are dry periods. During April and May there is hardly any rain. In September and October there is very little as well."

"What about the totals?" Ernesto asked.

"The two rainy seasons each yield about six inches, so there's an annual total of roughly twelve inches. On average, there are three or four heavy rains each year that total an inch or more. When heavy rains occur in the summer, they are less beneficial because the hard desert terrain causes a rapid runoff and evaporation is high due to low humidity."

"What's it like forty miles south of here? Do you have records for San Leandro?"

"No, that would be up to you. By all means do local measurements," she urged, "because desert patterns are localized, meaning the weather can be quite different only five miles away. If you want really good statistics, you'll need to set your own gauges and keep your own records. We can give you topographical maps, since elevation is a critical variable. Also pay attention to the existing vegetation, for it's the best clue as to the amount of actual rainfall at any specific location."

AFTER HIS RETURN FROM the weather station, Ernesto gathered the tools and supplies he needed for a long walk beyond the borders of Chris's two hundred acres. Equipped with a half dozen rain gauges and a topographical map, he followed the contours of the terrain that drained onto Chris's land, extending upslope for more than two miles. Ernesto covered all of it on his walk, including the stream itself, its surface, banks, and vegetation. He walked up toward the rim rocks, beyond which the plateau rose steadily toward the distant mountains of the Vermilion Range.

ERNESTO GATHERED INFORMATION ABOUT the entire drainage area, including the characteristics of its upper reaches: a flat section where the stream spread out and ponded; a clump of cottonwoods indicating more underground moisture; and a section of steeper ground subject to heavier erosion. By placing his rain gauges wherever conditions seemed to indicate a microclimate, he sought to learn the rainfall yield of the entire drainage area and an estimate of the runoff that could be harvested from it.

He tramped onward over the steeply rising landscape covered sparsely with juniper and pinon pine amongst the ever-present creosote, cholla, and prickly pear. Slowly the slope steepened even more, and the soil surface became harder and rockier. A glance at his map indicated an elevation of over six thousand feet.

Seen from here the broad valley of the Arena River spread far below to where the village of San Leandro was nestled along its banks. In the distant haze he could just make out the tall buildings of Gila Center. Below him wound the ribbon of the Sabine Highway, which appeared and then disappeared between intervening hills, and continued all the way to the border.

Caught in a wave of nostalgia he looked off into the distance, where Baboquivari Mountain rose in the purplish haze and the Altar Valley stretched off to the north. He tried to trace the route that he had taken with Jorge and Marcelino through the desert. Memories of his trek from

old Mexico returned as he gazed far to the south, but intervening hills obstructed any view of the way back to the village of San Jorge. His spirit rose
as he reflected on his new life with Chris; he wondered what the future held
in store for him.

His reverie ceased when he turned to survey the expanse of the Arena
Valley below. A red-tailed hawk caught an updraft and soared high above.
It captured Ernesto's attention as it dove down after its prey. He wondered
whether the hawk succeeded or whether its prey escaped. He pondered the
mysteries and uncertainties of life, his own good fortune, and the demise of
his companions.

After resuming his walk, he set the fifth rain gauge and continued up
to the very rim of the mesa, now less than a mile ahead. Following Vasquez
Creek upward, he reached the area where its water emerged just above the
rim rocks and flowed across the upper reaches of Switchback Trail. To his
right the trail squeezed between the menacing rim rocks, ever ascending
at a steeper angle until it emerged through an opening that led to the ruins
of the old Starret sawmill. Here he found a well with a hand pump that,
surprisingly, yielded fresh, cold water. Nearby were frayed strands of rusted
cable and a large ponderosa stump to which the cable had been attached
to winch wagons heavy with sawn boards down the steep beginnings of
Switchback Trail.

Ernesto returned to the creek and saw to his left the relatively level extent of the Kallisto seepage and the thick ponderosa forest that surrounded
it. Here he found a boulder and sat down to eat his lunch in the shade.

On his return Ernesto planted his last rain gauge. His annotated map
indicated that the drainage totaled about eight square miles. The gulley
which the stream had scoured out of the desert surface continued on past
Chris's land for less than a mile before its flow disappeared among the gravel
mounds and road cuts of the Sabine Highway.

8

NOT EVERY PROJECT THAT Yolanda Alonso undertook in the interest of San Leandro's prosperity succeeded. The present food bank was housed in what had once been the village's only grocery—it had succumbed to competition from the large chains in Gila Center nearby. The failed grocery became a no-frills warehouse in which sturdy metal scaffolds held pallets stacked with banana boxes filled with canned and packaged foods, destined for the poor.

Every day volunteers from various community service groups came to pick up boxes of food of varying sizes for households with different needs. The facility's volunteers filled these with appropriate amounts.

Claudia Gomez checked the to-do list posted near the lockers assigned to the regular volunteers. A bin of unsorted items culled from the shelves of a grocery chain needed sorting to eliminate anything unsuitable. Claudia sighed resignedly. By her lights, this job was the most disagreeable and unproductive task of all because it consisted of policing shelf-worn and expiration-dated stuff. She resented needing to toss items that should not have been contributed in the first place.

Claudia spent a couple of two-hour shifts every week at the facility by shuffling her teaching and administrative duties at the community college. Her interest and her longevity as a volunteer inevitably earned her some influence in setting the food bank's policies and practices.

Her status as a regular and her background as a nutritionist made her critical of food bank policies. She often found packing boxes for distribution a disagreeable task because she would end up tossing sugary items into a garbage bin in disgust, rather than sending them off as freebies to an unsuspecting client whose poor diet already contributed to obesity.

At the end of her shift she encountered Marvin Zehrer at the row of lockers reserved for volunteers. Marvin, as a longtime member and supervisor of volunteers, held a position on the board.

Claudia brought her concerns to him: "One thing that has always nagged me—and maybe it's just my issue, but you are surely aware of this too—I think we sometimes hand out lousy food. Much of what we get from groceries isn't really wholesome. It's loaded with carbs and high fructose corn syrup. Obesity is a serious health problem, especially for the poor, and we exacerbate it. Can't we figure out a way to do better?"

"I didn't know you felt so strongly about this. I guess we take a passive attitude about what is contributed to our pantry. If it's free, it is worth accepting, even if we wouldn't buy the stuff for ourselves."

"But that's just the point," Claudia said. "Should the poor be condemned to have food that we wouldn't buy for ourselves? I know I may be overstating the situation, but how many times have we delivered a food box loaded with carbs to an obese person who is as likely as not to be diabetic? We should provide fresh fruits and vegetables and more proteins."

"I'm afraid it's not that simple. We aren't licensed to be food handlers, so we can only deal with what's packaged or canned. We can't deal with fresh fruits and vegetables without more coolers and freezers. Besides, say what you will, most of our clients actually prefer packaged food to fresh produce."

"Of course they do, Claudia protested. "We've all been conditioned to like that stuff, even if it causes us harm. But do food handling regulations really forbid us from giving out fresh farm potatoes instead of chips encrusted with salt and soaked in fat? Couldn't we buy rice in hundred-pound bags, apples by the carboy, and pinto beans by the sack and repackage them in quart-sized plastic bags? And how about storing produce in coolers, like carrots, onions, lettuce, apples?"

"You're right, of course. But we live in an imperfect world in which the common good often is dismissed as unrealistic. Sometimes we need to accept what we can't change and try to do some good with the rest. The only way to escape to utopia would be to totally opt out. I prefer to fight the battles that I have a chance of winning."

Claudia wouldn't give up easily. "When I visit a home that has requested help, it is our practice to say a short prayer: 'Send forth your spirit and a new world will be created.' I'd rather not give up on that idea. At the very least, we should be pushing the envelope in the direction of integrity and try not to do harm."

Marvin, surprised by Claudia's intensity, said, "I will agree to do this. The board meets in two weeks. Before then I'll research food handling laws and see if there is an opening for what you are suggesting. If so, let's propose a change in our policy."

"Thanks. Marvin, I appreciate that. I've always had a professional interest in nutrition and public health. That's what my training is all about."

9

Deputy Unruh had risen through the ranks, and, when the sheriff announced his retirement, he was the natural successor. Despite his increase in rank (or possibly because of it), he still fretted about the missing migrant whom he had left dying in the desert. Reluctantly he had concluded that the migrant, while near death, had nevertheless survived. He couldn't dispel his nagging doubts about his exposure: Was the migrant conscious enough to have seen him? If so, would he still be recognized? Could he be held responsible for his death? This uncertainty created an accusatory voice that never ceased to rise up into his consciousness.

He turned over in his mind the various possibilities: Maybe the guy had already been apprehended and deported; Claudia would know about him, but approaching her would reveal his secret. He longed for closure and even considered whether he should resign and leave the area if he found that the migrant was still around.

Because of this uncertainty, the desert site drew him back as if it were magnetic. Driving down the two track he struggled to calm his nerves, even though he had any number of ready reasons for being there. After parking he walked the remaining distance and arrived at the site where the two corpses had lain. What he saw left him slack-jawed and frozen in mid-step: two gallon jugs of water! His mind raced to analyze what the jugs meant: whoever left the water knew what happened and had returned to mark the site.

Then it occurred to him that whoever placed the jugs probably knew about the third migrant . . . and probably had been his rescuer. He crept up to the other site. Yet another jug of water! Unruh's skin crawled as if he had just received a message from beyond this world. He hurried back to his cruiser and sped off.

Unruh drove directly to headquarters. He parked and ordered his staff not to disturb him while he secreted himself inside his office. First he opened his lower desk drawer and fumbled for a flask of whiskey. He took a long draught, sat back, and forced himself to make sense of his discoveries. His experience as a crime investigator helped him to analyze the situation. He reached a series of conclusions and a few fairly reasonable assumptions.

The two corpses had no bearing on his problem. Everything depended on the single migrant. If he were dead, there'd be no problem. But he did survive, almost certainly, because the call to the dispatcher came from near the clinic. That left two questions: First, is he still alive and living around here? Second, who was his rescuer and what does he know?

He recalled that he did have one advantage. Leaving water for migrants became a misdemeanor based on the new ordinance that was passed by the county commissioners. If he could discover who left the water, he could use this charge as leverage to investigate this person's involvement and knowledge. In this way he might be able to discover the third migrant's identity, his survival (or not), and consequently his own possible exposure.

Satisfied that he had analyzed the situation clearly, Unruh concluded that he had to identify who left water in the desert. A motion camera could do the trick if he aimed it directly at the right spot.

III

June 2016

10

"How much water have you captured today?" Chris asked Ernesto, who leaned on a shovel while pondering his labors.

"There'd be more if it ever rained around here," he responded darkly.

"When God created Arizona, he agreed to accept the devil's stipulation: no rain in April."

Ernesto retorted, "Not just April. How about May?"

Chris squinted at a cloudless sky. "The locals tell me not to expect any change until the summer monsoons in mid-July. Then you are likely to get flooded."

"I know," Ernesto said. "That's why I've got to plan for water storage."

"How much?" Chris asked.

"That's the question I'm trying to answer. Our drainage area is about eight square miles, and the average annual rainfall is no more than twelve inches. These are the raw numbers I've got to work with."

"Twelve inches of water over eight square miles. I can't even imagine that much water."

"But only a small fraction of that can be captured," Ernesto said.

"What fraction?" Chris asked. "How are you going to figure this out?"

"I called the county extension agent and asked him to help me," Ernesto said. "He will be here in a couple of days, and I hope you can be here when he comes because you need to agree with what I'm going to do. After all, it's still your land."

"Absolutely, I want to hear what he has to say."

Ernesto had something else to tell Chris and was reluctant to bring it up. "I took a job at Verde Gardens."

"Wonderful! I'm proud of you. When do you start?"

"Next week. I'll be an assistant to the grower who runs the greenhouses, and I'll also be helping in the orchard—probably because I can communicate easily with the field hands who are Latinos. Mr. Uribe, who's the manager, noticed my interest in desert agriculture when I talked with him after class."

"That's really a great break for you"

"It sure is. The grower is the head honcho, and I'll get the chance to learn from him. Verde Gardens uses hydroponics in one of their greenhouses."

"That job will give you lots of experience." Chris was delighted.

Ernesto finally got to the point. "I'm also going to be living there."

"You mean that Uribe wants you to move?"

Ernesto quickly added, "I've really been happy staying here with you, and I can't begin to tell you how lucky that has been for me. I will be grateful forever. But Mr. Uribe wants someone to be there overnight just in case something goes wrong. Besides, it's free; there won't be any rent."

Chris couldn't entirely disguise his disappointment. After a moment of indecision, he reached out to hug Ernesto. "I'm going to miss you, hermano, but I'm happy for you. You're on your way."

After his moving out was settled, Ernesto said, "I want you to be here when the extension agent comes."

"Sure. What are you going to ask him?"

"I want to talk to him about my estimates of how much water can be captured and how much is needed per square foot of garden area. Then I want to hear what he has to say about soil enhancement and the varieties and cultivars that do well in these desert environments."

Ernesto said, "Claudia is also interested in the garden. Because of her training as a nutritionist, she wants to explore growing organic produce. She also wants to introduce gardening to the needy that live around here."

"Good," Chris said. "That's enough for one meeting, and I'm looking forward to it. However, you're in charge, and I expect that you will take the initiative with the extension agent."

11

THE COTTONWOOD WAS BUILT with financial help from Yolanda Alonso, because she wanted the village to have a hotel. Similarly when San Leandro became the location of the southern branch of San Ysidro Community College, she saw to it that the campus included village offices.

In addition, she arranged for an apartment to be dedicated to her exclusive use at the Cottonwood. This is where she waited for Bill Starret's arrival.

She took considerable pride in keeping the apartment well-stocked to entertain her occasional guests. The refrigerator held the usual items: cheese, crackers, ice, beer, wine, and an assortment of soft drinks. The furniture consisted of a love seat at right angles to a comfortable recliner, and an end table where she set out snacks, drinks, and an ice bucket.

When Bill asked for the meeting he had been cryptic, even evasive, about its purpose. Instead he hinted that he wanted to surprise her. She agreed to meet but suggested her Cottonwood apartment rather than her ranch house on the opposite bank of the Arena. Bill had proposed his stately home at the edge of his Paradise Acres development, but she insisted on the Cottonwood.

The two of them had been pivotal in San Leandro's present growth. The vast expanse of the original Alonso Ranch, a spread that once encompassed the entire Arena watershed and hundreds of acres of high grasslands to the south, had once been hers. Of these extensive holdings only her original ranch house and the Verde Gardens remained in her name.

She deeded over to the village many properties in San Leandro that have become crucial to the village's survival.

Bill's connection to San Leandro began in the 1880s when his ancestors became prosperous by providing the Alonso Ranch with rough-sawn lumber for it's corrals. Since those early days, Bill's family had been the village's sole developer and road builder.

The receptionist buzzed, "Mr. Starret has arrived. May I show him in?"

"No, I'll come out to meet him." Yolanda was never outdone in extending courtesies.

She found Bill waiting just beyond her apartment's door. "Bill, it's so good to see you. Please come in. I always look forward to seeing you." Yolanda pointed to the recliner as she took a seat on the sofa.

Bill settled in and said, "And so do I. It came to me as I drove down here that we two go back a long way."

Bill had rehearsed how he could best flatter Yolanda. "You have been at the center of San Leandro since the village began. In fact, without you, we all agree, there would be no village at all. My family has been here to see you make it all happen, with just a little assistance from me from time to time." Bill minimized his family's role with endearing, false modesty.

"Thanks, Bill." She motioned with her hand, dismissing his artful remarks. "You give me too much credit. It's the people in the village that have made it all happen. I'm just around to help when a little push is needed.

"You said that you had a surprise for me. I can't imagine what it might be." She nudged the conversation along.

Bill didn't rush right into his proposal; instead he circled around and approached it step by step.

"You know that I still own the old homestead up on top of the rim rocks, where my grandpa cut the timber for the corrals that used to line the river."

Yolanda nodded; she was keenly aware of the history of the Arena Valley and the role of both of their ancestors.

"When Congress established the National Forest," Bill recited, "I kept my granddad's old place including the Switchback Trail, on which he carted the lumber down to the corrals that your ranch was building. When the National Forest approached me to sell the old place, I nearly did, but now I'm glad that I didn't. I have plans for a wonderful new development project, and my grandpa's place is the linchpin to make it happen."

Yolanda's suspicions were aroused and her remarks registered her incredulity. "Are you thinking of putting homes up on top of the rim?" She began to verbalize the problems she foresaw. "That would be quite a challenge. That trail with its switchbacks would hardly handle any construction traffic."

"No, no, not on top of the rim, but just under it, along the slope."

Yolanda's questions moved him to get into his proposal. He became animated while her doubts deepened.

"The project that I have in mind will transform the Arena Rim into a series of wonderful homes built snugly along the slope. They will capture the winter sun, but there will also be a series of gigantic rotating louvers for shade when it's needed. My inspiration comes from the thousand-year-old cliff dwellings of the Anasazi. I want to invite you to become a primary investor."

Yolanda was speechless as Bill's vision began to take shape in her mind. Instead of making an immediate reply, she temporized by fussing with the munchies on the table. She replenished Bill's ice water and found some salted nuts to add to the offerings. When she returned to her seat, she encouraged Bill to fill in some details.

"Who is going to move in to such elaborate homes?" she asked. "I don't think there would be many from San Leandro who could afford to do so."

Bill's face brightened. "No, not for anyone who presently lives here. That's the genius of the project. It will attract a new population that will increase the size of the village by attracting new residents, and quite wealthy ones at that. They will bring new money and everybody will be better off. They will be seasonal, snow birds as they're often called, stay here over the winter months, and go back north for the summer, so they will be hiring summer caretakers to maintain their second homes."

Bill waxed eloquent and his flow of verbiage ran on. He slowed to a halt when he noticed that Yolanda's expression did not match his enthusiasm.

"Bill, I have to tell you that I'm not convinced," Yolanda said. "I would need to see a detailed plan: the financing, the marketing, the way the construction would fit into the landscape—all this needs to be clarified. Do you already have title to the property? What do you think would be the cost of those homes? There are lots of questions. From your description it's clear that the construction will be very expensive. How much? How much would you want me to provide? What would be our legal relationship, if I were to be a part of this?"

Bill came to understand that Yolanda, in her own way, could be as skeptical as the Gila Center investment banker. But he pushed on undeterred.

"Right now I'm just exploring this with you. I don't have a fixed business plan yet. I still have to obtain some of the land up there.

"I will need some upfront money. That's why I've come to you first. By the way, this is all in confidence. I don't want this plan to become public knowledge for obvious reasons. Someone might just hear some rumors and take advantage."

Bill blurted out his ask. "I'm looking for an investor with five million. However, if your Verde Gardens property were part of the project, your investment would be decreased accordingly."

Yolanda stiffened. "Are you telling me that this project would extend as far as Verde Gardens?"

"It might. The size still needs to be worked out. The first step will be to get a slice of land from the National Forest in order to take advantage of the slope. Without this, the project can't be done."

Yolanda fixed her eyes on Bill and raised her index finger to emphasize her words. "Bill, I want lots more information: a business plan, an implementation timetable, and an assurance that the slope can withstand construction without creating a landslide." She paused. "Then I still need time to think this over. I appreciate that you came to me first, and I will agree to keep your project in confidence."

Yolanda's words as well as her tone of voice put the matter on hold. There was not going to be a decision at this time.

Bill sank back in his chair. "Please think it over. I prefer to handle it all locally, and I am reluctant to seek financing from banks."

"I understand. I intend to talk with my financial advisor in the strictest confidence. I'm sure you will allow me to do so."

"Yes, of course. But please don't delay too long."

Yolanda had already risen. Bill reluctantly recognized that the discussion was over. He left the apartment with mixed feelings. He realized that he could hardly have expected an instant decision in a matter of this magnitude. Yolanda had challenged him to flesh out his plans long before he had done so in his own mind.

12

A WEEK LATER YOLANDA Alonso returned to the Cottonwood and carefully edged her old Land Rover into her parking space nearest to the employee entrance. A private parking space that would always be open for her was another one of the conditions she requested in return for financing the hotel. She let herself in with her own master key.

The desk clerk jumped to attention when she entered. "The Paraiso Room is ready for your lunch. Mr. Weiser is on his way. When he gets here, we will tell him you are waiting for him. Is there anything else I can get you?"

"No, no, Rita. I'll be fine. I've arrived a bit early on purpose."

Yolanda even chose the name of the room, El Paraiso, a name she had also given to the valley when it represented the northern terminus of the Alonso Ranch. Here the cattle were corralled before they were driven to the rail heads and military camps to the north.

She named the valley "El Paraiso" because of its beauty and the abundance of water that flowed down from Kallisto Wells and the Arena Gorge. She even built her own ranch house along the river, where she continues to make her home. It is nestled by itself in its own box canyon surrounded by flowering vines, shrubs, and desert succulents.

El Paraiso was the smaller of the Cottonwood's two meeting rooms. It contained a couch and two comfortable chairs on one side, a desk with internet connections along a wall, and a table with four chairs. The table was set for two. Yolanda fussed with the contents of her briefcase as she arranged the papers that she would be reviewing with Leon. He had handled her insurance matters for many years and, over time, she had come to rely on him for financial advice as well.

The phone buzzed. "Mr. Weiser has arrived."

"Please have him come right in."

Yolanda opened the conference room door and greeted Leon warmly. "Thanks for making the time to meet me here."

She took his outstretched hand and held it with both of hers. "How have you been?"

Not to be outdone in pleasantries, Leon replied, "It is always a good day when I have the pleasure of visiting with you."

Yolanda waved off Leon's compliment, even though her eyes shone with appreciation. "This is not just one of our routine lunches. I have a question about an investment, for which I need your advice. The other party involved is eager for a quick answer."

Leon's insurance business had diminished since he retired, but he made it a practice to maintain a relationship with the clients he had served over the years and did so by meeting them at the Cottonwood for lunch.

"My days are not as crowded as they used to be, but I still look forward to meeting old friends here." After a moment he added, "And I always look forward to seeing you, whether there is business to conduct or not."

"Thank you, Leon. You always know the right words to flatter an old lady."

Leon's eyes twinkled at her kind words. For a moment he even imagined that she was unintentionally flirtatious. She certainly made a memorable impression with her svelte figure and piercing eyes. Her eyesight had not diminished over the years, and she had no need for glasses, so when she directed her gaze directly at him, Leon would inevitably cast his glance aside. He stood expectantly, as if at a kind of attention, waiting for her to introduce what would be the agenda of the meeting.

Yolanda took a chair and motioned for Leon to do the same. She placed her palm down flat on a stack of notes and began. "You know that I've always been cautious and conservative with the goods that the Lord has seen fit to place into my hands."

Leon interrupted, "And very wisely, if I may say so."

Yolanda smiled and patted his arm. "We do our best, don't we? . . . And the results have not been too disappointing."

"Not only that but you haven't fallen for fly-by-night schemes either." Leon offered his respect with earnest admiration. "I recall the frenzy two decades ago when lots of fools lined up to sink their money into an oil boom that turned out to be a bust. I think that's when the Masterson Ranch went under and Bill Starret bought it. Masterson became a tenant and still is."

A waiter knocked. "May I take your lunch order now?"

Yolanda said, "I will have a taco and a bowl of whole beans." Leon had just opened the menu when Yolanda suggested, "I recommend their burrito with a mild salsa."

Leon nodded as he closed the menu.

Yolanda continued, "But please give us a half hour. For now bring ice water and a bottle of your white wine."

She returned to the issue at hand. "Leon, you know that it has always been my first priority to see to the prosperity of San Leandro."

Leon agreed fervently. "Yes, the Cottonwood would not be here without your investment, neither would Lightner's sawmill, Verde Gardens, the food bank, and the open space along River Road."

Yolanda's intensity softened as she gratefully accepted the recognition that Leon gave her. "I've always wanted to use my money to keep the village moving and to provide meaningful employment for people here."

After a few moments of silence as if in regret for goals not yet achieved, she continued. "Meanwhile a couple of my municipal bonds are maturing and I need to find a place for those funds. You know that I stagger my investments, so there will be more next year. The recent crash has lowered returns so much that I'm thinking about better rates."

"Well there are any number of good stocks . . ." Leon said.

"No, no, Leon. I am staying away from trying to beat the market. Years ago I could invest in a company that actually made something useful and employed people to do so. Now they seem to be making a casino game out of the funds they manage. Nothing useful is actually produced, and the gaming makes the people whose money is being wagered even poorer. God did not entrust the goods of this world to my care so that I could squander them for no purpose other than greed."

Leon did not anticipate Yolanda's sudden fervor. "But you do have a right to a return on your investments," he assured her.

"I've always done well enough, I think. Often it has been with your advice. Whatever I own that is beyond what I need is put to beneficial use. It's sort of like surface water in a way. When you capture it and put to beneficial use, it becomes your right to have. But if it is just wasted, then that's wrong and your ownership actually ceases." She hoped to get Leon's agreement with this tentative argument, but he became silent as if he himself had been indicted.

A tap on the door signaled the arrival of the waiter with wine and water. After pouring both glasses, he added, "The chef is happy to serve a small salad if you like."

"Yes, but give us another fifteen minutes, please." Yolanda dismissed him with a wave.

"Leon, I have been approached by a local resident to become a principal investor in a development project. I would like your advice on his idea. I promised that I would maintain total confidentiality. I must ask you to do the same; otherwise I won't be able to tell you anything more."

"All our conversations are confidential. Does this go beyond the usual professional confidentiality?"

"It does in this way. He asked that I not only keep everything to myself, but also refrain from making any use of the information. You need to agree to this as well."

"Okay, I guess I can agree to that." After a short hesitation, he continued with a proviso. "Yolanda, I'm sure you're aware that I have a number of clients to whom I am bound to give my best advice. This includes the village itself, because I handle its insurance needs. I can't exclude the possibility that the interests of one of my clients might be in conflict with the interests of another at some time in the future. All I can commit to is that I won't make use of the information you give me to cause any disadvantage."

Yolanda appreciated Leon's careful remarks. "I can't ask for more than that."

After a moment Yolanda said, "The investment opportunity comes from Bill Starret."

"Really!" Leon's expression of astonishment was somewhat artful, for there was no one else in San Leandro who would be likely to launch a large development project. "I know him well. What kind of project does he have in mind that would need your investment? You know that he paid you a compliment by naming his development after your original name for this valley, by calling it Paradise Acres."

"So he did. As for his new project, it's a big one; probably larger than I can handle and I don't rightly know the full extent of it."

"Well, then Bill must really have big ideas in mind."

"He certainly does. I can't really describe it in detail because he hasn't figured out the details himself. He just gave me an overview of his concept. He plans to build upscale houses up under the rim rock of the Arena Valley escarpment. He said it would be designed to imitate the cliff dwellings of the Anasazi."

Leon uttered a low whistle. "That certainly sounds ambitious. How does he plan to anchor houses on that steep incline? That would be quite an engineering feat."

"It sounds crazy to me. But then I admit to being old fashioned. That's why I wanted to talk it over with you. I objected to the cost of these houses. I asked him if he thought that there would be any San Leandro residents who could afford to buy them."

Leon said nothing, but his expression made clear that Yolanda had hit upon the critical question.

"He replied that the homes would not be for locals but for wealthy seasonal visitors from northern cities. From his descriptions it became clear that a buyer's move-in costs would be in the million dollar range. He insisted that this would be a huge stimulus for the village economy."

"It would certainly be out of the price range of everyone that lives here now."

"Well, he wants me to invest. He said that he might want my Verde Gardens to be part of the project, so that it might actually disappear. He would offer to buy it or count it as part of my investment. In addition, he suggested that I commit five million at the outset and become a fifty-fifty partner."

Leon, who had been doodling on his notepad, dropped his ballpoint in astonishment. He gulped the last of his glass of wine and set it down carelessly so that it nearly rolled off the table. He recovered sufficiently to register his immediate reaction. "If you want my advice, don't commit a cent until you have a detailed business plan."

Yolanda felt reassured by Leon's reaction. "Well, that's exactly what has been my feeling as well. It's always been my practice to invest locally—you know that—but I have some trouble seeing how this project fits in with our local needs.

"Bill pooh-poohed this concern. His idea is that we need to open up the village to outside money; and he said that his project would bring in lots of wealthy northerners. What do you think about his reasoning?"

"I have to admit that I prefer the tried and true. So you can take my opinion with a grain of salt. But let me say what I think." Leon paused to gather his thoughts. "Proponents of artificial growth—and I call this artificial because it doesn't rise organically from within our village—never seem to factor in the longterm implications of expansion plans. There will be subsequent costs that the rest of the village will need to bear: infrastructure like roads, expanded village services, utilities, and so forth. In addition there's always the question of finding sufficient water for a big development. Finally there are the intangibles: the village will be different if Bill's vision comes about. Do we want that kind of village?"

The waiter appeared with their lunches. He refreshed the wine glasses and inquired whether anything else was needed.

Yolanda responded with a wave of the hand, "I won't need anything else." She turned to Leon who also waved his hand dismissively.

By now, Yolanda had come to a decision. "You've helped quite a bit, Leon. It's true that Bill's project would bring employment opportunities, but most of it would go to outside contractors. Certainly no one here could handle the specialized engineering that Bill's project would require. Then there's the fate of Verde Gardens, which is one of my favorites, and I am reluctant to see it sacrificed to make room for vacation homes. San Leandro needs a larger business base. I would like to see a grocery and hardware, but most people prefer to drive to Gila Center to shop. I am considering starting a hardware store with the funds that I have available this year.

"I will tell Bill that I will not invest in his project until I can look at a detailed business plan. Furthermore, I will let him know that I have misgivings about how well his proposed development will fit in with the present character of the village."

13

WILLIS CARR LANDED HIS chopper at the bottom of an arroyo that ran down from an eastern spur of the same ridge that overlooked San Leandro but eight miles to the north.

"Here we are," Willis turned to Tony Friedson, the owner of Two Gun Ranch, who had hired him.

Tony's calloused fingers struggled to loosen his shoulder harness. Tall, thin, and muscular with a deeply tanned face and furrowed brow, he gestured at the five-acre tank that lay in front of them. "See, there's only some mud and not a bit of water. I came down here last week on my ATV and found that it was drying up. I want you to take me up along these ridges to see if there is a way to capture more water. That's why I asked you to bring the chopper."

"Okay, tell me where to go," Willis said. "How much land do you have up here?"

"I've got twenty sections. Two of my own and the rest leased from the BLM. Normally that should be enough for 250 head of cattle at the rate of fifty acres each. There's enough range, but I'm short of water."

"That's a really big spread," Willis said.

"It is, but I'm already trucking in water to a steel tank. It doesn't take long before that eats up most of my profits."

"So you want me to fly over those ridges to see if there's an arroyo that can be made to drain into your earthen tank?"

"That's the plan. I know it will take a pipeline. The ridges are too high for surface drainage."

"When there's a good winter rain I've generally been able to make it until the spring calves can be moved to high pastures near the Vermillion

Range. Then I just need to bring in water for the brood stock until the monsoons start. But this year it hasn't worked out."

"There's another arroyo further up the slope and when we fly up there I want you to take elevations. If the ridge is not too high to bury a pipe under it, I'll ask Carmen Montez to give me an estimate."

"How about a deep well?"

"You'd have to go down five hundred feet to get water and even then it's still a gamble," Tony replied.

"So what are you going to do if the pipeline won't work?" Willis asked.

"Sell most of the herd. It's the only choice I've got," Tony lamented. "When the rains return, I'll try to build it back up."

IV

September 2016

14

BILL STARRET FIDGETED IN nervous expectation in the spacious waiting room of the Phoenix law firm of Mulcton, Killian, and Smart. He finished his second refill of coffee that a solicitous receptionist kept offering. The lobby was far more elaborate than the functional furnishings of Alma Fortner's, his hometown attorney at San Leandro. Bill tucked in his tie and brushed imaginary lint from the sleeve of his jacket.

His worry that a local attorney would put confidentiality at risk with even the possibility of a casual or unintentional disclosure of his plans led him to a big-city law firm.

The receptionist approached him. "Mr. Killian will see you now. May I take your cup?"

At the receptionist's knock Artemus Killian stepped around his tidy desk. Dressed casually but in excellent taste, he greeted Starret with an unctuous smile and grasped his hand while embracing Bill's arm with the other. Pointing to an ornate conference table with four chairs, he said, "On behalf of the Mulcton firm, I am pleased to welcome you. I hope that your trip here has been a pleasant one."

Bill, feeling embarrassed about his baggy suit, sat down without comment.

"I believe this is the first time that we've been able to represent you," Killian remarked to initiate the conversation.

Bill had rehearsed in his mind repeatedly how he would present his case, but now it seemed to be a jumble, leaving him without a sure way to begin. "Well, sir, I am here to request your help in obtaining . . . I'm a contractor and developer in San Leandro, a small town south of here . . . actually I have been quite successful over the years . . .of course, not in any way like the developers around here. . ."

57

Killian interrupted with a casual wave of the hand. "We have done a little research, as you would expect, in preparation for our meeting today, and we know about your impressive development at Paradise Acres. There is no doubt about your success in the business. Do you want to expand? Do you have another project, in which we could serve your needs better than the representation you have had in the past?"

"Yes, exactly." Bill finally got his thoughts in a row. "I have plans for an ambitious development project. The first step would be to identify properties within the Verde National Forest that are still in private hands and can be acquired by someone like me. My purpose is to do a land swap with the Forest. Therefore I need to present them with properties that are attractive, so much so that they would be strongly motivated to approve the swap for land I need overlooking the village of San Leandro."

"I see. Why would you choose our firm to represent you in this?"

Bill could answer this question forthrightly. "Quite simply because you are not local. I want to keep these transactions entirely secret because I don't want to take the chance that a local law firm might inadvertently reveal my plans. That could lead to a conflict of interest with other parties, which a local firm might also be representing."

"Are you saying that the mere disclosure of your plans has the potential of interfering with their accomplishment?

"Maybe. I'm concerned that some villagers don't want any changes."

"If local opposition is a concern, then I must insist on total candor on your part or we may not be able to represent you. Why is confidentiality so important that you would seek the services of a firm unfamiliar to you and many miles distant?"

Bill was caught. He hoped to gloss over explicit details for now, so he replied in a way that kept his reasons for confidentiality conventional.

"Well, you know that in real estate when a project is rumored, the news spreads magically and prices rise accordingly. In fact, I want to make these acquisitions through a shell company called Star Holdings, which you can set up for me as another measure of anonymity. Of course, the ultimate reason to keep this quiet is that I expect some people in the village are likely to oppose my plans."

"I believe I'm beginning to get the picture." Killian pushed back in his chair and raised his hand for emphasis. "Two questions come to mind. First, why would there be opposition to your acquisition of this Forest land? Second, how much do you expect to spend?"

"The anticipated opposition would probably come from the usual suspects," Bill said. "Those who oppose development on principle and who want to retain the small town atmosphere they profess to love. Surely you are aware of the usual objections that are made to developers."

Killian listened closely to catch any hints of what Bill might be trying to conceal. "In this area you will also need to guarantee a hundred-year supply of water. Is this a problem that you might be facing?"

Bill said, "I own property from which I can draw water. This shouldn't be an issue. As for the value of Forest land for the swap, that's hard to say. Once word is out that a development is underway, prices tend to double. I hope to manage with about a million."

Killian continued with his fact finding. "Will there be a need for improvements in infrastructure? Do you anticipate any difficulties in obtaining roads, sewer connections, electrical service, etc.?"

Bill anticipated this question, and by now his mind was agile and sharp.

"That's really a zoning issue and is a part of any development project. I have been in this situation before. My company does the platting, does the engineering, and strikes a compromise with city government about the installation of roads and utilities. It's always a dance in which each side tries to come up with the best possible deal, but both sides want the project to go through. The village wants a larger tax base; the developer wants to sell lots. It's just a matter of coming to a win-win compromise."

Bill noticed that this little recitation caused a smile of recognition from Killian.

Killian summarized his take on Starret's proposal. "I believe we will be able to assist you. I will present it to the partners at our weekly meeting. The search for salable Forest land will be subcontracted to our usual realtor. The document that spells out our relationship and also sets forth the proposed fee schedule will be sent within a few days. Since you are new to our firm, we will require a retainer of two thousand dollars payable whether you accept our services or not. It would be advisable for you to make that payment today so that we can get started."

Starret gathered that Killian would make a positive recommendation to the partners. He rose, accepted Killian's hand, and left the room. As he passed the receptionist, she beckoned him to wait. She put down the phone. "Mr. Killian suggests that you will be paying your retainer now?"

Bill signed his credit card slip and received a smile from the receptionist. He left with a brisk gait that matched his confidence.

15

AFTER CLASS ERNESTO WAITED to speak to Chris. "Can you drive out to the desert with me to replace the water jugs?"

"Sure. After you're done working at Verde Gardens, I'll pick you up. Maybe Claudia will come along too."

"I hope so."

They visited the desert rescue site once again and left jugs of water to mark the place where Ernesto's two companions had died. Then they meandered a little further into the desert than usual. Ernesto noticed something tied to the branch of a juniper.

He called Chris and Claudia over. "Look at this. There's something tied to this bush."

Claudia peered at the contrivance. "It's a camera. Not a point-and-shoot, but a motion camera."

Ernesto, still bewildered, asked. "You mean it's supposed to take a picture if something moves in front of it?"

"Exactly," Chris said.

Ernesto doffed his cap. "If I wave my cap in front of it, will we hear it click?"

"Try it."

"I didn't hear anything. Maybe there isn't supposed to be a click."

Claudia suddenly grasped the significance of the camera. She grabbed Ernesto's arm and pulled him away. "That camera's here to take your picture. See where it's aimed? Right where we left the jug of water last week."

"Why? What's special about a jug of water?"

"Not the jug," Claudia said. "Somebody wants to get your picture!"

"Who?"

"When Chris found you, did he mention anyone else?"

"No, I don't think so." Ernesto still hadn't drawn the obvious conclusion. "If we took a good look at the camera, would that give us a clue?"

"No, that's not going to answer my question," Claudia said. "But take a look."

Ernesto leaned in close. "There's the brand name. But look at the strap. It's blind stamped with a pattern of suns and moons."

Claudia became insistent. "Make sure that you never face it." She grabbed the sleeve of his shirt to move him aside. "Stay here and don't move. I'm going back to get my sun hat with a flap in back."

Claudia returned while still adjusting her hat. "Do you have a bandana or something to put over your head?

"I do." Ernesto replied. It began to dawn on him why Claudia became obsessed with covering up. "Somebody is interested in the place where Chris found me?"

"That's right. Always keep your back to the camera. Whoever left it will be more confused than ever, because he'll only see our backs and won't know who we are."

16

Ernesto changed his work schedule at Verde Gardens to meet with the extension agent from the university at his proposed garden site.

He stopped at Claudia's clinic. "I've invited Colin Foster from the extension service to go over the garden plans. Can you be there too—tomorrow at ten?"

"Definitely."

"I know you are interested in making plots available for the community; but this meeting will be mostly about water and soil enhancement. Nevertheless, you should be in on what we decide."

Claudia agreed. "Water's the critical issue. If you can't solve that, nothing else matters."

Because Colin Foster was unfamiliar with San Leandro, he arrived at 9:30 to get a feel for the location. His directions led him to a barren high desert scene that seemed unsuitable for any kind of agriculture, so he decided that he must have missed a turn and rechecked his directions.

While Foster puzzled over his directions, Ernesto and his companions arrived. Foster asked, "I'm supposed to meet Ernesto Ramirez about a garden project. Can you direct me, I'm lost."

"I'm Ernesto. You must be Colin Foster." Ernesto held out his hand. "Meet Chris O'Brien and Claudia Gomez."

Foster, still confused, said, "Pleased to meet you."

He assumed that he would be led to more promising ground. "Let's take a look at the land that you want to convert to a garden," Foster began. "I want to see the site so that I have a better idea of what you have in mind."

Ernesto waved his arm to encompass the desert underfoot. His optimism resided in his imagination rather than in evidence on the ground.

Foster restrained himself from giving voice to his disappointment. Their walk took them to the banks of Vasquez Creek, whose flow was diverted to irrigate a small kitchen garden.

Foster inquired perfunctorily in a way that hid his misgivings. "Where does this creek come from? Is its flow constant and dependable?"

"There's going to be a lot more water than this," Ernesto said hurriedly. "When we are finished out here, I want to detail my plans for water harvesting. Obviously, it will be the main problem we need to address."

"That's an understatement," Foster said. He kicked the soil with his boot to expose a dusty inch of coarse sand. "The texture of the ground is your next problem, maybe equally as difficult as the water supply."

"I know," Ernesto replied, as if subjected to an oral exam and found to be wanting. "I have a plan for soil enhancement that I would like to go over with you as well."

Foster's skepticism remained high, but he could not help but be impressed by Ernesto's spirit. "You do have one advantage; your site lends itself to terracing, so you can maximize whatever supply of water you may be able to obtain." Foster made this small concession, even though he couldn't imagine that the site could be adequately irrigated.

Ernesto's reply remained spirited. "Exactly, that's why I intend to do laser leveling. All the available water will be put to use; nothing will be lost to overflow."

"How big is this going to be?"

Chris spoke up. "I've got two hundred acres and I've made half of it available for this project. I'm sure that's more than enough."

Foster chuckled in agreement with the obvious.

Ernesto clarified, "We're going to start small, if for no other reason than the cost. I am interested in developing a production garden, but we will also be using the site as a demonstration project, in which we can introduce people to growing their own produce."

These words caused Foster to shoot him an incredulous look. Charitable motivations were not something he ordinarily encountered. It solidified his determination that Ernesto would need a realistic business plan. He fully expected that the recognition of economic necessities would spell an end to the whole idea, so he replied guardedly, "Your plans need to address how you expect this project to be financially viable."

Hardly dismayed, Ernesto said, "I have a job at Verde Gardens. I know that this garden won't be self-supporting right away, so I'll be investing in it from my salary and especially with my own labor. However, I do think that it can break even, once it's established."

"I need to see your projections on costs and income," Foster remarked dryly.

Foster's clients were typically agricultural, forestry, and ranching industries whose business models involved large-scale operations with enormous assets. For them issues of sustainability and organic practices—to say nothing of concerns for the poor—never entered the discussion.

He was also aware that recent research had shown the limitations of exploitive practices, though he was hard-pressed to come up with any project in which such concerns had been forthrightly addressed. Ernesto's vision was a novel experience for him, and possibly an eye-opener. By the time they returned to Ernesto's former room in Chris's shack, which he had converted into a work room, Foster had decided to hear Ernesto out and give the project a chance. If a market garden was possible on this site, he felt it could be done almost anywhere.

They made their way inside, where Ernesto had cleared some working space. There were maps, drawings, calculations, and action plans spread over the table. When they were settled, Ernesto addressed the issue of water first.

"We have a two hundred acre piece of land here, which Chris acquired years ago. At present, except for a small kitchen garden, where I'm experimenting, this land does not produce anything of value. However, it does have potential. I believe that there will be enough water if the supply is managed effectively, namely by capturing all the runoff. The soil quality is typical desert and needs considerable enhancement. Water harvesting and efficient water usage will be the key." Ernesto had Colin's attention. "May I go through water harvesting calculations step by step? Interrupt when you have a question, or if our plans seem to be misguided."

Foster responded guardedly, "Okay, let's see what you've come up with."

Ernesto began systematically, "Two figures are crucial: the total annual rainfall and the extent of the drainage area. The annual rainfall figure which is most often given for this area is twelve inches. For my purposes, I have taken a more conservative figure, namely eleven inches."

"Do your figures come from weather service records?" Foster asked mainly to get an impression in his own mind about how thorough Ernesto had been.

"Yes, I looked at the fifty-year records from Gila Center just north of here; they report an average annual rainfall of twelve inches. About half of this amount falls during the summer monsoons, and the other half during the winter months. I have set out some rain gauges on the property to get local readings. These have not yet yielded results, but I expect that they will be about the same as Gila Center."

Foster said, "Tell me about that little creek, does it have a continuous flow, and how large is the drainage area which flows into it?"

"Vasquez Creek is continuous because it comes from a naturally flowing spring just beyond the Arena Rim. Its source is at the southernmost extreme of a half-mile seepage called Kallisto Wells. For the rest of the drainage area, I used a topographical map and hiked the slope above us. My calculations show eight square miles."

"Okay, that gives us the critical figures: eleven inches of rainfall and eight square miles." Foster slowly became comfortable with Ernesto's thoroughness.

"There is a far more critical calculation that needs to be made," Ernesto said. "What percentage of the water that falls on the drainage area becomes actual runoff?"

How Ernesto articulated this variable impressed Foster, who said, "You need to go one step further, what percentage of the runoff can also be harvested and put to use?"

"I came up with some numbers that seem reasonable to me. I would like you to review them with me."

"Sure, let's hear it," Foster said.

Ernesto continued, "Runoff is only a percentage of the total rainfall, and this percentage figure is determined by lots of variables: the type of precipitation—rain or snow—how heavily the rain falls, the amount of rain in any given event, how long the rain continues, the distance the water must flow to get to the harvesting point, the amount of existing soil moisture when the rain falls. I'm sure that there are still other variables."

"I think you have the main ones," Foster said.

Ernesto put special emphasis on his next calculations by pointing them out one by one with the eraser of his pencil. "Of all these variables the most important is the amount of rainfall at any given time. I have examined Gila Center records and made these assumptions when calculating runoff: There will be one rain event each year that totals one and a half inches, three rains of one inch, eight rains of one-half inch, and about ten events of a quarter inch or less."

Foster nodded appreciatively while fumbling in his pocket for a calculator.

Ernesto said, "I am assuming that an inch and a half rain will yield a runoff of twenty-five percent. Similarly I assume a fifteen-percent yield when it rains one inch, and a five-percent yield when it rains a half inch. There will be no runoff at all when it rains less than a half inch. By comparison, the

U.S. Geological Service estimates three tenths of runoff for every inch of rain. That's why I think my figures are conservative."

Foster's expression indicated his respect for Ernesto's research. "These look like reasonable numbers."

His words of support lit up Ernesto's face and urged him onward. "We have an eight square mile drainage area. According to my calculations, this will yield an annual runoff of about 250 thousand gallons. The maximum single runoff would be 10,890 square feet in the case of an inch and a half event. So the reservoir that we need should be that size, namely twenty-five by sixty feet with a depth of seven feet. This amounts to 10,500 square feet. Hopefully, the tank will be replenished by rainfall at about the same rate that it is being used up."

Foster interrupted, "Have you factored in any water loss from leakage and from evaporation?"

"I haven't done so because all our calculations have been conservative. I wanted to keep the reservoir as small as possible, because it represents the most expensive part of the construction. Furthermore, an overflow from the reservoir would not actually result in a loss of water because it would be channeled to fruit trees, which will be planted outside the leveled plots of the garden area. There is one further conservative feature of our estimates. I don't include the continuous flow of the Vasquez." Then Ernesto asked, "Does the university extension have statistics on the percentage of runoff specifically for desert conditions? I'm under the impression that desert soils result in greater levels of runoff. If the USGS cites a three-tenths percentage figure, could it be even greater in the case of desert conditions?"

"I'll look into it," Foster said.

Ernesto said, "I'd like some help with the design of the garden. Should the beds be six feet wide with an access path of three feet between them? The length of the beds will depend on the size and scope of the total garden project.

"Drip lines will be buried and run the length of the beds. Two questions occur to me: how many parallel drip lines are needed in beds six feet wide, and how deep should they be buried? Would the depth differ depending on the type of crop? I would appreciate help on all of this."

Foster felt challenged by the detailed data that Ernesto requested. "That sort of information is usually gained from experience. I don't think that any experiments explicitly address your question."

Ernesto had still other questions. "Does the choice of the crops we grow make a difference? Is water usage significantly different depending on the crop? We assume that our soil is alkaline. What is the best plan for soil enhancement? Naturally we will need to do soil testing. What else do we need to know about our soil?"

Foster agreed to find out what he could. The project fascinated him, and he decided to give it serious attention. "Let's meet again in two weeks. When do you plan to start the development work on the site?"

"We expect to begin work on water harvesting when the winter rains begin. But first, the size of the earthen tank has to be established. That's why the water research has to come first."

"Okay," Foster agreed. "There's not much time to waste. In two weeks then."

Foster departed, and as he drove along the dirt road to the highway, he muttered to himself, "You never know what's going to come up next."

V

OCTOBER 2016

17

BILL STARRET CHOSE TO drive his F-350 Lariat rather than his usual vintage Lincoln to sell his development plans to a local rancher whose shortage of water had become a critical concern for him. The truck was his construction vehicle and construction was on his mind. His boot already rested on the truck's running board, when he looked up to the rim rocks that loomed high above. In his mind he already saw how the summit would appear from below, after his houses had been built. A wave of self-confidence washed over him as he began the trip that would make or break his plans.

When Yolanda Alonso disappointed him by saying that she would not become an investor, only one person remained who had the means to become a partner in Anasazi Vistas.

The clattering of the 6.7-liter diesel engine pleased him as he rehearsed how he would convince Tony Friedson to become his partner, and his confidence rose as he reflected on his strong closing argument based on Tony's water shortage.

His drive took him along the banks of the Arena River, where the cottonwoods were turning color and lent a yellowish hue to the entire roadway. While the fall of the year was usually without rain, the ancient cottonwoods that populated the river bank always found moisture, even though there would be no water on the surface, by seeking it underground through the underlying river rock and gravel.

Bill Starret passed the short circular drive called River Street and pulled off to the side to indulge his nostalgia. Here, along the river were the rotting remains of the ponderosa posts that his grandfather had set in place to hold the Alonso Ranch corrals.

Bill's pride of accomplishment was aroused as he looked downstream at the results of his first construction project, where he had confined the river within a straight ditch, had removed the obstructing river rock, and had drained the lagoon that had once served as the Alonso Ranch's water tank. He turned around again to survey the rim above and visualized the construction that would transform the view.

Bill could not fail to notice the majesty of the cottonwoods. Under their shade rope swings had been fashioned for the delight of the village's children. Bill mused that his life has never been as effortless as this scene represented. He always struggled to subdue a reluctant nature rather than revel in its enjoyment.

The purpose of his trip today underscored this philosophy. He believed that while God created the natural world, he left it undeveloped, and the owner of every patch of dirt should strive to enhance it to achieve its highest potential.

Bill's guiding principle held that the pursuit of profit squared completely with the fulfillment of life's purposes.

He resolved to convince Tony Friedson at Two Gun Ranch to buy into his latest development plan. There was no time to waste because he had received papers from Mulcton, Killian, and Smart that required his signature.

Bill approached the gate to Tony's ranch with its two distinctive uprights in the shape of Winchester rifles. These supported the crossbeam with the legend "Two Gun Ranch" fashioned out of wrought iron. Then came a long driveway lined with alligator cedars. Bill had made the drive many times, so he knew to circle the ranch house and park next to the small building that Tony called his bunkhouse, where he preferred to conduct his business.

At the bunkhouse door Bill lifted a device shaped like a miniature post maul that clanged down on the head of a stylized metal fence post.

"Come on in," commanded a gravelly voice from inside. "If you're a friend and come in peace, you don't need to knock."

Tony's greeting, while unconventional, was entirely sincere. Tony regarded a handshake as being as sacred as a notarized deed.

Warmly welcomed, Bill smiled broadly when Tony pointed to a chair at the head of the table.

"I know you're here on business, but I don't want to be rude by not offering you something. Can Bonnie bring some tea and lemonade? You know that I don't keep alcohol."

"Yes, I remember well. That's why I brought some bourbon."

Bill knew that Tony's grandfather had paid dearly because he had been addicted to the hard stuff, and this was the reason Tony held firmly to sobriety.

Tony used an intercom to have Bonnie bring the refreshments from the ranch house. Dressed in western gear, she brought an ice bucket, a pitcher of iced tea, and assorted snacks. Tony poured a large tumbler of tea while Bill helped himself to two fingers of bourbon over ice and corralled some cashews.

"I have a business venture to propose." Bill paused for emphasis and then continued cryptically. "It's not something that I would share with anyone else, and you'll soon understand why. I know I can count on your discretion, but nevertheless I must insist that none of this conversation pass beyond the walls of this room."

Tony nodded eagerly but said nothing.

"I'm launching a housing development that is far and away the largest I've ever undertaken. It requires resources beyond my means. I hope you will agree to become my partner. There are risks involved but, I assure you, the rewards will be considerable."

Tony still made no reply but leaned forward with heightened curiosity.

With another sip of bourbon Bill took a deep breath. "I will sign a contract with a Phoenix law firm to obtain parcels within the Verde National Forest in the name of a shell company I'm calling Star Holdings. I want to use these properties to do a land swap with the Verde National Forest for property along the Arena Rim above San Leandro. When I combine this Forest land with the holdings that have been in my family for generations, I will have what I need for the development project I'm planning. Naturally the Forest land I intend to acquire to swap for the Arena Rim must be of sufficient acreage and value that the National Forest people will not hesitate to make the swap."

"This sounds like an ambitious project," Tony said, voicing his interest.

Bill played his trump card. "Listen to this. I am holding out the possibility that you will be able to restore your ranch to its original borders, and also bring back access to water from the Kallisto."

Tony's face flushed with a rush of emotion. "Bill, don't say that unless you mean it! You know that my grandfather made me promise on his deathbed to put his ranch back together again. It's a promise that I haven't been able to keep. Are you sure that your plan might actually get it done?"

"Yes, I am, Tony. But you will need to listen to the whole plan before I can expect you to believe me."

Tony settled back in his chair, absorbed by Bill's boosterism. "Okay, my friend, tell me more."

Bill refreshed his glass with more ice and another finger of booze. He outlined the complexities of his plan while minimizing the juggling of many variables that needed to fall in place one after the other. "Like I said, I need to acquire land within the National Forest and use it to make a swap. The Phoenix law firm will use a realtor to identify this property. The legal owner will be Star Holdings and the cost will be in the neighborhood of a million.

"Completing this swap is the first critical step, and I may need to rely on some political influence to get it done. I know that the Forest Service is always suspicious when they are approached about a land swap."

Tony's face clouded. "So if it all depends on the Forest; can we rely on them?"

Bill ignored Tony's comment and pressed on. "Once we complete the swap, we do the platting and the marketing. I have a tentative name for it. How about something like Anasazi Vistas?"

Tony's face flushed with enthusiasm. "That's brilliant, Bill. I can see your ads. Live in the style of Native Americans—all wholesome and natural—but with every amenity that money can buy. That's a great marketing brand, and it will appeal to the folks with money who are searching for something trendy and original. Bill, you amaze me. I can just see the Arena Rim transformed from a barren waste to a showcase for people who want to own something really special."

Tony's enthusiasm had reached a peak, and it left no doubt that Bill had won him over.

Bill turned aside the compliment and had another splash of bourbon while continuing his sales pitch. "The relationship and timing between funding and development will be like the timing of a trapeze act. We raise money from sales at the same time we start construction, if not before.

"This is where it gets tricky. Cash flow will be critical, but I have a plan that I will get to in a minute. Fortunately my grandpa's homestead is blessed with an extraordinarily shallow water table. So there will be no problem about water. All we have to do is drill a bigger well and bury a pipeline to the edge of the mesa."

"You've even got the water problem licked," Tony said.

"Yep, it's a piece of luck that I owe to my granddad, Josiah, and his homestead."Bill grabbed a plat map. "Let's look at the land holdings from here to there. Your ranch borders Masterson's, next to him is Verde Gardens; then Paradise Acres; beyond that is the Forest land I want to acquire. I hope to eventually get control of all of these properties."

Tony became pensive. "Bill, I've got to tell you how my ranch and Masterson's came to be. Two Gun Ranch used to own everything from here to Verde Gardens—that's before the Gardens even existed. My grandfather lost the best part of the ranch in a hand of poker. He was into his liquor at the time, so he wasn't clear about just what he had wagered. In the lawsuit that followed some of the witnesses maintained that only a portion of the ranch was at risk, but naturally no records existed. After all, it was just a card game. Our attorney tried to make the case that he wasn't *sui compos*, legal jargon for being able to make a legally binding decision. Everybody could see that he was drunk.

"The judge asked the lawyers to try for an out of court settlement. In the end he lost what became the Masterson ranch, and it included the water rights to the flow of the Kallisto Wells. He had paid five hundred dollars for those water rights in the 1890s—a tidy sum in those days. He lost all of the Kallisto water, and what I have left is range land that has no flowing water, so that during dry spells I'm forced to buy it."

Bill knew all this history and had tailored his proposal to capitalize on it. "Tony, the key lies not in the Masterson Ranch, but in Verde Gardens. I've done some investigating and believe we can get Verde Gardens by quietly buying shares in it. The Alonso family took the company public about fifteen years ago, and the major stock holders are still family members. Yolanda Alonso actually owns forty percent of it. She is now eighty-six years old and has not been active in its management for a long time. I suggest that we purchase any stock that becomes available. When we gain a substantial interest, we can approach Yolanda to make an offer." Bill continued, "One more detail and a key one: we can use Verde Gardens as a cash cow by borrowing against it to fund our development costs. We park all our debt there, and eventually we let it go bankrupt and walk away."

Imperceptibly, Bill had begun to speak in the plural, as if there were no doubt that Tony was on board as a partner.

Tony struggled to put all of Bill's plans into perspective. "Let me get this straight. We get control of the Gardens and convert it into a cash cow. You already have the assured water that you need. When the project succeeds, you will return the Masterson Ranch to me, and I can fulfill what I promised my grandfather."

"Right. There will be some tricky times when we need to funnel funds from one corporation to another. Those legal minds in Phoenix can handle that kind of stuff; they're charging me enough. We might even consider cutting them in on a percentage basis instead of a fee for services."

The whole scheme inflamed Tony's gambling spirit, a character trait that he clearly inherited. "Bill, we're both experienced in business. Let's say we spend some time putting down what we think our partnership should be like. Let's meet again a week from today. Then we'll see how things look. If both of us think we have a deal, we go on to the next step."

"That's fine by me," Bill agreed. He finished his bourbon.

Tony rose from his chair and smiled broadly. "I will see you next week, my friend." He stretched out his hand, and Bill was sure that Star Holdings would soon be a reality.

18

In the evening after the sun had set, and a pink glow still shone in the west, Claudia and Ernesto drove to Chris's shack. They could see a light in his bedroom, and his pickup was parked by the front door, so they were certain he was home. Claudia had a great deal of respect for Chris and tolerated his every idiosyncrasy, but the thought came to her that he was best living by himself. His habits would be a problem in any tidy neighborhood with homeowner covenants. After Ernesto got his own place at Verde Gardens, the appearance of the shack became, if anything, even more disorderly. Though Ernesto was grateful for the hospitality the shack had provided him, he was relieved to have his own place.

The discovery of the camera raised baffling uncertainties about what had gone on in the desert. They both suspected that Chris knew more than he had told them and could solve the mystery of the camera.

Ernesto put it straight-out. "Chris was the only one who was there; if there's any reason for the camera, he would be the one who would know what it is."

Claudia agreed. "He probably knows who has a reason to get your picture."

Claudia knocked on the door and waited patiently for him to answer.

Chris was not accustomed to visitors; he opened the door a crack and peered out cautiously. When he recognized them his face brightened. "Come in. It's great you came here, instead of me coming to your place all the time," he said. "Of course, you have more room than I do. Pardon the mess here."

Chris cleared some tools off the small couch and pulled up a folding chair for himself. "What's up?"

"We went out to the desert to leave water like we usually do. You may remember a good sized juniper just a little ways from where you found me. When we noticed something unusual, we walked over to take a closer look, and found that someone had hung a camera on one of its branches. We didn't touch it. It was aimed directly at where you found me, and where we have been leaving a water jug. Claudia recognized that it was a motion activated camera."

Ernesto asked, "Do you know anything about who would want to go to the trouble to get a picture of us out there? And why?"

Chris knew that this day was bound to come sooner or later. Originally he hadn't told Ernesto everything he knew, for he didn't want to give him any reason for anger or revenge, not yet sure that he could trust his temperament. However, by now he was confident that Ernesto could handle the entire story. Even so, he decided to proceed carefully, for he knew that the officer who had abandoned Ernesto, Unruh, was now the sheriff of San Ysidro County. Chris began with a question.

"Maybe you have the answer to this mystery yourself and aren't aware that you do. Was there anyone else out there other than you, Marcelino, and Jorge?"

Ernesto was puzzled. "What do you mean? I was unconscious when you found me; at least that's what I have always thought, and I have no memory of stopping, lying down, or anything like that. The last thing I remember is being tired, hot, and thirsty."

"So no one approached you, talked to you, or you to him? Do you recall anything that might now seem like a dream or a ghost? You could have been lying there for a long time.

"Claudia, you're a nurse, do you think that he could have been calling out for help, that someone might have heard him, but would have no memory of it now?"

"I suppose it's possible, but then why would someone who heard him not make any effort to save him?"

There was no logical response to Claudia's question. Chris knew that it was time to reveal what he knew.

"I didn't tell you everything about your rescue because I wanted to make it easier for you to adjust to life here. Remember, you were a stranger to me when I found you. I didn't know how you would react if you knew everything that happened. Now I know that you are not a person who would want to get even or take revenge." Chris was about to say more, but decided to hold off.

Ernesto sat motionless and stony-faced. "Chris, you have something terrible to tell me, don't you? I think that I can promise you that I can handle the truth. Please tell us what you know."

Once he had decided to reveal what he knew of the events in the desert, Chris could only blurt it out. "Ernesto, you did try to speak to someone when you were lying in the desert; and he heard you. He walked over to you, but then he hesitated and walked away. He got into his truck and drove off. He abandoned you and left you to die. I watched all this from far away with binoculars. After he drove off, I went to you. It was about ten minutes later."

Claudia was astounded and expected Chris to say more, but his eyes were now lowered in silence. Ernesto seemed cemented to the couch, speechless. He extended his hand to Chris, for they were not sitting far apart, and muttered, "Now I understand why you didn't tell me."

The three of them sat in somber silence until Ernesto broke the spell, incredulous and dismayed. "You mean he just wanted me to die there."

Chris replied as calmly as he could. "He didn't do anything to save you."

Claudia knew from experience that when horrible things are told it takes time to cushion the shock. She said, "Let's go over to my place and talk this over."

They all squeezed into the front seat of Claudia's SUV, Ernesto in the middle. They made the eight-mile ride mostly in silence, but Claudia clasped Ernesto's hand in support.

When they arrived, Chris said, "I think we could use a glass of wine. Do you have some?" he asked Claudia. "I have some questions about the camera."

Claudia was now in her nurse's take-charge mood. She poured wine for Chris and Ernesto and got out some crackers and cheese.

Ernesto was deeply subdued and asked Chris in a soft voice, "So you know who it was who left me to die, don't you?"

Chris merely nodded and said nothing more.

"Ernesto, do we really need to know?" Claudia pleaded. Ernesto didn't answer. She turned to Chris. "Would it do us any good to know?"

Chris ventured the best answer he knew. "Remember I asked you both whether you could overcome anger and could forgive? I think that's the answer. If you aren't sure, it's better not to tell you whom I saw. Besides, keeping this secret a little longer doesn't mean that I can't tell you later on."

Ernesto said, "Keep your secret, at least for now. Later I may be more certain about myself. Someone took my life, or at least he wanted to. This is too much for me right now. I am only a simple man; I can't pretend to be a saint. My future is in America now. No one can take that from me, and I will not put it at risk by doing something stupid."

Ernesto was done. Chris debated whether it was time to call it a night. However important his role had been, at present the drama centered on Ernesto alone.

Ernesto said, "We still have to decide what to do about the camera. We now know that whoever left me to die is now trying to get my picture. Why? Does he want to get to know who I am and what I am doing? But why should he care, if he expected me to die anyway? Or is he worried that I might harm him? Does the fact that he set up the camera mean that he has regrets? There are so many questions. I have a crazy idea. Suppose we use his camera to speak to him.

"Maybe he is feeling guilty. Why wouldn't he feel guilty, unless he is an animal? If he feels guilt, he could wish someday to express his regret. If he would do that, then I could forgive him. His apology would also save him from himself and would save me from any thought of getting even."

Chris said nothing but marveled at the incredible words of wisdom he had just heard. He felt tears coming to his eyes, as all of them were wrapped in silence.

Finally Claudia spoke up. "Ernesto, talking to him is a good idea. He probably thinks that we haven't discovered his camera, and so he would think that anything he captures would be by accident. Let's send him messages."

"The camera means that he is obsessed with who I am. Even subtle messages won't be missed. Next time we go out there, one of us should wear a t-shirt with some sort of message on it."

"What kind of message?" Chris asked.

"I don't know, something about water, maybe. How about a Bible passage like Moses striking water from a rock?"

Chris suggested something straightforward and simple. "How about a t-shirt with the words 'water is essential for life'?"

"Good," said Claudia. "I can get it printed at the college."

19

CHRIS ARRIVED EARLY FOR breakfast, as he usually did, clutching his newspaper and relishing the prospect of devouring the paper along with strong, hot coffee. Diana greeted him with her usual gusto. "I see you made it again, like an old penny."

"Yeah, I don't have anything better to do than to spend time here."

"I try to welcome all types. I serve good coffee whether you deserve it or not."

Chris unfolded the paper, elaborately pretending that he barely noticed the abuse he accepted so undeservedly. "Let's see what tragedies are being perpetrated today by the rich and powerful."

Diana made another stab at a smart remark as she spun around to leave: "When you run into some good news, let me know."

"Sure will," replied Chris, who was already into the lead editorial.

Diana appeared again to replenish his coffee. "You don't let this stuff cool off do you? You must have an insulated tongue."

Chris allowed himself to be lured into more nonsense, even if it made him appear ridiculous. "You know you could save yourself lots of shoe leather if you just set me up with two cups. You could cut your trips in half, and you would also stop interrupting my reading so often."

"No, I have a better idea. I'll talk the management into getting a bucket for you from the hardware at Gila Center." Diana knew she had scored a knockout, so she sailed triumphantly away preventing any response from Chris. He ruefully acknowledged that he had been bested.

Carmen appeared at the entrance and found, as usual, that Chris had arrived ahead of her. Diana intercepted her with a cheery greeting and motioned dismissively, "He's over there in his usual booth. Don't know why you bother with him. You could do a lot better."

Carmen laughed. "He'll do for now."

Carmen rushed right in with the news which she suspected Chris already knew, "Claudia told me about the camera in the desert, and Ernesto's plan to leave a message for him on the back of his t-shirt. Is he hoping for an apology from the person who left him for dead?"

"I don't think there will be an apology," Chris said with finality.

"Why?" Carmen challenged. "Can't you give the possibility of a good outcome a chance?"

Chris struggled to come up with a good reason without sharing what he knew about Unruh. "What would be the advantage for that fellow to come forward and reveal that he had left someone to die?"

"I suppose so." Carmen allowed with a look of resignation.

Diana reappeared to take their orders, transformed for the moment into a dutiful waitress. Their breakfast appeared shortly thereafter and the coffee cups were topped off as well.

Chris changed the subject. "I see you're wearing Dickies coveralls. Did you drive your front-end loader here from that rock quarry of yours?"

Carmen ignored him and took a bite of toast.

Chris stopped his teasing and expressed what he really felt. "Actually you look wonderful in work clothes."

This remark surprised and delighted Carmen, but she deflected his remark, "Is that supposed to be a compliment? I just try to dress as slovenly as you do."

Chris enjoyed her friendly insults and kept the flirting going. "I can't really afford decent clothes because of the inflated price you demanded for that useless land you sold me. It has put me in the poor house."

"It was a bargain. Besides you were in no shape to live anywhere near a decent neighborhood. You were just lucky I had some remote place to sell you."

Chris had no ready reply but corralled a wayward slice of potato on his plate and changed the subject. "Maybe Ernesto's arrival will put the land to some good use. He's working with the university's extension agent, and he has some elaborate plans. Eventually he will need your machinery to create a large water tank."

"He hasn't talked to me about it yet. Actually I just came from the quarry. An outfit called Samson Industries stopped by. They wanted to know if I could provide five hundred yards of crushed rock, and what I would charge for it. They must have a big project in the works."

"Really! That's a lot of rock. You have any idea what they want it for?"

"No. But an inquiry like that is not unusual. When an outfit plans to make a bid on a project that requires rock or gravel, they try to find the nearest possible supplier in order to decrease their costs. It has an impact on what their bid will be. It does mean that whatever is underway, it's something local. Otherwise, they wouldn't have approached me."

"So who is Samson and what would they do with five hundred yards of rock here in San Leandro?"

"Good question. The most likely use would be road building. But I can't imagine where. The only possibility would be to improve Bill Starret's old Switchback Trail. But that begs the question, why would Bill want to do that?"

"Can you supply that much crushed rock?"

"Sure. But it does take about all I have on hand."

The conversation came to a lull, so they both sat in silence, but were not ready to depart. Their easy rapport allowed for disarming candor, so he mused, "You've always faulted me for being a loner, haven't you?"

"No, no, it's not a matter of finding fault. It's who you are . . . and it's what I've learned to admire about you." Carmen hesitated to go on, but blurted out. "It's just that you're so . . . angry. When you lament about the world's ills after reading the paper, that's your anger coming out."

Chris snapped, "Don't try to get inside my head; you're not my shrink."

She winced and retreated. He regretted the outburst. A sullen, suffocating curtain descended between them.

Diana perceived their wary silence. She grabbed some coffee. "Here's some dark mud left over from last night. It's free."

Chris offered his cup and briefly caught Carmen's eye. She found words to soften the tension. "I've been angry too," she said. "Arturo and I had never been a pair. I don't know what he really wanted. It wasn't love. He finally just ran off and left me with nothing but a broken down trailer in a rocky canyon. I don't remember what was worse, my rage or his rejection.

"Returning to my family in the east was out of the question because when I left them I had burned all the bridges. I had no income, just some river rock that Bill Starret had scooped out of the Arena River when he straightened it. This I could sell but it wasn't enough to pay the groceries. San Leandro didn't have a realtor, so I took it on.

"Then one day Yolanda Alonso showed up with Mr. Uribe driving a used front-end loader. She said they didn't need it anymore at Verde Gardens. Then they simply left. She didn't hover over me. She knew I needed the machine, and that I also needed my space."

"I never heard that story," Chris said as he took her hand. "I'm not angry at anyone here; I love the people here. I'm . . . angry at . . . God?" It turned into a question.

Her face softened. "I know, Chris, I really do." She squeezed his hand. Arturo just left me; but Angela died seated next to you. They're both gone and anger won't bring them back. I can remember Arturo now without feeling the anger anymore . . ." She left the sentence unfinished—*because I met you.*

Chris saw the look in her eyes and understood, but was afraid to acknowledge it. Instead he cast his eyes down. She saw his discomfiture and read it accurately. He fussed with the folds of the paper and made motions to leave.

"It's my turn to pay." she said

Carmen went her separate way. She recognized that, in spite of herself, she had come to regard this village scold with affection.

20

In the week following Foster's visit, Ernesto, Claudia, and Chris met in the evening at the proposed garden site.

Ernesto unloaded an armful of wooden stakes and a sledgehammer, while assessing the contours of the area. "It's time to mark out where our garden is going to be."

"First we need to decide how large it should be," Chris said.

"Remember when Foster was here," Claudia said. "You wanted to start small because you didn't have the money for anything bigger. But shouldn't we plan for growth? How big could it eventually get to be, and what would be the ideal size?"

"Working at Verde Gardens it's amazing how much one can grow on a small, well-managed plot," Ernesto said. "I think we should start small, no more than five acres."

"Suppose the garden is spectacularly successful; is there a limit beyond which we would not want it to grow? Chris asked.

"I couldn't imagine a garden bigger than fifty acres. Verde Gardens isn't even that big." Ernesto said.

"Okay, it's five and fifty," Chris concluded. "Now let's decide what needs to fit into that space."

"Obviously growing beds, a water tank, a covered workplace to prepare produce for customers, an equipment shed, and an irrigation system. What else?" Ernesto asked.

Claudia made notes on a scratch pad.

"A place to start seeds, eventually a greenhouse; a sun-screened area for plants sensitive to direct sun; a space for fruit and nut trees; and finally a hydroponic operation for tomatoes and cucumbers. We're talking long-term, aren't we?" Ernesto added.

Chris confronted them. "That's quite a litany! I wonder if it will all fit on five acres."

"We're planning for whatever the future brings," Ernesto said. "Maybe it will not grow at all, but we have to be open to the possibility that it will. I haven't even mentioned individual plats for people who want to do their own gardening, which is your main interest, isn't it, Claudia?"

"Yes," Claudia said. "But I have no idea whether that project will catch on, so it's hard to guess how much room it would take."

"We're only staking out five acres today, growth—if any—will come later," Ernesto said.

Chris assembled his surveying equipment. "Let's locate a stretch of land with a gentle slope so that our irrigation will flow naturally. Once we've got the site, the location of our water tank will follow and so will everything else."

Ernesto sketched out how he visualized the growing beds. "They need to spread laterally from a central pathway, about fifty feet on either side. Each bed should be six feet wide and a few inches lower than the above it on the slope. So the growing area will be about 120 feet wide and as long as the eventual expansion of the garden will require. Any sheds, workplaces, and access roads should be along the side."

Claudia added, "Plats for individuals should be on the far side of the central path; depending on the demand, those spaces can be converted to commercial use. I don't know how many people I can recruit to take up gardening."

While Chris did the surveying, Ernesto pounded stakes down to mark the extent of the growing beds. This amounted to about two acres. Then the outline of the water tank emerged, as well as a channel for the flow of Vasquez Creek.

"What about the fruit trees?" Chris asked.

"Along the far side of the growing beds, but a little farther down slope so that any overflow irrigation will naturally find its way to them."

When the stakes had been set, Claudia wondered about future expansion. "Where will you put your greenhouses?"

Ernesto pointed to the near side of the growing beds. "All the specialized facilities will be along here, because they need to be near the road. If the garden is really successful, we will need a good-sized place to prepare and display produce for customers. Eventually starter greenhouses and hydroponics will be on this side as well."

Ernesto pounded in more stakes and painted them in different colors depending on their purpose: the water tank in red, the growing beds in white, fruit trees in blue, and water channels in yellow.

Exhausted by his efforts, he dropped the post maul at his side and visualized the garden outlined by his stakes. "Next comes the landscaping," he mused. "I'm going to see Carmen Montez tomorrow."

21

ARTEMUS KILLIAN DROVE HIS BMW to San Leandro well before his scheduled meeting with Bill and Tony. The firm did not ordinarily see new clients outside its offices, but in this instance Killian made an exception.

Bill had sketched for him the general outline of the plans that he and Tony Friedson had worked out at Two Gun Ranch. While this was not yet a formal business plan with an implementation calendar or a cash flow schedule, it did set out the basics: income from the sale of lots, the estimate of a twenty percent profit over construction costs, and interest on the financing of mortgages.

All of this piqued Killian's interest, and when Bill hinted that he would consider offering him an investor's share in return for his legal work, Killian was intrigued and decided to make the trip to see for himself. He alerted his partners in the firm to the extraordinary potential for substantial profit with the stipulation that they could still insulate themselves from any loss by the language of their contract with Star Holdings

When Bill learned that Killian planned to visit, he sought to impress him with elaborate arrangements at the Cottonwood.

"The bunkhouse is where we should meet with him," Tony insisted. "It's got the informal atmosphere that a fellow from the big city will expect when he visits the desert. It will be a reception totally different from what he's used to with deep pocketed developers. The charm of the bunkhouse will work marvels. He's been wined and dined by rich developers many times. He's used to that. Let's make this a totally different experience for him."

Bill had trouble imagining Killian at the rough plank table, with the straight-backed chairs and the log roof supports. "Do you really think so?"

"Sure," Tony said. "He should experience San Leandro for what it is—and us for whom we are. If he doesn't like it, we're better off finding out right away."

"Okay, Tony," Bill relented. "I hope you're right." He remained skeptical, but he had to listen to Tony. There was no other partner in sight.

"What kind of percentage do you think we need to offer him?" Bill asked. "Is ten percent going to be enough? It seems like a lot just for his legal work."

"It's not about the value they place on their legal work," Tony replied. "If Killian makes a deal, it will be because he sees a chance to make a killing."

Bill fretted that his project was in danger of being divided up and dissipated. "Remember, they're into us for two thousand already."

"Are you saying that you expect them to give back the retainer?" Tony objected. "If we even brought that up, he'd be convinced that we're hopeless skinflints."

"No, it seems that we are giving away our profits piece by piece."

Tony scratched his head and made another comment that Bill found a little far-fetched. "He should not get the impression that we're well heeled—of course, by his standards we aren't. If Killian thinks we're strapped for cash, he will be inclined to believe that we're offering him a sweet deal."

"This guy's experienced," Bill said. "We're not going to fool him."

Tony turned the argument on its head. "Let him think we're bumpkins and totally transparent."

"I hope you're right," Bill finally agreed.

During his recent Phoenix trip Bill had painted his project in the most colorful hues, including a marketing program that capitalized on the extraordinary landscape. He mentioned that he already had a well-heeled customer who had promised that there would be many more.

Bill waxed eloquently about the exclusive cliffside properties fashioned after Anasazi dwellings with the most elaborate amenities. He proposed three separate construction phases ranging from relatively conventional homes that still had spectacular views to multimillion-dollar kivas clinging to the steep slope just below the rim rock. Finally, Bill laid out in detail the complex series of steps involved in the project's implementation.

Bill knew that the grandiose plans he had laid before Killian didn't square with the meager amount of funding they had available.

"I agree that we need to avoid giving the impression that we're rolling in cash," Bill said, "but suppose he asks us about our reserves. We've got to tell him that we're both into this for at least three million. Otherwise he will think that we're just dreaming."

"Sorry," Tony shook his head. "I just don't have that much cash and I won't mortgage the ranch."

"I don't either," Bill admitted. "Neither one of us is going to risk that much. But that's no problem; the two of us will always be in control."

Bill had arranged to meet Killian in the Cottonwood parking lot, but Killian had arrived early and had spent a half-hour surveying the village and its environs. It was his first visit, and it reminded him of alpine settlements he had seen in France. Impressed by the Arena Rim that hovered over the eastern limits of the village, he pictured what it would be like with the upscale kivas that Bill proposed.

He found the meandering Arena River charming, and contrasted the relaxed lifestyle in San Leandro with the dogged persistence of Phoenix commuters who endured its heat and sprawl. *This is a paradise*, he mused. If Mulcton could get in at the ground floor of a really great development project here, he thought it might bring them rich returns and would enhance his standing in the Mulcton firm. After viewing the scene, much of the selling job had already been done.

Bill spotted Killian and exclaimed enthusiastically, "Welcome to Shangri la." It was a greeting that Bill had considered and rehearsed. Killian's reaction led him to believe that his hyperbole was not over the top.

Killian declined Bill's offer to drive to Two Gun Ranch with him. Instead Bill led the way through the ranch entrance, then along the long driveway, the circuit around the ranch house, and the entrance to the bunkhouse. He invited Killian to sound the post maul knocker, which elicited Tony's usual response from inside: "If you come in peace, you have no need to knock." Killian was fascinated.

Tony followed his usual offer of hospitality. "Would you like something cold to drink? There's iced tea and lemonade."

Killian found himself on foreign turf, but he was intrigued and far from being offended. He asked for lemonade, while Bill opted for iced tea, for he suspected that his usual bourbon would be out of place in Killian's presence. Tony used the intercom and soon Bonnie appeared with tumblers and pitchers. Killian accepted his drink with exaggerated gratitude.

Tony's table was entirely covered with topographical maps, and Bill explained the Star Holdings' succession of projects, as he made comments on one map after another. Killian's normal critical judgment, already considerably eroded by his introduction to San Leandro, was influenced even more at the prospect of participating in an exciting, if risky, development project.

When Bill had finished his meticulous presentation, he subtly suggested that Killian consider an equity interest. "I'm sure that you can see the potential of Anasazi Vistas. If it is successful—and I have no doubt of that, otherwise Tony and I would not be investing in it so heavily—your firm will be involved in an incomparable project the likes of which has never been attempted." Bill halted his spiel and allowed his words to have their effect.

Tony spoke as if on cue. "We'd consider a greater level of participation on the part of Mulcton."

Killian would have brought up the issue on his own. "I believe that our firm would be prepared to become a participant of sorts. We would handle all of the legal work and assist in developing your marketing and public presentations. Of course, I will need to run this by the partners."

Tony chimed in, "We're delighted to hear it. I'm sure that we can come to an arrangement that would be agreeable."

"I will bring it up at our next meeting. May I suggest that in exchange for our firm's legal services, our equity in the project be set at ten percent?"

Bill shot Tony a glance and noted his smile of satisfaction. "I believe that those are terms we can accept."

Killian expressed his appreciation and indicated that he would be looking forward to a long-term association with Star Holdings. As a final indication of his positive impression, he hinted that he would consider some personal investment beyond that which Mulcton would be making.

22

Once Unruh had decided to mount his camera at the site where he had encountered Ernesto, he kept checking it to see whether he had captured his prey. The first couple of times the pictures on the chip were disappointing. There were images of birds, rabbits, and deer. The second time he was astonished to see a cougar sniffing at the water jug. He would have reported this sighting, but could not reveal the circumstances.

Finally he captured two persons leaving a fresh jug of water. One of them was wearing a black t-shirt with white lettering, "Water is essential for life."

Unruh remained puzzled. He wondered whether he had the answer he was looking for. Was this the very person he had found lying in the desert? And who was the woman with him? Was she Claudia from the clinic? If so, that squared with the fact that the call to the sheriff had come from the phone near the clinic. And the words on the t-shirt, were they meant for him? How could they believe that he would get the message? That would mean that they were aware of the camera. But if they had discovered the camera, wouldn't there be a picture of them approaching the juniper where it was mounted?

Unruh pondered how he could get answers to all these questions. The more information the camera gave him, the more uncertainties remained.

23

On the morning of Colin Foster's second visit to Desert Gardens, Ernesto fussed compulsively with his preparations. There were drawings to scale of the entire site, a meticulous detail of a typical growing bed, and a sketch of the irrigation conduits.

The stakes outlined the boundaries of the garden. Ernesto took Foster on a tour: the location of the water tank, the outline of the growing beds, and finally the extent of possible expansions.

Foster set his papers down and, after some pleasantries, got down to business.

"I have some data that you wanted me to check on," Foster said. "You also had some homework to do. What have you come up with regarding your purposes and goals?"

Ernesto summarized the results of their planning session. "We are dividing the growing area into two sections, one for production and the other for individual plots. They will be designed so that each side can be converted to the other depending upon demand."

"Excellent," Foster said. "I am always suspicious of a proposal that doesn't make provision for change. This sounds like a good compromise."

"Now for the research I did for you. Your runoff percentages are a tad conservative, just like you said they were, but they aren't far off. Your numbers are sound for another reason. Like it or not, the desert will become even drier in the future because we are in a long-term warming pattern. Your conservative runoff figures factor in the likelihood of reduced rainfall in the future.

"Next, I checked into the dimensions of growing beds and the depth of the irrigation lines. Six-foot-wide beds are fine, assuming that you intend to access them from either side. The advantage of that width is obvious: it gives you better use of the land, and you save a little on water as well. The depth of your irrigation lines depends on what you are growing. Deep-rooted vegetables such as carrots will do fine with an irrigation line that is six inches below the surface. Lettuces do better with less depth."

Ernesto said, "Actually my plans have changed after reading about different ways of starting seeds. I think we need shallow irrigation when seeds are sprouting and deeper irrigation during the growing period."

"Exactly," Foster said. "Your fixed irrigation lines probably should be four inches below. That's a decent compromise that will work for most crops. For sprouting seeds, irrigation should be on the surface and needs to be sustained by some kind of sheet mulch."

"And the need for this sheet mulch is different depending on the crop," Ernesto said.

"Yes," Foster said, "and there are guidelines for this. Some seeds only need a bit of wetting; others are better put into the ground when they have already begun to sprout. In this, science yields to art. The experienced gardener generally knows best."

Foster looked over all the sketches and drawings. Ernesto's work impressed him. "What about soil supplements? Any thought about that? You know that you are dealing with desert soil, which means high pH, lots of gravel and sand, and a low percentage of organic matter. Of course, you're going to need a soil test. Tell me what else you plan to do beyond that."

Ernesto fished out a schedule of soil supplements. "Here is a quick summary. We plan to get a truckload of wheat straw in oblong bales. We will lay straw over the entire surface about three inches thick and allow it to decompose over the winter. In the spring we will rototill the straw into the soil about eight inches deep. This is the plan for the beds that will be put in production immediately.

"The beds left unplanted for another season will get a seeding of a legume ground cover that has been inoculated to fix nitrogen. This ground cover will be turned over as green manure halfway through the summer, and will then be top dressed with additional wheat straw.

"Depending on the results of the soil tests, we will be adding appropriate amounts of hard rock phosphate and gluconite. Once the soil has been stabilized and is ready for planting, soil amendments will be entirely organic: biochar to increase carbon, wheat straw, mulch, and compost generated from the plants that are grown on-site."

Foster said, "You've done a sound job of planning and research. I have spent most of my time advising factory farms, and I must admit that I have done so with some misgivings. What you have done is different from what most of the people I have dealt with have done, and it has been new to me.

But sustainable practices have emerged to be at the cutting edge of small farm practice. I'll be stopping by to see how it's going, whether you call on me or not."

VI

November 2016

24

As the days shortened and the heat of the summer receded, implementation of Desert Gardens began in earnest. Chris and Claudia's circle of friends became key contributors, and they gathered on a Saturday morning to launch the project, which would take several weekends. Chris borrowed surveying equipment to shoot elevations, while Ernesto directed the earth moving.

Carmen provided equipment: a front-end loader, a rig to sort stones by size, a supply of crushed rock and gravel, and a cement mixer. Ernesto devoted most of his salary at Verde Gardens to the effort, while Claudia became an investor to supplement his expenditures.

Ernesto directed the excavation of a reservoir sufficient to hold over ten thousand square feet of water and lined it with heavy plastic to prevent loss by absorption.

With the reservoir in place, he excavated a spillway that directed overflow to a line of fruit trees.

Ernesto dug the beds down to twelve inches and removed the rocks. Next he began the work of constructing the growing beds with downslope walls built of rocks fixed in concrete.

He put down wheat straw and covered this with four inches of loam. After mixing these layers with a rototiller, he built the soil level up to its original level with a mixture of the existing ground and imported top soil enriched with biochar.

The next weekend they assembled the tubing required for drip irrigation and buried it four inches below the surface.

On top of this he added a surface layer of chopped straw that was wetted down to stabilize it. A topping of cow manure from a local feed lot was spread as a final layer to provide the nitrogen needed to encourage decomposition.

Finally Ernesto was able to concentrate on the selection of seeds, planting sequences, and the acquisition of additional soil enhancements. He began to scan the skies for the arrival of winter rains.

25

EDGAR MOON, SPECIALIZING IN wilderness properties, attracted an unusual mix of clients. Many were individuals who cared little about infrastructure such as good roads, convenient shopping, schools, or hospitals because their interest was in an inexpensive, rustic site that would serve as a hunting camp or a personal retreat.

His most recent client, the legal firm of Mulcton, Killian, and Smart, placed him on retainer to identify parcels bordering the Verde National Forest with the proviso that these parcels be available for purchase and not already restricted by covenant with the Verde Forest.

Edgar examined National Forest maps and made note of any gaps which indicated private holdings. The next step, a laborious one, involved matching those open spaces with the identity of their private owners. Some of these were already listed for sale; if not, he tracked down the owners in order to determine whether they would entertain an offer. Mulcton's client did not necessarily want a single contiguous parcel but was willing to buy separate plots that taken together could be swapped in exchange for other existing National Forest land

The Verde National Forest had been established more recently than most. When the boundaries were drawn and approved by Congress, they enclosed many tracts held by private individuals, who had the option of selling to the newly established Forest but were not required to do so.

Moon first looked at a four-hundred-acre parcel owned by a church-related organization and used as a wilderness camp and retreat. Fortunately he drove a high-clearance vehicle, because the access road was washed out in a number of places. After he managed to traverse this half-mile access strip, the property broadened out to form a rough square. After another half mile Edgar came to a large building that showed the signs of several successive additions.

The entire facility had the appearance of abandonment. Disclosure statements provided by the listing realtor indicated that the well on the property had failed. Edgar surmised that this was the reason for the camp's demise.

The property held an impressive stand of ponderosa pine. It had potential for development as a primitive campground, if the Forest Service could obtain a source of potable water. The stated asking price was a thousand an acre. Edgar made a note that an opening offer of a quarter million would be reasonable.

Edgar's next stop took him to an extensive piece owned by the privately held utility Upland Energy Corporation. This was once the site of a lumber mill that produced utility poles for an earlier utility that Upland had acquired through merger. Upland shut down the mill because it had its own supplier of poles. It retained the property for decades, even though it made no use of it and hadn't even offered it for sale. He noted that it shared a boundary with the Verde Forest, and as he tramped over the landscape for a couple of hours, he was impressed with its value, even though the old mill was a ruin.

The former owner had practiced positive forest management by thinning and culling, so that the present stand of ponderosas was straight and tall. It was largely immune from wildfire danger because sound management assured that a ground-level burn would not reach the tree tops. The entire fifteen hundred acres only needed twenty years of growth to produce a wealth of saw logs. He estimated that the property should be worth nearly a million. An inquiry at the corporate offices of Upland would give him some idea of what the opening bid should be.

26

Artemus Killian called Bill Starret to inform him that Mulcton, Killian, and Smart had agreed to an equity contract with Star Holdings at ten percent. He suggested that both he and his partner, Tony Friedson, along with any legal advisors, come to the Mulcton offices to review and to sign the required papers. In addition Killian informed Bill that their agent had identified two properties for the anticipated swap with the Verde Forest. Finally, the incorporation documents of Star Holdings were ready.

Now that a fateful decision was looming, Bill's decisiveness failed him, and he called Tony for reassurance. "Killian called me and told me that all the papers are ready for us to sign. I know that it's time to commit, but I'm nervous. What if it's a big mistake?"

Tony suspected that Bill's hesitation was a simple case of cold feet. "Come on over and we'll talk."

Bill arrived with his usual supply of bourbon, and Tony suspected that it was not his first drink.

Tony said, "So they've got the papers ready for us to sign. Tell me why you're uneasy about it. I thought we had gone over all this."

"I can't put my finger on it," Bill said. "It's just that I feel like I'm on the edge of a cliff, and someone's asking me to jump."

"Yeah, I think I know how you feel. We're standing at the gate. We have to be sure we want to pass through it."

"I know this shouldn't faze me," Bill fretted. "I've done lots of business dealings, and they've always turned out okay, but this seems different. I've never had to deal with big-city lawyers. They're probably straight shooters, but they still make me feel like I'm a sucker. Working with Alma Fortner here was always a lot simpler. She's someone I knew I could trust. The Mulcton firm just doesn't have a comfortable feel."

"I suppose we could talk to Alma Fortner. She wouldn't let us get into trouble."

"No, no. I don't want our plans to get out. That's why I went to a Phoenix lawyer to begin with."

"Well, Bill, one way or another you've got to settle your mind about this. We can't go on if you're going to be looking over your shoulder all the time."

"Tell me, Tony, be honest. Do you think it's a crazy idea? Is it a stupid gamble?"

Tony furrowed his brow, for he had never seen Bill this wobbly. "Maybe we do need to get a second opinion just to get some reassurance. I have dealt with some Phoenix lawyers in the past, Stewart and Williamson. Maybe we should ask them to review the documents prepared by Mulcton."

Bill fought with his trepidation. "It's a shame that when it comes to legal matters, I turn into a befuddled turkey. Sometimes I think they deliberately make these contracts so complex that the ordinary person can't understand them."

Tony was worried that Bill's jitters would put his hopes for an enlarged ranch in jeopardy. "No time to get paranoid now, Bill. We've got a good plan; we just need to be sure that there isn't some trap that we're unaware of. It isn't that we can't trust the Mulcton people, but there's always the possibility that some essential detail is left out."

"Have you contacted Stewart and Williamson already?"

"No, I wanted to wait until we could talk."

"What kind of relationship have you had with them? Do you feel secure in your dealings with them?"

"Sure, I've used them a number of times; mostly about family matters," Tony said. "And they represented my grandfather years ago when he had to part with a third of the ranch."

"Okay, Tony, let's call them now and ask if they'll help us."

Tony made the call while Bill listened in nervously. Tony explained the situation as succinctly as he could and received, in turn, an invitation to make an appointment to visit the Stewart offices. Tony cupped his receiver. "They want us to come to their offices; otherwise they won't take on our case. Is that okay with you?"

"Sure, go ahead," Bill said.

WHEN THEY ARRIVED AT the offices of Stewart and Williamson, Bill had mostly shed his doubts and misgivings. Josh Marshall questioned both of them in detail about their development project. He indicated his discomfort with the Verde Gardens takeover.

"Have you had any meetings with the San Leandro community about your development plans?"

"No, not yet," Bill replied. "Our development plans can't be anything but tentative until we have an agreement with the Forest Service on the land swap. After this is completed we will present our plans to the village. Any public disclosure prior to that time would be premature and would give more time for the usual opponents of development to rise up."

Josh hesitated before responding. "I'm sure that you recognize that the longer you delay the more suspicions will arise. The timing of your decision is up to you, but you need to be aware of the consequences of delay."

"You aren't suggesting that we have bad reasons for keeping this under wraps, are you?" Bill protested. "After all we don't own the property yet. Can we be expected to make our plans known before we even have the land on which we could implement them?"

Josh replied evenly, "No, not normally. But it is a project which profoundly affects the village and its character, and obviously there will be objections."

He made the dilemma explicit. "Once you go ahead and make the swap with the National Forest, you'll have made a substantial investment. Is it only after this that you intend to notify the community? Aren't you risking this investment, if strong local opposition emerges?"

Bill squirmed in his chair and glanced at Tony whose expression was blank. He found it difficult to negotiate between community interests and his own private property rights. He believed that personal advantage in business should not be encumbered by any third-party interests.

"We are only interested in the law as it pertains to this project," Bill said.

"Very well," Marshall responded in a flat voice. "We will represent you by reviewing the suitability of the Mulcton documents for your purposes, as we understand them. We will take no responsibility for the purposes that underlie the documents themselves. Our fee for this service will be five hundred an hour."

Even Tony became sobered by the tone that the meeting had taken. "Do you think we are doing something wrong?"

"I have already responded to that question. We will not advise you on ethical questions, except to the extent of having warned you of the legal hazard you are exposed to regarding prevailing community interests. The choice you make is entirely your own."

"Would you give us a few moments?" Tony asked.

"Sure, take your time. I'll be in the office next door. Just knock when you are ready."

Tony complained, "Does Marshall think we are crooks?"

"No, he's just skittish about anything that falls a little short of his standards," Bill said. "Our only question is whether it's legal. What we do is our decision alone, just like he said. Let's ignore his quibbles and proceed with our plan."

Bill's words settled Tony's resolve. His hopes for fulfilling his dying grandfather's command overcame all his doubts and scruples. "You're right, Bill. We don't have to sweat this."

They returned to Josh's office. "We want you to review the Mulcton documents to determine how well they protect our interests. Your fees are acceptable to us."

"Thank you," Marshall said. "Please sign this. It retains us as your representative, sets our fees, and requests that Mulcton forward a copy of the legal work that they have done on your behalf. We expect that our review will be completed within the week. We will be in touch."

Bill remained uneasy, but he couldn't put his finger on it. Tony, on the other hand, gladly accepted Josh's extended hand as they were leaving his office.

Josh Marshall of Stewart and Williamson called Tony within a week, as he had promised he would. "We have reviewed the documents from Mulcton and we find that they are reasonable and do not adversely compromise your interests."

27

CHRIS HOPPED DOWN FROM his pickup, and entered the Pancake House. He headed to his usual booth, even as he was scanning the front page headlines in the paper. Diana had seen him coming and had coffee already waiting.

Chris was surprised that she had gotten to his accustomed booth before he did. "Careful, I'm not used to this kind of service."

"You better be happy with whatever you get. I saw you coming and thought I could get your coffee for you before you had a chance to complain."

"I've never been known to complain, especially with people I know and love."

"That would certainly exclude me," Diana retorted, though she secretly appreciated his remark.

"Not at all, you know you're my favorite person," Chris replied with a wink.

"Oh, Puh-leeze," Diana replied, uncertain about what facial expression she should assume. She artfully concealed the fact that she was actually in awe of him, and cherished his sidewise remark.

Chris surveyed the paper's headlines and then immediately turned to the opinion page. He had already moved from the columnists to editorials and finally to letters to the editor when Carmen arrived.

Diana greeted her warmly, "A little late today, young lady. Was it a flat tire, or did you forget to set the alarm? Of course, I wouldn't blame you for delaying your meeting with him as long as you can." She pointed dismissively at Chris without even turning towards him.

Chris overheard and, inspired by this insult, rose dramatically to greet Carmen. He took her hand, put his arm around her shoulder, and then— without having planned it—kissed her resolutely.

Carmen was startled; Diana was speechless; Chris was embarrassed. Both sat down not quite daring to catch each other's eyes while Diana hastened to grab Carmen's cup without a word.

An awkward period of silence ensued. "What's new in the paper?" Carmen finally broke the silence.

Chris was grateful for a neutral subject. He was railing about the mortgage crisis and the greed and heartlessness of lending institutions when Diana reappeared to take their orders. "What would you two lovers want for breakfast?"

She said it as blandly and flatly as she could, as if her choice of words was in no way remarkable. Carmen was not caught at a loss; rather she responded with equal flatness. "I'll have my usual whole grain short stack with maple syrup and a quarter melon . . . with coffee," she added purposelessly while smiling at Diana. "I can't speak for Chris," as she looked at him and noticed his discomfort.

Chris was at a loss for any smart remark. "One egg over well, dry multigrain toast, some ham," he recited. "And coffee," he added in empty mimicry. Carmen smiled sheepishly, while Diana turned and kept her smirk to herself.

Carmen decided to acknowledge the elephant in the room. "Don't be embarrassed, Chris, I appreciate your kiss, and I have no regret about it. I think you are a really neat guy. Why do you suppose I spend my Tuesday mornings with you here? I'm not saying that this is a romantic thing, but I do admire you."

Chris was relieved by the sudden candor, "I guess I would say the same for you." Chris's response wasn't especially original or personal, but Carmen accepted it gratefully.

Diana approached stealthily, afraid of interrupting, then became uncharacteristically business-like, setting down the plates without a word. "More coffee?" was the extent of her comment.

"How about later, for me," Chris responded. He had recovered some of his usual crustiness. "We can depend on you to interrupt our conversation. Whenever the spirit moves you, bring me a refill."

Carmen was delighted that Chris had recovered his composure. Diana ignored him. "How about you, Carmen?"

"I'll hold off until later too. Thanks, Diana."

As Chris was slathering his toast with orange marmalade, Carmen inquired about Ernesto and Claudia. "Has Ernesto renewed the face of the earth yet?"

The allusion was not lost on Chris. "He's busy bringing new life to the desert." Chris continued with a description of the county extension agent's expert assistance. He filled her in on their intention of designing the garden as a production operation, with small plots for individual gardeners. Finally he explained the rain harvesting, the drip irrigation, and the soil enhancement.

Carmen commented, "You know one of Bill Starret's favorite remarks is 'God may have created the earth, but he left it undeveloped.'"

"That's really an interesting statement. What he means by it—bulldozing the hell out of the desert to make room for more development—I couldn't disagree with more . . ." Chris halted mid-sentence. "But then Ernesto is doing some earth moving too and I agree with what he's doing," he said.

"But he is doing it for a good purpose," Carmen said.

"I'm not sure that just having a good purpose is the critical difference," Chris said. "It leaves open the critical question: who gets to decide what purpose is good and what isn't?"

"Sorry, Chris, you're making it all too complicated. It's just common sense, isn't it?"

"No there's got to be some clear marker. For instance, you just can't do whatever you want in this valley. The slope of the land, the kind of stuff that grows here, the lack of water, the climate, everything we live with . . . all of it places limits on what we should do."

"Sure, and I think that's what I mean when I say it's just common sense."

"No, common sense is too slippery, too subjective, too easily made to fit someone's short-term advantage. For instance, if someone decided to level the desert to make room for a large cotton farm that requires lots of water, it might seem a common sense decision in terms of short-term profits, but the ill effects of that decision would endure for centuries. It would use up all of the underground water, and would eventually be unsustainable. See what I'm getting at?"

"So you are saying that the land itself has a say in what one can do or not do."

"Exactly," Chris said. "Such decisions must also factor in how it will impact the people who live here. Ernesto has done careful work to make sure that he can develop a garden with the water that the site provides. It will be sustainable. And his purpose will benefit others. These two considerations are the critical issues.

"Ernesto's project is an example of ethical caring for the earth. It encompasses a social purpose. It is consistent with maintaining the land's value because it enhances its inherent productivity without exploitation. Finally his actions are consistent with the land as he found it."

"That's an exacting standard," Carmen said.

"Sure it is, but nothing less will work in the long run."

"Breakfast with you always ends up being a lesson in civics, but I'm not complaining."

"I think it's my turn to buy. I noticed that Diana has looked our way a couple of times."

"Let me leave her a fiver for a tip. You can buy the breakfast."

"Okay, Carmen. Next week, same time?"

"Unless you hear differently."

28

AT CLAUDIA GOMEZ'S URGING, Martin Zehrer proposed a change of policy at the food bank to provide fresh fruits and vegetables and to repackage staples into smaller containers. Claudia also attended the meeting.

Martin said, "I've checked into food handling regulations. The food bank must designate at least one individual with supervisory authority to acquire ANSI certification as a food handler. When we get this certification we can repackage any processed items and handle perishables."

Martin volunteered to obtain ANSI certification.

Claudia added, "I have a source of fresh produce at a very reasonable price from Verde Gardens, because they will sell at a steep discount anything that isn't perfect in appearance. I will make this my personal project, so the people that we visit will always get fresh produce."

She also revealed her plans for an additional supply of produce from Ernesto Ramirez, as soon as Desert Gardens got underway. Additionally, she outlined her ultimate goal of providing the community with individual garden plots, in which they could provide for their own needs and learn to become successful gardeners themselves.

Finally Claudia proposed a series of workshops on food preservation and storage under the sponsorship of the community college.

The committee approved these proposals and ordered their implementation as soon as Martin had obtained certification and the food bank made the necessary changes.

AFTER THE MEETING OF the board, Claudia immediately drove to the food bank for her two-hour volunteer commitment. In response to an insistent knock on the door, she opened and found the sheriff confronting her.

Startled and unsure, she said, "Come in. . . . How can I help you? . . . Is there a problem?"

"I came by to check on your security," Unruh said. "There have been reports of some illegals passing this way. I want to be sure that this place is secure. Mind if I take a look around? I'm going to check out the exterior first."

"Sure. Go ahead."

Unruh took a walk around the outside of the building, came back inside, and examined the interior doors and windows. "This used to be a grocery a while back. Now it seems to be a storage shed. What do you do here?"

The question was unexpected, for surely Unruh was acquainted with the purpose of the facility. She made a straightforward answer. "We hand out food boxes to people who ask for our assistance."

Unruh made no comment, but announced, "I've got to ask you to improve your security. The windows should be covered with metal grates, bolted to the walls. The doors need metal enclosures on sliders or rollers. You need an exterior light on a timer, so that the area is never in the dark."

Claudia answered cautiously, "We've never had a problem here."

"You've been lucky. The sorts of people that your hand-outs attract are precisely the ones you should worry about."

"Actually I know most of our clients quite well. I can't imagine any of them giving us any trouble. What you are suggesting is going to cost us some money, and that means we have less available to help our clients."

Unruh voiced his discomfort with the entire operation. "You shouldn't call them clients. They're just taking advantage of you. You aren't doing them any favors either. Helping those people is a trap. It confirms them in their dependency and victimizes you by causing you to think you are actually helping them. It doesn't do anyone any good."

Claudia had heard enough. She began to move toward the food pantry's door. She opened it, and motioned to him with a gesture toward the outside. "Thanks for your visit. You've made your purpose quite clear. Now, if you'll excuse me, I must get back to work."

Unruh was not used to being shown the door and would not be deprived of the last word. "I know what I'm talking about. There's a reason why I wear this uniform. Just recently I've noticed that some fools have been leaving water in the desert, and I don't think they were leaving it for the deer." He kicked the dirt and made his way to his cruiser.

Claudia folded into a chair, and sank her head between her hands while her throat tightened. Now she knew for sure who had left a motion camera in the desert. She also knew who had left Ernesto to die.

29

ANTON WEHRLI HAD BOUGHT a five-acre ranchette along the eastern shore of the Arena just north of San Leandro. The term "ranchette" was surely a gross hyperbole, for its size would not support enough desert vegetation to keep even one goat alive. Real ranches in the area required at least ten sections of land—each section was a square mile, or 640 acres.

Of course, Anton had no visions of keeping livestock when he bought his place. Instead he had just retired from a small northern city, where he had been city manager. He had found it stressful because he reported to a city council that routinely inserted itself into the details of management, instead of restricting its role to matters of policy. Anton and his wife, Petra, arrived looking forward to a stress-free retirement.

But the village of only seven hundred residents could not overlook his experience and his level-headed demeanor. Almost by acclamation the village elected him to a two-year term on the village council, and—since the office of mayor alternated among the council's three members—he became mayor as well.

San Leandro was a small village, so its governance was uncomplicated. There was no village manager, only a village clerk, Stella Mantilla, the only paid employee, and she was only part-time. Wehrli found her service invaluable, for she was the village's institutional memory and was generally the first to know of any problem. What served as village headquarters was found at the San Leandro branch of the San Ysidro Community College—a spartan office for Stella and a meeting room that was also used for workshops and short courses by the college.

Nothing in San Leandro happened that did not come to Stella's personal attention. The board members met only quarterly, and Anton kept their role to matters of policy: the approval of the village budget and the assessment of property taxes. Everything else was handled by Stella. She received the mail, answered the phone, kept the books, and—in all routine matters—ran the village.

"What's new today?" Wehrli greeted Stella as he arrived for his weekly meeting with her.

Stella pointed wordlessly to a side table where she had arranged the items that Wehrli needed to see: the usual stuff—checks to approve and blurbs to look at. She said, "There is one unusual item; I'm sure it will be obvious when you see it."

She had everything arranged. On top were bills to be paid by the village, with checks already cut awaiting his signature; letters of inquiry and complaints, each with a slip for Anton's comment about any action that should be taken; purchase orders arranged by number, each with a space for him to initial his approval.

At the end there was an array of blurbs, announcements, or information pieces—the biggest stack. Each had an action slip attached: "discard, file, take action____?"

One of the information papers carried Stella's handwritten note: "This needs review and decision by the board." Her note was enough to cause Anton to give it special attention.

When Stella noticed that Anton had picked up this mailing, she mentioned, "That's from the ADWR, the Arizona Department of Water Resources. They are reminding us about the provisions of the Arizona Groundwater Management Code (AGMC). It's something we need to look into. You'll see that it's going to have an impact on the village."

Anton grunted a reply and buried his nose in the mailing to learn what it was all about.

The ADWR alerted the village that it needed to comply with its 1994 regulation, which designated Santa Cruz County as an Active Management Area (AMA) for the handling of water resources.

He mumbled as he kept reading. "We're in the Santa Cruz AMA, it says; an Active Management Area defined as place where the 'magnitude of overdraft of water is most severe.'"

Stella summarized, "That's right. Overdraft is the rate of water withdrawal in excess of its recharge. Recharge is the replenishment of an aquifer, either naturally or artificially."

Anton read on. "The primary management goal required by the code is to attain 'safe-yield' by 2025, which is defined 'as a long-term balance between the annual amount of groundwater withdrawn in the AMA and the amount of natural and artificial recharge.'" Anton sat back and let the document slip down onto his lap.

Stella waited for Anton's reaction, for she had already determined what needed to be done. When he looked up she gave him a knowing look. Anton asked, "Are we in violation of 'safe yield?'"

She said, "We are."

Anton said, "Maybe we should invite someone from ADWR to meet with the board. Maybe this will help us figure out what we need to do."

"Do you want me to set it up?"

"Yes. Find a time when ADWR can send someone; then notify Angel Benevides and Bill Starret. The entire council needs to be in on this. Set it up at the Cottonwood."

30

Stella mailed a folder of handouts to each of the councilors. She enclosed a copy of the mailing from ADWR, its four page governing document about securing Arizona's water for the future, and finally a detailed statistical analysis of the Santa Cruz AMA. In addition Stella added her own report on the history of San Leandro's water usage, which indicated that the local aquifer was receding at the rate of twelve feet a year.

In the mailing she concluded, "The ADWR is sending Tom Montrose, the hydrologist who oversees the Santa Cruz AMA. He told me that he's delighted to come to explain the code, and I provided him with a copy of my report on our water usage."

The El Paraiso room was set up as Montrose requested with a whiteboard and PowerPoint.

"This board's not going to be unanimous about water," Anton said apprehensively. "Bill is a developer. His family's been around here forever, and he's not likely to welcome anything that limits his business."

Stella tried to be optimistic. "He doesn't have any plans right now—at least I don't know of any. Maybe he won't clash with a conservationist like Angel."

"I'm going to let Montrose take the lead. The board has your report on the village's water usage and the fact that we're out of compliance with 'safe yield.' You are probably going to be challenged about those figures."

"Those usage figures are firm. The twelve-foot loss in the water level of the aquifer is also beyond question."

Wehrli introduced Montrose, who gave a fifteen-minute PowerPoint overview of the hydrology of the Santa Cruz AMA. He summarized the thirty-eight-page report issued in 2007 that documented the fifteen-foot level of subsidence among the 110 wells in the AMA area. Then he welcomed comments and questions.

Wehrli got the discussion underway. "Why did the ADWR designate certain places as 'Active Management Areas'?"

"Because these are the areas that are most critical. They represent seventy percent of water overdraft, eighty percent of the population, and the greatest risk of calamity. Originally there were four AMAs: Phoenix, Pinal, Prescott, and Tucson. Santa Cruz was separated from Tucson in 1994. The primary goal of each AMA is to achieve 'safe yield' by 2025, namely a balance between water use and natural or artificial recharge."

Starret kept his participation to a minimum, and his secret development plans made him wary of any limitation on groundwater usage. He asked obliquely, "What about sources of water that existed before the establishment of the Santa Cruz AMA?"

"Take a look at the ADWR document that is in your folder. It affirms that any irrigation that existed between 1975 and 1980 for horticulture, human consumption, or feed may continue. Secondly any land retired from agricultural irrigation retains its water rights, though this can't be transferred separately from the land and is limited to three acre-feet. Finally a well used for non-irrigation is grandfathered but may not be pumped beyond what it produced during the 1975–80 period. This right can be leased or sold, but can't be divided."

Starret followed up. "So the code regulates groundwater, but not surface water or a flowing stream?"

"That's right," Montrose allowed. "In the case of surface water traditional rights and limitations remain that are grounded in case law."

"What about areas which are outside an AMA?" Benevides asked.

"The code also establishes three Irrigation Non-Expansion Areas, INAs for short, where groundwater depletion has arisen. These are usually agricultural areas where alfalfa, cotton, and nuts are grown.

Stella said, "I have heard that groundwater depletion in an area east of here has been so severe that private wells have gone dry."

"Yes, that's true. In fact it has caused many wells to be deepened to a thousand feet."

Benevides asked, "Am I right in assuming that 1975–80 is the time period governing any grandfathered right?"

"That's right," Montrose said. "I should have mentioned that a grandfathered well is still limited in how much can be drawn from it. In most cases this is thirty-five gallons per minute, and this yield has to be metered.

"A well which existed before 1975–80 is considered an exempt well. This means that thirty-five gallons per minute can be pumped provided it is for non-irrigation purposes. A private lawn or garden is limited to two acres, and a new well, not grandfathered, requires a permit from the ADWR."

Starret was worried how this would affect new developments. He approached the question obliquely. "Does the code address population growth?"

Montrose answered in detail. "Anyone who offers subdivided—and not subdivided—land for sale or lease within an AMA must demonstrate an assured water supply for one hundred years. A certificate to this effect is issued by the ADWR. It requires that the applicant demonstrate: 1) that water of sufficient quantity and quality is available to sustain the proposed development for a hundred years; 2) that the use is consistent with the AMA's water management goals, namely that it meets conservation requirements and does not conflict with the achievement of safe yield by 2025; and 3) that in the case of a development, it has the means to provide water delivery and treatment of effluent."

Starret asked, "What about a source other than groundwater?"

Montrose said, "It could be surface water or a flowing stream or even an aqueduct such as the Central Arizona Project. The purpose of the code is not to restrict growth or to limit freedom but to secure the future, because water is a finite resource."

Benevides came right to the point. "What do we need to do in San Leandro that we haven't been doing?"

"Stella's report gives most of the answer," Montrose replied. "Maybe we should have her review the research she has done."

Stella held up her report for all to see. "We billed 1,125 acre-feet last year, in addition we used another 51 acre-feet for village purposes that were not billed. This means we consumed 1,176 acre-feet. Over the past ten years our usage shows an average annual increase of just above four percent. At this rate, within five years we would be using 1,398 acre-feet.

"Our deep well yields about 900 acre-feet; the balance of our water comes from our share of the flow of Kallisto Wells, namely 425 acre-feet. The agreement we have with Verde Gardens and Masterson Ranch, who also draw water from Kallisto Wells, allocates a third of its flow to us, while the rest is shared equally by Masterson and Verde Gardens. The total flow of Kallisto is estimated to be 1,300 acre-feet. This means that the maximum village share is 430 acre-feet.

"Regarding our deep wells, the availability and sustainability of their supply can be calculated by measuring the water level of the aquifer. We have a serious problem because the level has been receding at a rate of twelve feet a year. Without a hydrological study it is impossible to translate this number into acre-feet of supply, but it is beyond question that our present level of use is more than what the aquifer can supply on a continuing basis. In other words, we are in violation of the requirement of 'safe-yield'. We are slowly running out of water."

Benevides listened carefully and grimaced. "Thanks, Stella. I guess we do have a problem."

She had an additional concern. "We need to factor in the steady decrease in rainfall. Of course, this decrease is not predictable, and there are even some who deny that there has been a drop-off, but records indicate that trend lines are heading downward."

Starret could not resist showing his distaste at the mention of climate change and challenged Stella. "Let's hear about a solution, not just the problem."

Stella replied evenly, "There are no easy answers, unless we can lasso an iceberg from Antarctica and park it over by the Kallisto." There wasn't any laughter, so she added hurriedly, "However, the adoption of conservation policies could reduce our usage by a third.

"Our deep well is obviously exempt," she continued. "However, its level is receding; therefore we know that it will not provide us the water we will need in the future."

Starret had become increasingly uncomfortable. "Why don't we just sink another well? That should solve the problem. I assume the ADWR would issue a permit, because we need the water."

Montrose replied, "It's not that simple. If you drill a well that draws from the same aquifer, nothing's changed; you're still in violation of safe-yield. If you move out to another aquifer, you are still subject to the same requirement of safe yield there."

Bill was subdued but not defeated. "My family's lived here for over a hundred years. We've always had plenty of water. There's got to be a solution," he affirmed defiantly.

Montrose held his tongue. Anton didn't want to confront Bill. Benevides waited for someone else to speak up.

Stella did. "I can think of two solutions. We can buy water. Or we can cut down on our use. Either choice will bring us to safe yield."

Benevides asked, "What's the price of water?

Stella had done some research. "In an INA east of here, extensive plantations of nut orchards which require flood irrigation have caused the aquifer to fail. Residential wells have gone dry. Commercial wells are now drilled a thousand feet deep so that they cost about $25,000 each. An agricultural conglomerate can afford this, but private individuals can't. A market for residential water service has emerged. It costs up to $200 monthly for a five-hundred-gallon weekly supply."

Her recitation cast a pall of gloom and reduced everyone to silence. She confronted the discomfort. "The price of water is entirely disconnected from reality. Our normal attitude is that water is free. When the village charges for water, it's understood to cover the cost of its delivery, not the water itself. In the California central valley, water for agricultural irrigation costs about $75 per acre-foot. The same amount of water obtained by reverse osmosis would cost over two million. Water is more precious than gold because without it the recovery of precious metals is impossible, and life itself can't continue even for a few days without it."

These remarks did not elicit any comment except for a broad smile from Montrose. "There is another option. It's conservation. You can cut your usage by a third without any lessening of your lifestyle."

Benevides brightened markedly. "I like that approach, but how can we get people to buy into it? As soon as I mention conservation around here, faces darken."

Wehrli finally spoke up. "We need to achieve community consensus, and has to start with us right here. The board needs to support lower use with monetary incentives and by subsidizing the adoption of lower-use plumbing fixtures."

Montrose commented, "I agree with the conservation approach. When faced with a dilemma the best path is the one that offers the least resistance.

Only Bill remained opposed, but he kept it to himself. The water issue put his development plans in jeopardy, but he couldn't easily object without revealing the reason.

Wehrli moved the issue forward. "In my position as mayor, I'm asking your support to propose a conservation effort within the village. The best way to build consensus is by having a town hall. So I propose that Stella and I present a conservation plan to reduce our water usage sufficiently to achieve safe yield."

Benevides agreed enthusiastically, while Starret meekly raised his hand in favor.

Wehrli wasn't done. "There are some additional issues that we need to consider. First of all, how will we respond to lot owners who want to build and ask us to provide utilities? Surely the lot owner has a reasonable expectation that the village will honor this request."

Benevides said, "What if we refuse to do so? Do we incur any responsibility for any decrease in property value due to our refusal to provide water? What if the village actually doesn't have the means to honor the request for water service? Surely we couldn't be held liable in that case."

Wehrli replied, "That's a real conundrum. Let's talk to Alma Fortner to get her advice. We don't need a formal legal decision yet, and I hope it never comes to that."

Stella brought up the obvious. "I've got another suggestion. We are assuming that the Masterson Ranch and Verde Gardens wouldn't sell us all or a part of their share of the Kallisto. Maybe they would. Shouldn't we approach them with an offer?"

"We need to look into that," Wehrli said.

"We have to pass a village ordinance to implement conservation," Stella said. "It would require that outside water use be forbidden unless it is captured from rooftops. Many people have gardens; we'd have to limit their size and type of irrigation."

"The village would need to provide a public car wash," Wehrli added.

Bill listened with growing distress. "If we do run out of water—and I doubt that it would happen in my lifetime—we won't face this alone. The whole state will have the same problem and there will be a solution that will save all of us. For instance, we might rely on desalinated water from the Pacific, like San Diego. Finally, if the Rio Grande and the Colorado are all used up, there are still the Great Lakes. A pipeline from the north would bail everybody out."

Benevides was dismayed but kept his cool. "The Colorado is a hundred and four percent spoken for because effluent is recycled back in. I don't think I'd look forward to the costs of a pipeline from Chicago."

Angel continued, "Who else draws from our aquifer? If it's receding twelve feet a year, the village shouldn't be required to deal with the problem alone."

Stella had looked into this. "Most of the water from the aquifer is drawn by the copper mine in Nudoso Hills. They have a variance which allows them to draw as much as they need.

Benevides was alarmed. "How did that come about?"

"The legislature took that action before the mine opened."

Benevides spoke with an air of finality. "Let's have Anton and Stella work out the details, flesh out a conservation proposal, and call a town hall to present it to the village."

31

STANLEY UNRUH MADE ANOTHER trip into the desert. As usual he parked on the two track and walked into the arroyo where he had mounted his camera on the branch of a juniper. He no longer felt the tension that had accompanied his earlier visits, yet he continued to be uneasy about the meaning of the jugs of water, which kept appearing at the site of the migrants' demise. He hoped that his hidden camera would finally reveal the identity of the migrant, even if he still hadn't determined exactly what he would do if it did.

He had come to the conclusion that the migrant he abandoned must be the same person now leaving jugs of water. Otherwise why would he be wearing a shirt inscribed with words that referred to water as essential to life? Maybe this time the camera would reveal something more, or even capture a clear image of his face.

Unruh saw nothing unusual at the site. There was a gallon jug of water just as he had anticipated. The camera was undisturbed. He exchanged the chip with a fresh one, took another look around, visited the site of the two corpses, and found two jugs of water just as he expected. He retraced his steps to his pickup and returned to his office.

Unruh sensed the tension of anticipation when he read the chip on his computer. Once again he saw the fleeting image of a coyote and the fluttering wings of passing birds. Then fully in view, clearly posing for the camera was the back of a man wearing a black t-shirt. The shirt read "Mt. 10:42." He grabbed his copy of the Bible and read, "And whoever gives even a cup of cold water to one of these little ones in the name of a disciple—truly I tell you none of these will lose their reward."

Stanley sat back to reflect on what all this meant. No doubt he was being addressed by someone who knew what he had done. It was also clear that the person wearing the t-shirt knew that he was being caught on camera, and actually posed for it. Now Unruh was convinced that the person on the picture must be the same person whom he had left for dead.

He pondered his options. What if he left a message suggesting that they meet? But that would blow his anonymity, and he would have no assurance that he wouldn't be exposed and denounced, which would spell the end of his career in law enforcement. Even worse it could put him in danger. Suppose this guy was out for vengeance. He had no choice but to keep his secret. Maybe the next message on the camera would solve the dilemma.

32

Bill received a report from the Mulcton firm. Edgar Moon of Mountain Properties had identified two parcels adjacent to the Verde National Forest that would work as a trade for the Arena Rim near San Leandro.

Mulcton wanted to proceed with negotiations to acquire both of them for Star Holdings. The asking price of the first parcel was $400,000 and the realtor, Edgar Moon, proposed an offer of $250,000. The second parcel was much larger and the realtor proposed an offer of $750,000 with an upper limit of a million. The realtor's commission was set at eight percent.

When Bill received this message he made another trip to the bunkhouse at Two Gun Ranch to see Tony. The meeting followed the usual ritual.

"It looks like we have to commit some money," Bill said. "I feel like I'm caught in a vise. We still don't know if the Forest will agree to the swap. We could be buying land that we can't use and won't be able to dump. I've never gone out on a limb like this."

Tony had inherited something of his father's gambling spirit. "Nothing ventured, nothing gained, my friend. It looks like that Moon fellow is suggesting that we cough up somewhere between a million and a million four. Suppose you were to make an offer for the Arena Rim from a private owner. What would you expect to pay for it? Wouldn't it be about that much?"

"Who knows? Maybe about a million. But suppose they think it's worth more than that. What if they turn us down and don't make the trade at all and we're stuck with a million in distant lands for which we have no use?"

"Yep, that's possible. We could be left with just sour apples. We would be stuck with two options, and we'd have to choose the least harmful. We could make use of whatever political connections we have to get the Verde Forest to reconsider. If that doesn't work, we would need to dispose of the two properties, very likely at a big loss."

"I know," replied Bill with obvious discomfort. "Would it be possible to draw up a contingency clause that would make the purchase conditional and not reveal our plans—a contingency such as 'based upon the acquisition of properties on the Arena Rim'? This would protect us without actually giving away our intentions."

Tony squinted thoughtfully. "You know, that might work. Let's talk to Killian and see what he can come up with. These legal guys can invent all sorts of escape clauses when they have an interest in doing so."

"Are we comfortable with the prices Moon proposes? Do we need to get an independent appraisal?"

"I can't imagine what good that would do. We could hire an appraiser to report to us directly without Killian's or Moon's knowledge, but whatever he would tell us isn't really what we need to know. The only issue is whether the Verde Forest people think these parcels are so valuable that they would be willing to make the trade. There is no way we can get an answer to that question ahead of time."

"So we depend on Moon's judgment about the value?"

"I guess so. But let's try to purchase them with an escape clause."

Bill continued, "I'm in no mood to make another trip to Phoenix. Can we arrange a conference call with Killian?"

Tony agreed. They made the call and Killian agreed that the purchase offer could be drafted so that it allowed for a contingency based on the Forest Service's willingness to do a swap.

Three weeks later Killian came to terms with the owners of the two parcels for a total of a $1,200,000 with the contingency language which Tony and Bill requested. Star Holdings entered an agreement for the Upland property for $900,000 and the abandoned church camp for $300,000. The commissions to Mountain Properties added an additional $96,000. Bill and Tony agreed to pay this much for land they never intended to use.

33

Torn between dread and expectation Stanley Unruh ventured again into the desert in order to retrieve yet another message from his camera. He was desperate to learn something new. The mystery of the missing body and the enigmatic t-shirt messages encaged him and placed him in the vise of his own torment.

He approached the site with unseemly caution, even though he could clearly see that there was nobody around and nothing seemed out of place. Once again he found water jugs where they had been before. He replaced the chip in his camera and headed back to his office.

After watching the usual images of birds and varmints, the camera captured a man and a woman who were careful never to face the camera. They replaced the jug of water with a fresh one. They lingered for a time and seemed to utter a prayer while keeping their backs to the camera. Clearly they wanted the camera to capture the words on his t-shirt. Again the message was biblical: "Lk 17:3." Unruh checked his Bible. "Be on your guard! If another disciple sins, you must rebuke the offender; and if there is repentance, you must forgive."

Unruh pondered the import of these words. Surely the mandate to forgive couldn't be directed at him, for the messenger surely thought that he was the one in need of forgiveness. Does it allude to a promise of forgiveness? On what basis? Should he reply and invite a clear request? But how could he without revealing his identity? Then what? One thing was abundantly clear; this t-shirt fellow was a master at torment.

VII

December 2016

34

THE VERDE NATIONAL FOREST headquarters in Gila Center had a varied staff. "A land of many uses" was the motto which was emblazoned on the Forest Service signs. The least of these, as it turned out, was the production of timber, which was part of the head forester's duties. He finalized agreements for the sale of timber to private companies—"stumpage" as the contract was usually termed. He also monitored compliance, including the reduction of slashings to within two feet of the ground, the measurement of harvested timber, and the provision of logging trails. But most of the forestry's business actually fell to others.

An assistant forester was in charge of recreational activities within the Forest, a "use" which had become increasingly important. This included all public access, the maintenance of recreational trails, and the management of campgrounds and cabins. In the case of the Verde, she also managed the Forest watershed, an issue of critical importance in desert lands, since most surface water originated within Forest land.

Another was in charge of wildlife management, including claims made by adjoining landowners for damages by deer or other predatory animals, the harvesting of animals by hunters, if any, and monitoring the health and wellbeing of all wildlife.

A swap of Forest land for adjoining properties was in the hands of the chief forester. Very often these swaps were mutually beneficial to the Forest and to the private land owner, especially when the Forest was able to obtain private holdings within its boundaries or desirable properties that adjoined it.

When National Forests were established, inevitably privately owned parcels remained within their boundaries. The Forest Service placed a priority, when doing property swaps, on obtaining these properties so it could manage an entire seamless expanse. In many instances, covenants based on eminent domain required a land owner whose property was entirely surrounded by Forest land to offer the Forest the first right of purchase.

Bill and Tony, dressed in suit and tie, waited to meet with the head of the Verde Forest. They were seated on grungy back-to-back plastic chairs in a wide hallway which served as the waiting area. The Forest Service did not present itself as a prosperous business but as an unpretentious public utility.

Miles Stanton, the Verde head forester, stepped out and called out loud, "William Starret and Tony Friedson? Come on in."

Startled, Bill and Tony rose to see a fellow in work boots and a blue work shirt motioning them to follow. When he noticed that Bill carried a tube of drawings, he changed direction. "On second thought, let's go to the conference room where we have some table space."

Miles dispensed with all formalities. "I understand you have a land swap to propose. You can spread things out here. Let's see what we've got."

The informality of their reception by Stanton astonished Bill. Somehow he had imagined an inner office guarded by at least two tiers of receptionists, one more intimidating than the next. He did not expect to be greeted by an easy-going person in a blue work shirt with an open collar.

"You fellows are from San Leandro, aren't you?" Without waiting for a reply, he went on. "I love that area, one of the nicest valleys in the Verde Forest. How long have you been living there?"

Tony spoke up quickly, "My family has been ranching there for two generations. Bill here has been a developer in San Leandro all his life, and his family lived in the valley when all of it was still a part of the Alonso Ranch. You might call us village fathers, except that the earliest families go back to Spanish days."

"San Leandro wasn't a village until the early twentieth century," Bill added helpfully, "but it was on the migration routes of Spaniards from the seventeenth century. There are still some families who trace their heritage back to that period."

Bill unrolled his charts, maps, and photographs and handed Miles a copy of his proposal. In Bill's eyes the magnitude of the transaction he proposed wasn't being matched by the head forester's demeanor.

Nevertheless Bill had prepared a systematic presentation and he launched into it. "We are here to propose a land swap with the Verde National Forest of 1900 acres for a 200-acre strip of land above San Leandro. What we are offering consists of two parcels, one of 1500 acres, the other of 400. Their boundaries are marked on these topographic maps. Here are photos of these properties taken from two thousand feet, which will provide you with much greater detail.

"As you can see, the smaller property is a former church camp with fairly extensive facilities that remain serviceable. The larger parcel is a former lumber mill that made use of the acreage to produce utility poles. The mill has been removed, though traces of it remain. Both properties are wooded with good stands of ponderosa pine. The former church camp is almost entirely surrounded by Forest land, with only a neck that served as an access road, while the former lumber mill property lies adjacent to the Verde Forest on its longest side."

Bill had hardly stopped to catch his breath, when he noticed to his dismay that Miles hadn't been paying attention to what he was saying, but was focused on the aerial photos.

Miles still hadn't made any comment, but examined the maps and photographs closely, making note of their location relative to the rest of the Forest and their accessibility to existing Forest roads.

Finally he allowed, "These are certainly properties which the Verde would consider. As you have pointed out, they have good stands of pine. I'm sure you understand that I can't make a decision like this on the spot. There are procedures to which I am bound, and there are consultations that I prefer to undertake on my own. We also conduct the usual notifications of neighboring property owners, and will have at least one hearing in San Leandro.

"As you can imagine, a major part of the decision will be based on an assessment of the relative value of these parcels. In the eyes of the Forest Service, this decision isn't based primarily on monetary value. We base our decision on how it contributes to the Forest and how it fits in with neighboring properties. So we look at the parcel with considerations that go beyond their value as real estate holdings."

Bill, who already harbored uneasy feelings, took this remark as a dark cloud of uncertainty, but he soldiered on with his proposal at the point where he had left off.

"Here is a map of the two hundred acres we want to acquire, and a photo from a thousand feet. As you can see it is on the slope below the Arena Rim, which is nearly bare of all vegetation. At the east end of the plot it extends slightly above the rim and intersects with the access road to my existing property. You will note that virtually none of the property is forested at all. It is not within but at the boundary of the actual Forest. We are interested only in a strip of land, roughly a half mile wide, at the edge of the Forest. Our interest in it lies in its great potential for development as highly attractive residential parcels." Bill's monologue petered out.

Miles studied the map, the photos, and especially the development plan. By consulting the topographic map, he made note of the steep slope

down from the Arena Rim. "You will have a challenge to avoid any damage
to the rim if you disturb this site. If the slope of the rim were to erode, it
would affect the quality of the Forest beyond the boundary."

Bill hurried to offer reassurance. "We are equally concerned about
maintaining the rim as it is. In fact, the rim, in its present shape, is an essential feature of the site and its most attractive one. We plan to name the site
Anasazi Vistas, which makes sense only if our building sites can be situated
against the rim without any loss to its stability."

"I see," Miles replied. "You are surely aware that choosing this site
for construction will sharply increase your unit costs. Is there an adequate
market for this? These matters are not our prime concern, yet we do have
an interest in the viability of any developments that border the Forest. For
instance, will utilities be provided by the village of San Leandro? This will
certainly be one of the issues that will be of interest to the village, and we
will be in contact with them about your plans."

Bill became uncomfortable, as Miles edged onto some issues he did
not want to clarify at this time. He intended to obtain water by substantially
enlarging the existing shallow well on the Starret homestead but didn't want
to open this question until later. "The development agreements will come
later once we have the property in hand. It would be futile to enter into these
discussions now." Bill hoped that this remark would close off any further
discussion of access to water.

"Yes, of course," Miles replied. "I am concerned that the building sites
you are planning, which fit snugly into the steep slope, will require extensive
substructure. This will double or even triple the construction cost per unit.
Whether there is a market for such expensive residential construction is
your problem. My problem is that I do not have any assurance that you will
really spend what is necessary to protect the integrity of the rim. How do
we know that the slope of the rim, which through erosion has settled at the
maximum sustainable angle, will be retained?"

Tony hurried his reply. "We can only reassure you that it is in our interests to maintain the slope. If we don't, our entire marketing and development plan is not sustainable. We have an even greater interest in this than
the Forest Service has."

"Okay," Miles replied. "We will take your proposal under consideration. As I mentioned, there are procedures which I must follow and people
I will consult on my own. Naturally the Forest Service always makes it a
practice to notify neighboring property owners whenever a swap such as
this is being considered. They will have the opportunity to express their
concerns. After these consultations, we will base our decision on the relative

attractiveness of the properties relative to the rest of the Forest. Obviously we will not ignore the interests of third parties, but these are never primary."

"Can you give us a time frame? When would you think that we could expect a decision?"

"I never mention a date because the process is never entirely in my hands. I can only tell you that we will pursue the proposal. We will not be sitting on it."

Miles began to gather up papers. "May I keep your maps, photos, and the other papers?"

"Of course," Bill replied. "Thanks for considering this proposed swap. Let me urge you to move the process along as quickly as you can." Bill said this as he was already moving toward the door.

At the door he stopped abruptly. "Just out of curiosity . . . when you notify neighboring property holders of the proposed swap, does this include just the adjoining property holders, or do you include more distant owners as well?"

"Just the adjoining owners, has been our policy."

Bill nodded, "I will be awaiting your decision." Relieved that the Forest Service would only be notifying Yolanda Alonso and himself, the only adjoining property holders, he did not anticipate serious opposition from the village. Yolanda had already agreed not to reveal his plans.

35

DURING NOVEMBER THE CONSTANT repetition of bright, sunny days with humidity readings in the teens came to an end. High clouds arose in the West announcing the promise of rain. The jet stream began to shift southward and the cloudless days of fall gave way to higher humidity and high cirrus overcast.

A dark descending smudge of rainfall began to appear in the west, called "virga," rainfall which dries up in the air before it reaches the ground, the first sign of change in the weather pattern.

Watching the Weather Channel at Verde Gardens, Ernesto followed the movement of a massive cold front approaching the west coast, stretching southward parallel to the Baja Peninsula. Its steep plunge drove the center of low pressure deeply to the south, eventually cutting it off from the movement of the front itself. Spinning by itself, it steadily deepened and picked up more and more moisture from the sea, even as it continued its southward path.

Finally the front slammed onto land at the south end of the Baja Peninsula, and—because it no longer moved along with the larger weather front from which it arose—it advanced slowly while dumping enormous amounts of rain onto the parched desert. Ernesto awaited the arrival of the first big rain of the season. His spirit rose as the atmospheric pressure dropped; for him the imminent storm called for fervent anticipation and rejoicing.

The humidity shot upward as the clouds thickened, the temperature dropped, and the dew point surged as a steady drizzle began. By nightfall it poured, and a wind-driven torrent with lightning and crashing thunder lasted until morning. At dawn the entire desert landscape carried a covering of water, which gathered into streams and filled dried-up arroyos.

The cut-off low moved slowly, so that the downpour persisted throughout the next day. Breaks in the cloud cover only began to show in the west by late afternoon.

Chris called Ernesto. "Get your raincoat; you've got to see the Arena Gorge. It's really awesome when it's running this high. I'm calling Claudia to join us."

The gorge was a notch in the Arena Rim that released water from a twenty-square-mile area of grassland and scattered pine and formed the headwaters of the Arena River. Usually the thousand-foot waterfall carried only a trickle, and during the dry months there was only seepage from the rock formations at its banks. After downpours like this, it became a raging torrent.

Ernesto and Claudia arrived at Chris's shack. He pointed enthusiastically at the water tank that had just been excavated. "Look, it's overflowing."

The overflow even filled the circular catchments around their newly planted fruit trees. The mulch which covered the growing plots was battened down and saturated. Ernesto ran around the tank like a kid released to play in the water.

As they approached the Arena Gorge, its roar became ever more deafening. A safety fence along the perimeter of a protruding rock shelf protected them and allowed them to approach the torrent in the relative safety of the overhang. The noise was awesome and fearful; the spray was so thick that the opposite bank, only fifty feet away, was barely visible. Boulders the size of barrels crashed with explosive force and hurtled down the incline. The threesome stood entranced and speechless, totally engrossed by the force of nature. Time passed without notice. After a half hour, which seemed like only minutes, they left the viewpoint reluctantly, but turned around at intervals to prolong the experience.

Once back at his shack Chris became introspective and shared the deep significance which the falls carried for him. "When I first got to San Leandro I brought a lot of troubles with me. It was on a day like this that I walked over to the falls, when it was crashing as loud as today. I stood transfixed by the noise and the spray, soaked to the skin, because I hadn't bothered to take a coat. It didn't matter. The force of the waters had a healing effect on me. I sensed Angela's presence and seemed to hear her voice calling to me above the roar of the water. She seemed to say to me that she was restored in body and happy in spirit. She urged me to find healing as well. I made many drives into the desert in those days, but nothing soothed me more than the time I spent at the gorge. I have gone there when the flow was high and also when there was just a trickle. I've scrambled over its boulders, and investigated its pools and eddies, and I always felt restored."

Ernesto nodded knowingly. "I know exactly what you mean, when you speak of encountering Angela there. I have often sensed the presence of Marcelino beside me. He was such a generous leader to us as we tramped our way across the Altar Valley. He gave up his share of the little water we had. It was because of his generosity that I gained the edge to survive.

"When the three of us crossed the border to begin our trek we each carried two gallon-jugs of water. This was intended to last only two days. We had paid a coyote to make a cache for us along the way. But our two-gallon supply had to be dropped because we were fleeing the helicopter. When we arrived at the rendezvous site, we searched in the heat of the day to retrieve the cache. Our efforts were in vain because our coyote feared the helicopter as much as we did and did not leave anything for us. Marcelino tried to make the most of a dire situation and altered our route, so we ended up near the Arena Valley.

"A nearby village had water, but we couldn't risk asking for it. The coyote had even told us that there was a flow of spring water in a nearby meadow, but it was in full view of the village and we didn't dare to be out in the open. Besides we had no containers left, except a single jug that was half empty. There was no choice but to keep going as quickly as we could; we had to get to safety before the desert would seal our fate. Obviously we didn't quite make it.

"Marcelino blamed himself for our trouble for he had chosen the coyote, and he held himself responsible. He insisted that we should each receive a little extra from the last half jug. I'm sure that his sacrifice was just enough to give me the margin I needed to survive. We walked that night and all the next day, most of the time after the last of the jug was dry. I can't remember when it was that we stopped; I guess I was too delirious by that time to know.

"Remember when I told you that I didn't want you to tell me who abandoned me for dead? I sensed Marcelino near me at that time, and I seemed to hear him saying to me, 'It is not for you to know this now, but you will know later on. Then you may be ready to hear it, when your anger is gone.'"

Claudia was listening in. "I'm not into esoteric ideas like you two are. Maybe you're just experiencing that age-old tradition of guardian spirits. I've always felt that the boundary between the living and the dead is not as impenetrable as we have been led to believe."

Ernesto did not return with Claudia, but hiked uphill to read the rain gauges that he had planted the previous month. They revealed a pattern of rainfall intensity which increased at higher elevations. At the garden site with an elevation of thirty-five hundred feet, his gauge registered an inch and a half. His gauges higher up near the rim at close to seven thousand feet showed over two inches. The estimates of runoff were confirmed: twenty-five percent in the case of a rainfall event of one and a half inches for a total of just short of eleven hundred cubic feet—the total capacity of his tank. He noted with satisfaction that his rain harvesting had captured nearly all of the runoff. There was no erosion downstream.

36

SEVERAL WEEKS LATER, BECAUSE of the ADWR mandate, Anton Wehrli decided to inspect Kallisto Wells personally, to familiarize himself again with its water channels and their headgates. He parked his pickup at the top of Switchback Trail and hiked a quarter mile along the crest of the rim.

The flow of the Kallisto oozed out of the rock formation along a line that stretched nearly a half mile. On the north end the seepage it formed a small pond approximately two feet in depth. This fed an outflow that was split by the headgates in three directions. It was clear that at earlier times the pond overflowed into a creek that found its way down to the Arena, but now this creek bed was dry. All three headgates were fully open, but none flowed at full capacity because of the reduced water level of the pond itself. The entire works depended on gravity.

Anton spent a few minutes sketching the scene with special attention to the lateral channels and their headgates.

He walked south to the farthest extent of the seepage and made note of another small stream that flowed over the rim and continued down the slope until it disappeared where the highway builders had excavated a gravel quarry. He recalled that this little flow was named Vasquez Creek.

Anton returned to his pickup and drove home. His inspection of Kallisto Wells reminded him that he needed to touch base with Bret Masterson, who also received water from the Kallisto. Since it was early in the afternoon, and he had nothing else scheduled, he decided to give Brett Masterson a call.

"Brett, this is Anton Wehrli. I wonder if I could stop by for few minutes. I can be at your place in ten minutes."

"Sure, what's this about?"

"We both draw water from the Kallisto. I have been reviewing the village's water use. It seems to me that the total flow from the Kallisto is diminishing from year to year. I would like to hear what you know about it, and what your experience has been."

"Okay, Anton. Come on over. Or would you like to meet at the Cottonwood?"

"Naw, not today. Maybe some other time."

Anton found Brett lounging on his sun porch. He had a couple of cold beers waiting. "I decided that a beer would be welcome at the end of the afternoon. I hope you feel the same."

"Thanks, Brett. I just took a walk up to the Kallisto, and the exercise has made me thirsty. You know, it's been quite a while since I've taken a look at those headgates. I found that none of them are running at full capacity. This leads me to think that the flow has been slowing down gradually. Have you noticed any decrease?"

"I can't say that I have. Of course, I've never done any metering. We use some of it to water our stock, and I use of the rest to irrigate some of our best pasture."

"The village does metering because that's how we get paid for our water service, and that's why I know that we are not getting quite as much as we used to. As a result we are pumping more from our deep well, and its water level is going down year by year. This means that we are using more water than our sources can supply indefinitely.

"This brings me to ask a question. This is just to broach the subject with you," Anton added sheepishly. "I wonder if you would consider making up our shortfall from your Kallisto allotment. Of course, like I said, I am just exploring this matter at the moment."

"Any loss of water would seriously affect the value of the ranch, and the owner would never allow it.

"I thought you were the owner."

"I used to be, but I made a big mistake when I put the place at risk during the oil boom a while back. Bill Starret bought out my creditors. The ranch belongs to him now."

Anton had the answer he was looking for. The Masterson ranch was not available and neither was its water.

37

Stella Mantilla used the village pickup for a short drive to Yolanda Alonso's old ranch house. While it was not far, it was not without its challenges, and she gripped the steering wheel firmly when, at the edge of town, the dirt road dipped down into the Arena for a low-water crossing. She splashed through a four-inch current, a water level much reduced from the four-foot flow that the recent rainstorm had caused. Yellow traffic barriers were still there but had been moved to the side. Within the crossing, depth gauges stood and gave warning to unwary drivers.

Rising out of the river bottom, the road turned sharply to the left and followed the river upstream, clinging precariously to the bank. After a quarter mile of hugging the cliffside, the road veered into a box canyon that opened up to the right. From here a well-surfaced narrow lane led to Yolanda's old ranch house. Stella arrived at a parking circle, which was both spacious and inviting.

A weather-worn ocotillo fence deterred not only human intruders but also all manner of wild desert critters. Inside the enclosure Stella admired a meticulously kept flower garden, now past its seasonal prime, surrounded by an assortment of garden ornaments and found-art statuary. Next to the house she admired a vegetable garden with orderly rows of raised beds with assorted greens and root crops. Irrigation came by way of a pipe that captured Arena River water a quarter mile upstream and emptied into a reservoir. Yolanda's plantings explained the necessity of the tightly closed gate that prevented the incursion of hungry mule deer, rabbits and javelinas.

Stella negotiated the stone steps leading to the gate and confronted a neatly painted sign: "Welcome to Alonso hollow. Close the gate. Chickens want out and javelinas want in."

Stella did as instructed then followed a stone walkway and knocked. She heard a voice from inside, but she couldn't make out the words. Stella hesitated, not wishing to knock again but not knowing what else to do. Suddenly a small panel in the door opened from the inside and a deeply wrinkled face with piercing eyes appeared in the opening.

"Stella, what a surprise! Just wait a moment while I unlock the door. You know I live alone out here, and I have to be cautious." When the dead-bolt slid open, the heavy door swung noisily on its wrought iron hinges. "I'm delighted to see you. You know I don't get many visitors; when I need to meet someone, I usually do so at the Cottonwood. Please, come in?"

Yolanda motioned Stella to take a chair. Meanwhile she settled into her own stuffed recliner with the aid of a cane. She spoke with a strong voice, "Now what brings me the pleasure of your visit?"

Stella came right to the point. "I want to talk to you about Verde Gardens. I believe you are the owner?"

"Well, I own a part of it." Yolanda failed to elaborate.

Stella filled the lull by commenting on the garden. "You have lovely flowers. Do you take care of the garden yourself?"

"The flowers keep me company. They give me much joy because they always look pretty, whether I notice them or not," Yolanda remarked cryptically.

Stella explained the purpose of her visit with short, direct statements: "You know that I work for the village, and my boss is the mayor, Anton Wehrli. I am interested in the water that you get from Kallisto Wells."

Yolanda understood perfectly. She fixed her eyes directly upon Stella. "Mr. Uribe manages Verde Gardens, and I would not make a decision about its water supply without consulting him. All of the water comes from Kallisto Wells."

"Do you need all of the water from the Kallisto? If not, would you consider making some of it available to the village? I'm just exploring options on behalf of the village."

"Oh, I believe that the entire flow is put to use. Once again I would need to talk to Mr. Uribe."

"Mrs. Alonso, have you ever given any thought to selling Verde Gardens?"

"Verde Gardens isn't privately owned anymore. I'm only one of the stockholders now."

"What's the price of the stock now, if you don't mind my asking?"

"I don't keep up with the value of shares anymore. Furthermore I'm only a part owner, and I have never considered selling. It's one of my best properties because it is such a benefit to the village. It used to be listed on the Pacific Stock Exchange, but I believe it's traded privately now."

"I came here just to make an inquiry about Verde Gardens. I gather from what you are saying that you would not consider an offer from to village."

"I'm sorry to disappoint you and Mr. Wehrli. I haven't considered selling. That's why I don't have any idea what it's worth."

Stella had her answer, but did not wish to leave abruptly. "I know you have an apartment at the Cottonwood. My place is at the college. Would you like to meet me for lunch sometime? I often eat at the Cottonwood when I'm too lazy to pack a lunch."

"That's a wonderful idea. But you have to let me know ahead of time— at least by mid-morning." Yolanda braced herself on the arms of her chair as she was about to rise.

Stella rose quickly to give her a hand. "I'll leave my card. You can call me any time. Thank you for your time."

Back at the village Stella made some notes for Anton: "Mrs. Alonso has no intention of selling. She depends on Mr. Uribe, the Verde Gardens manager, for advice and seems to have placed the whole operation in his hands. She hasn't even kept up on the value of the property."

38

ANTON FOLLOWED UP ON the suggestion made by the village board to contract with a hydrologist, Arch Minter, from Water Consultants of Gila Center to advise the village on its water problems.

"We'll need to cover some ground to get a good look at the situation. Leave your car here and let me take you," Anton said.

"Whatever you say."

"Our village draws water from a deep well. We're aware that the water level is receding at the rate of twelve feet annually. Can you tell us how many acre-feet that represents, and how deep the aquifer goes?"

"There is no way we can look underground and do an accurate measurement of how much water a given aquifer may hold. We can map out with considerable accuracy the size of an aquifer in surface distance. Without exploratory wells, we have little ability to measure its depth."

Anton said, "The copper mine ten miles west of here draws from the same source. I asked them about their usage, and they said they don't meter it, and they have a legal waiver from the state that allows them to take whatever they need."

Arch said, "Their usage is almost certainly more than yours."

"Is there any way to negotiate with them?"

"Probably not. They are not likely to reveal their usage, nor consider any decrease. Without water, they're out of business." Arch noticed Anton's disappointment. "The information you have given us is still helpful. You know how much you have been pumping. You also know that your water level recedes twelve feet annually. What we don't know is how much water other users of the aquifer draw from it; nor do we know the amount of natural recharge. This recharge, whatever it is, is also being used up. In general, as aquifers go, yours is a small one.

"I also researched Kallisto Wells, since you mentioned that the village draws water from it. In my opinion, Kallisto is not groundwater, but surface water because it is actually an underground stream that surfaces just above the rim due to an impermeable rock formation below. This means that, if a new well were sunk, the flow from the Kallisto would most likely be compromised, and that would be contrary to prevailing water law.

"We also know that wells not too distant from San Leandro have a much shallower water level. This indicates with virtual certainty that they can't be drawing from the same source as you are. In effect this fact defines the surface extent of your aquifer. It's entirely possible that it could be really deep, but we don't know how deep."

"So what are you telling me?" Anton inquired with increasing alarm.

"I'd have to be honest with you. You have a problem, just like everyone else around here. At the present rate of extraction from the aquifer, if I were a betting man, I certainly wouldn't give you much more than fifty years. Even that time frame is questionable."

"What are our options?"

"Simple. Find another source of water. Recharge your aquifer as much as you can by recycling your effluent. Do serious conservation right away. There is no magic bullet. It's a finite resource; when you use it up, it's gone."

Anton brought up one other possibility. "Would you take a look at the source of the Arena River above the gorge? We had a tremendous flow from up there after the recent rainstorm. What would it take to dam it up and create a spillway and a treatment facility?"

"Did you say that the drainage area is about twenty square miles?"

"Yes, that's about right."

"And your annual rainfall is about twelve inches?"

Anton nodded but added, "Rainfall here is very sporadic and very local. I would guess that we probably get less than ten inches in town, but there is more at the top of the plateau."

"How much you can impound depends on how much rain falls at any given time. If it rained a quarter inch every week for a year, that would be fourteen inches. However, you probably wouldn't be able to harvest a drop because all of it would be absorbed and there would be no runoff at all. But if you have four rainfall events of two inches each, you would be filling a substantial lake each time. It all depends on the amount of runoff."

"Well last week there was a two-inch event up there."

"How often does that happen?" He continued without giving Anton a chance to answer. "Of course, we have no way of predicting the future. Let's assume that, out of your twelve inches of rain, you actually would acquire a ten percent runoff. That would be a reasonable amount." Arch stopped to run the numbers on his hand calculator. "To retain that much water you would need to create a huge dam and an elaborate spillway.

"This brings up another issue that must enter into your planning. If you impound the waters of the Arena at its source, you are also reducing the recharge of your aquifer. It is impossible to know how much the river replenishes the aquifer, but there is bound to be some."

Anton brought up an even more serious problem. "If we dam up a pond that size, it would need to be really secure. Our village could not be asked to be a couple of miles downstream from a lake that could release a flood. It would wash away the entire village if the dam gave way. In any case we would need a spillway, a conduit down to a treatment plant, and so forth. How much would it cost—just a rough estimate?"

"It would be millions, of course. I couldn't give you an estimate off hand. But with a few hours of research, I could give you a good ballpark figure."

"Yeah, I think we need some kind of estimate," Anton replied without much enthusiasm. "When we get back down to the village I need to have you look at another possible project, the creation of an injection well so that we can recharge the aquifer with our effluent water."

"Sure thing. But if you replace your evaporation pond with an injection well, you will also need to upgrade your treatment plant from a primary to a secondary level."

Anton became discouraged, as every possible solution turned out to be so expensive that it would exceed the village's resources. "I guess we need an estimate on the injection well and updating the treatment plant. But forget about a dam up above the gorge. We can't afford that."

39

WHEN THE MULCTON LAW firm became an equity partner in Star Holdings, they took added interest in the viability of Bill's planning. Killian had suspicions about the availability of a hundred-year water supply and engaged a consultant from Hydro Resources to make an assessment of how much water a larger well on Starret's homestead might yield. He was concerned whether it would be enough to supply Bill's development. Carson Fowler, a hydrologist, arrived at San Leandro with a four-wheeler in tow. He unloaded at the Cottonwood and made his way up Switchback Trail to the top of the Arena Rim.

Fowler immediately took note of a potential problem. The Starret homestead was less than a quarter mile from Kallisto Wells. Did the two share the same source of water? Did Bill's well draw from the same underground stream which broke the surface at Kallisto Wells? If it was the same stream, then Starret's expanded water usage would inevitably cut into the Kallisto flow. He noted that the headgates at the Kallisto split its flow three ways. Each of these three would almost certainly contest Bill's new well, if their flow were compromised.

When Fowler returned to his office, he sketched out his report to Killian and did not mince words. His report read: "The total annual flow at Kallisto is approximately fourteen hundred acre-feet. The seepage extends about two thousand feet and is concentrated in only a few spots. This is consistent with an upwelling caused by an impermeable substratum of rock. There is no indication of a surface flow above the site; but that doesn't mean that the Kallisto isn't by definition a surface flow, only incidentally underground. This means that it is not groundwater by law, but a surface flow."

Fowler's report alerted Killian to the prevailing laws governing water rights. In the case of groundwater, the owner of the surface land had first rights. But the Kallisto was surface water, in which the right of prior appropriation held sway. This meant that whoever put the water to beneficial use obtained rights to it, as long as that use persisted.

Fowler's report concluded: "A certain level of ambiguity persists because the law does not recognize an explicit linkage between surface water and groundwater, even if an aquifer can be linked unquestionably to a surface water source. A surface owner owns all of the underground water, if that is how the source is defined. He is entitled to sink a well, but, if this compromises the supply of another existing source of water, he will probably face a challenge. His rights hinge on whether his well draws on a source that is unquestionably groundwater."

He concluded his report by stating, "Your client should be advised that if he chooses to enlarge his well and if this action adversely affects the three present users of Kallisto water, he would almost certainly face legal action.

"In our opinion, though we recognize the greater competence of your law firm in these legal matters, your client should be advised to acquire water rights by purchase from the present users of the Kallisto."

Killian studied the Hydro Resources report and came to the conclusion that Star Holdings faced some very difficult challenges in obtaining an assured hundred-year water supply. This steepened the Mulcton firm's gamble in becoming an equity partner. Nevertheless Killian felt that all was not lost, and it was too soon to bail out. After all, the Forest Service had not yet made any commitment to the proposed property swap.

40

"Have you noticed any drop in the amount of water coming from the Kallisto?" Anton questioned Arturo Uribe, the manager of Verde Gardens.

"Yes, there's been some decrease. I can tell because our overflow isn't nearly what it used to be."

"Overflow? Are you telling me that you actually have more water than you need?" Anton's face registered surprise and heightened expectations.

Arturo hastened to elaborate. "Sometimes, but not always. Our water usage isn't constant. When we flood new plantings, the tank usually runs dry, but when there's no special need, we will have some overflow. It goes down a culvert to the Arena below."

Anton's replied enthusiastically. "Suppose we change the direction of your overflow to the village; would that work out for you?"

"It would just be a matter of putting in another pipe, but it's something I would routinely bring to Mrs. Alonso's attention."

Anton became uncommonly animated, for he saw a deal in the making. "Of course, your costs would be covered by the village," he added hurriedly. "Would Mrs. Alonso agree? What do you think?"

"If it's for the village, she would probably waive the costs, but I wouldn't let her be that generous."

Anton entertained hopes that the village's water problem might be solved after all. "Just estimating—how much water overflows from your tank?"

"Naturally, we don't meter the overflow, so I can only give you an estimate. I would say maybe ten percent." Arturo hastened to mention that this amount could not be assured. "When the college relocated their horticulture program, they did so largely because Verde Gardens was local and a valuable teaching resource. Inevitably this will have an effect on our water usage. We are in the early stages of developing the curriculum, so the impact is still uncertain.

"Because of collaboration with the college, we have had to take a look at our entire operation. We'll need to diversify; enrollees in the program will each have an experimental plot. As the enrollment in the horticulture program expands, so will our array of plantings. We will concentrate our commercial output on just a few crops that we can grow year-round and in quantity, most likely tomatoes, cucumbers, carrots, radishes, and cabbages.

"Finally, as Mrs. Alonso always says: 'modernize and specialize.' This will require that we move aggressively into hydroponics, especially for cucumbers and tomatoes."

Uribe emphasized that he faced an uncertain transition. "The challenge for me is how to manage these changes with limited resources. I'm taking a lot of time getting to the point. If you take our excess water, I have to insist that we get paid for it. We will need greenhouses for hydroponics, structures to provide sun screen for sensitive leafy plants, and spray nozzles to reduce high temperatures. Without these improvements we can't expand our commercial side."

Anton nodded vigorously. "Of course, the village will work with you. Let's meet again next week. Meanwhile, I will consult the village council and you talk to Mrs. Alonso."

Anton was immensely pleased when he left Verde Gardens, since it gave promise of an additional forty acre-feet of water—not enough to achieve safe yield, but it was better than nothing.

WHEN ANTON AND STELLA met with Angel Benevides and Bill Starret, the options available to the village were already clear. The estimated cost of an injection well and an upgraded water treatment plant seemed within reach. But an impounding of the Arena above the gorge was out of the question. Conservation was the only reasonable way to achieve safe yield as required by the ADWR.

Bill Starret remained silent. He found the village's preoccupation with water troubling and a potential threat to his plans, but he had no way of countering it.

Benevides reported on his conversation with Fortner, who advised that the village plan on providing water to owners of undeveloped lots. While a right to water service on the part of lot owners was ambiguous, it was Fortner's advice that the village make every effort to provide it.

41

STELLA ARRANGED TO USE the auditorium of San Ysidro High School on Saturday morning. She ran off a hundred flyers for distribution throughout the village; took out a half-page ad in the local shopper; and recorded radio spots which ran twice daily during the week before the meeting.

Wehrli opened the town hall and introduced the participants, then stepped aside to let Stella explain the basics of the water problem. It took her only ten minutes to outline the discrepancy between supply and usage. She ended with a forthright statement of the stark choices that the village faced and presented an outline of the board's recommendations.

"First, the village board proposes upgrading the effluent treatment facility and the construction of an injection well. A bond issue for this investment will be submitted to the voters for their approval.

"Second, water usage will be reduced by conservation. The board will propose changes in water rates based on usage. Rates will be higher for heavier usage and this increase in village income will be used to subsidize installation of low-flow plumbing fixtures.

"Third, outside watering will be permitted only with rainwater captured on rooftops. The village will provide a carwash. A vegetable garden no larger than twenty feet by forty feet will be permitted as long as it is equipped with approved drip irrigation."

Leon Weisner approached a microphone. As an insurance agent he was well known in the village, and he was accustomed to speaking in public. "You have made clear that our present supply of water does not meet our future needs. The obvious solution, it seems to me, is to increase our supply. Surely there must be water available somewhere. I can't imagine that we'd actually run out, unless we just don't make an effort to find any."

Wehrli took the question. He related the report of Arch Minter on harvesting the flow of the Arena, its cost and loss or recharge to the aquifer. Then he explained his estimate on the probable size and capacity of the aquifer. He went on to explain the history of the Kallisto and the complex legal issues relating to surface and groundwater and concluded by explaining the law of prior appropriation and the requirement of safe yield in the case of any water resource.

Weisner's expression indicated that he remained unconvinced. Next at the microphone was a woman who didn't bother to introduce herself and simply blurted out, "You can't be serious. You can't tell me that there isn't any water anymore. I'll just drill a well in my backyard."

Wehrli replied, "We've always taken for granted that we can take care of ourselves and that the resources we need are there for the taking. But I'm afraid the fact that we live in a desert has to be taken seriously. If you drill in your backyard you will be drawing from the same aquifer as the village and the safe-yield requirement will apply to you as well. At the present time the water level of our aquifer is at 220 feet, and it is going down twelve feet every year. We could acquire surface rights to underground water by buying land outside the boundaries of our own aquifer, but if we do we'd still need to observe the same rule of safe yield. The facts remain the same: we can't take more water than the aquifer gets from natural recharge."

Benevides at the councilors' table grabbed the microphone. "I want to say a word to back up Anton. When he first brought this problem to our attention, I didn't want to believe him either. But I'm convinced this isn't some nightmare that goes away when we wake up. There is only so much water in the desert, and eventually you do run out. I've lived here all my life and I remember when the Kallisto overflowed all its headgates and ran down to the Arena River. That flow has diminished over the years just like our aquifer has."

Bill Starret, who had kept his development plans in total secrecy, took the microphone and tried to minimize the problem. "The aquifer's water level is now at 220 That's quite a ways down, but I know of wells north of here that are much deeper. We can just keep deepening the well. At the rate of twelve feet a year, that gives us quite a few years before we would run out. By that time there will be a solution that we can't presently foresee."

Wehrli did not relish taking on Starret, who had developed Paradise Acres and who was the one most likely to request water service for a new development. Stella recognized Anton's dilemma and approached the microphone herself. He was surprised and relieved.

Stella proceeded with a dry, factual recital. "We've focused on the very same questions you bring up. We asked our consultant, Arch Minter, to give us an idea of the size of our aquifer. He said that for a definitive answer we would need to sink a series of test wells. That's a lot of expense, which I think we can avoid. He established that the surface size of our aquifer is relatively small. He did this by comparing the depths of neighboring wells. If a well ten miles to the north draws water at a hundred feet, then it is a separate source from ours.

"That establishes the surface size. It doesn't tell us how deep it goes. There's no way to tell for sure. The water down there isn't like a lake; it's rock or gravel with water all around. If it is rock, the water capacity will be less; if it is gravel, there will be room for more. Nobody really knows without sinking deep shafts to find out what's down there. What we do know is that the resource is finite and that it becomes more expensive to bring up the water the deeper you go.

"The ADWR doesn't impose a sanction automatically if we don't achieve safe yield, but it has the option of imposing one. The real sanction we face is not a fine but what we have to live with if we don't take this seriously. A village without water is the real sanction."

Angel Benevides took the microphone. "I want to follow up on Stella's remarks. She is right in what she is telling us, but we must not come to the conclusion that we don't have any hope of solving this problem. We do have a very attractive option, namely reducing our water usage. I hope that we can get to that subject before long."

As if on cue, the next speaker asked how the village could reduce its water usage. "I would like a list of options. How much good would they do? Would they add expense for each of us? Would I have to buy new appliances? Could I still have a garden, if I need to water it?"

Angel Benevides replied, "We've let Anton and Stella carry the water (pardon the metaphor) for us. Let me try and tackle this and give a lot of the credit to Stella, who has done most of the research.

"The village will reimburse you if you replace wasteful fixtures and appliances with water conserving ones. How we will get the money to do this, I will get to in a minute. You asked for a list of possible conservation options. Here are some obvious ones: no outside watering, except for a small vegetable garden; a restriction on outside water use except for what you can capture from your own roof; a public car wash run by the village; no irrigation of grass except with captured rain water; converting any lawn to desert landscaping.

"There will need to be an increase in water rates for two reasons: first of all, to help the village subsidize the installation of low-use fixtures and secondly to encourage less use. The list can be expanded, but this much will be enough to give you an idea. We believe that we can reduce our water use by a third simply by conservation."

San Leandro did not have a chamber of commerce, but there was an informal group who met weekly for lunch at the Cottonwood. Their chair, Marcy Woodson, had been waiting at the microphone. "The general impression I get from your remarks today is that there is little or no chance for growth or development unless the water issue is resolved. Even worse, your solution assumes that it can be solved only by reducing use. You're not giving any hope for any business to start up or to grow. You're giving us a formula for a ghost town. I know that's not your purpose, but can you convince me that it's not the inevitable result?"

Wehrli began a reply and invited the panel to add to his remarks. "The scenario you describe is one that we want to avoid for obvious reasons. First of all I want you to imagine a different outcome. Suppose we don't solve the problem and we really do face a sharply reduced supply; what would the prospects for business and development in this village be in that case?

"We don't want to sugarcoat anything here. Life can't go on as before. This meeting is being held to motivate us to reduce our water use. I would say that lower per person use of water does not necessarily result in a reduced lifestyle. The average American uses an astounding eighty to a hundred gallons of water each day. By comparison the average European, whose lifestyle is not inferior to ours, uses much less. We could cut our use in half and still seem wasteful to most people on the earth.

"Neither should we assume that reduced water usage will limit all growth and development. Obviously there are some water-intensive enterprises that we won't be able to support. The challenge which we face is to encourage developments which do not incur excessive water usage. Anyone want to add to this?"

An attendee unexpectedly stepped forward. "I moved here some ten years ago from a town in Pennsylvania. We faced a similar situation, for we had a city dependent on a single industry. When this local plant was taken over by a large corporation, they quickly closed it and left our town in the lurch. Obviously they only wanted to acquire the plant in order to eliminate a competitor. The result was that we were left with homes we couldn't sell, a plant that was rusting away, and a population living off sparse retirements. We couldn't change the facts, but we could change our planning. More importantly we had to change our attitude.

"The city leveraged its assets, many of which had not previously been recognized, and developed an entirely new business base. Instead of being a glass products producer only, it developed a diversified base."

The next to approach the microphone was a shrunken old man who leaned heavily on a cane. "I've gathered from Mr. Benavides's remarks that water rates will need to go up. He said that this was necessary to get the funds so the village can force us to change to newer fixtures and appliances. Is that the only reason? If my appliances meet the new standard already, would I still have to pay a higher rate? I want to tell you that I can't afford it."

Stella approached the podium. "Since I do the billing for water, this is a question that I should take. The reason I would favor a gradual increase in water rates is twofold. First is the one you mentioned: to provide funds to assist with the replacement of wasteful fixtures and appliances.

"But there is a second reason as well. The advice that I have received from other communities is unanimous. Nothing works better than a monetary incentive. You will never get total agreement on a policy, and even if you did, there will always be someone who will make an exception in his favor. An appeal to the common good or civic duty, or whatever else you wish to call it, only takes you so far. A more effective incentive toward conservation is cost. When waste becomes expensive, we will have less of it. I don't want to sound too cynical, but human nature is what it is."

The next speaker approached the microphone sheepishly. Her voice was low and gave evidence of tension and anger. "Will the village be able to provide water service to lots which have not yet been built up?" She seemed to have more to say, but only stammered briefly, and then stepped back awkwardly.

This was the question which Anton dreaded, but knew it had to be addressed. In fact, he had decided that he would bring it up on his own, if no one else did. "That is probably the most difficult problem we face. Once again, I hope others will help me with this answer. I expect that we would make every effort to provide water to existing lot holders within the village limits. This does not mean that we will be able to honor every development project. New development plans, termed highest use, will not be possible.

"We recognize that someone who purchases a village lot does so with the expectation that its value is dependent upon its eventual development, even if this is not written explicitly in a sales agreement or constitutes a legal right in a strict sense."

Bill remained silent but listened intently to Anton's answer. He was worried that his silence, even as he sat with the other councilors, would be noted.

A young fellow in his twenties approached the microphone. "I can't accept that there really is no water available. Everything has a price. I'm sure that there is always water for sale, though we may not be willing to pay the going rate. Is there an established water market? Do we know what it would cost, if we really wished to buy our water?"

Stella took the question. "There isn't an established market like there is for commodities like corn or soybeans. Water has not traditionally been traded, and we have not thought of it as scarce until recently.

"I have heard of water purchases, specifically effluent water that has gone through secondary treatment. The prices that I'm aware of have been surprisingly high—in the ten thousands per acre-foot. My suspicion is that these prices are artificially high because they reflect what a developer is willing to pay in order to meet the requirement of a hundred-year assured supply.

"Of course, we would be interested only in drinking water, not treated effluent. I have had contact with homeowners east of here whose wells have gone dry. They are paying up to $200 a month for a 500-gallon weekly supply. Conservation will be ten times cheaper than the purchase of water on the market."

Wehrli approached the microphone. "While all of you may bring up any additional issues, let me address where we might go from here. I'm sure you all know that I don't personally set policy in the village. I'm only one of three board members. The three of us are your elected representatives, and together we set village policies. We could have chosen to resolve this water problem on our own, but we decided to hear from you first. However, eventually we will meet and will arrive at appropriate decisions."

Angel Benevides moved to the mic. "We hope that this town hall has been informative and useful. It has been helpful to us. Now I would like to propose the following options. We, as your councilors, can proceed immediately to draft a series of proposals much like the ones Stella has already outlined. We could simply enact them and instruct Stella to implement them. But we would prefer to present them to you first so that we can profit from your comments and suggestions. We propose to do this at a similar town hall within a month. If you think that we should first have another discussion like we had today, we can do that as well.

"May I have a show of hands of those who want us to proceed now to draw up a series of proposals and to bring them to you for comment within a month? Is this question clearly understood? How many of you support this? May I have a show of hands now?" A clear majority indicated a vote in the affirmative. "I believe that we have strong support for a follow up meeting within a month. Before leaving here, I want to invite all of you to talk to us. This is a small village. We can proceed with a certain amount of informality. Any information you may have will be welcome." With a broad smile Benevides continued, "If you know of some available surface water that is ours for the taking, by all means let us know.

"As a final comment, I want to publicly thank Stella Mantilla for her diligent research and for arranging this town hall. Please join me in this round of applause."

Anton went to Stella's side and raised her hand with his. They both lingered in the auditorium while various townspeople circled them. Comments and questions continued for a half hour, even as the crowd slowly filtered out into the parking lot. When the last of the attendees had left, Anton congratulated Stella on her work.

Benevides said, "When we meet again to draft proposals, please invite Stella to join us."

VIII

February 2017

42

CHRIS MANEUVERED HIS PICKUP into the parking lot of the Pancake House for his usual breakfast with Carmen. The morning was unusually crisp and bracing. A massive high-pressure dome had intensified over the desert, resulting in a cloudless sky with scarcely a trace of wind. The warmth of the day escaped skyward and cold air settled into the valleys. The temperature in San Leandro dropped into the upper twenties, even though four thousand feet higher on the Arena Rim it remained in the forties.

Chris bundled up for the occasion, remembering that dressing in layers is the most effective barrier against the cold. He put on a long-sleeved flannel shirt, which he had brought from Montana and had hadn't worn since then. Over this, he wore a down vest and finally a fur-lined hat with ear flaps.

He pushed into the eatery, to the usual booth where Diana was already pouring coffee. "Here's something to warm up your frozen innards."

"Thanks, Diana. The cold actually makes me feel more bright and alert."

"Thanks for the warning. I'll stay clear."

He ignored the remark. "My innards are fine. It's my skin that has goose bumps."

"Really, have you managed to unfreeze your heart?"

"I have. Like it says in Isaiah, the Lord has changed it from stone."

"When someone quotes the Bible at me, I've learned to give him a wide berth, and you are no exception."

"Good advice, most times. It depends on the source."

The baseboard heaters along the walls were making crackling noises as their metal fins expanded with heat from the furnace. Chris began to shed his layers. He draped his vest over a chair from an adjoining table and dropped his hat on the seat. His plaid shirt was too warm as well, but he couldn't very well shed it, for it would have revealed his torn undershirt. Within a minute his unlayering was accomplished and his nose was buried in the newspaper, oblivious to his surroundings.

Chris had been checking his watch in anticipation of Carmen's arrival. When the door opened he was immediately alert and was the first to greet her. This attention was a sign of his newfound attachment.

Diana approached to take their orders, but decided to do some teasing. "I've been letting you two overdo it long enough. It's time to get something healthy into your stomachs. If this sounds like your mother talking, you're not far off. Both of you show the bloated appearance of people who have allowed a lousy diet to become an ingrained habit."

Chris and Carmen were both amused by Diana's spiel. Their appreciation encouraged her to prolong her harangue. "As for you, young lady, I would recommend that you change to oatmeal with raisins and a side of ham for protein. You've done enough carb loading for a lifetime. And for you, old man, you've got to unplug your sluggish arteries. I suggest you have oatmeal too and some dry toast. This will help you put some discipline back in your life." By now both of them were doubled over in laughter.

Carmen finally recovered enough to place her order. "No thanks, mom, I'll have the usual. Do you remember?"

"Of course I do: overly sugared hotcakes, high-caloric maple syrup, and a fructose-rich melon." Turning to Chris, she cajoled, "I'm sure you won't listen to good advice either. That will be ham and an egg smothered in grease, with toast, thankfully dry."

After Diana had departed, Chris said, "I didn't see you at the village town hall about the water problem. What Stella Mantilla and Anton Wehrli said about the laws that govern water usage was quite a challenge."

"Oh, I was there, but I got there late because I had to load a truck with gravel. When I got there I was sitting on some bleachers in the back while they were explaining the difference between surface water and groundwater. It turns out to be a critical distinction." Chris nodded while Carmen elaborated. "For starters, water rights aren't like the ownership of a commodity like corn because water is essential for life.

"Ernesto's rescue makes that clear," Chris said. "He only had two days without water and barely survived. So water is, by definition, a common resource and its ownership can never be absolute."

"I remember last year, there was a story about an incredibly rich entrepreneur who proposed to sink deep wells into the Oglalla aquifer in order to transfer water by pipeline to a large city. He expected to make a lot of money off this venture. Isn't that theft, pure and simple?"

"It would be in my judgment," Chris said. "It brings up the old maxim: what laws allow isn't necessarily ethical. What is ethical can't always be enforced by law."

Carmen said, "The reverse is also true. What laws forbid isn't always unethical and what is unethical isn't always illegal."

"Right. A law, sanctioned by a community, is an agreement to accomplish a just outcome. But because a law must be universally applicable, it can never totally address every conceivable situation that may arise between individuals. An obligation may arise that the law should not recognize or address. Hence the saying, 'what laws allow isn't necessarily ethical.' This is the reason why the immediate standard of behavior is always the individual conscience, while any ethical system or standard is always one step away from being compelling in individual instances."

"You're getting too abstract," Carmen said.

"Not at all. Let's take water law. It recognizes the right of a property owner to underground water. This legal principle works out to be ethical in most instances, but not always, as your example about the Oglalla shows."

Carmen pondered his words and saw in them a broader application. "I think that every organization finds it difficult to avoid making best belief and best practice the subject of legislation. The reasoning goes something like this: Once we determine that a certain practice works out well, shouldn't we make it an obligatory standard, namely a law? But when this happens, we sanction permanently something which owes its existence to a transient, cultural situation."

Chris was pondering how an ethical standard, whether based on civil law or a religiously sanctioned system, was consistent with the sovereignty of the individual conscience. "Is there any external standard of moral behavior which is really compelling and directly applicable in individual instances?"

Carmen was startled by how sharply Chris posed the question. "Now you really are getting down to basics. Surely every moral code is only as good as the system upon which it is based. Some may be better than others."

"Exactly," Chris said. "The ultimate standard has to be altruism, which is never a do-don't command, but an enduring stance of benevolence."

"How about the golden rule? Doesn't it apply universally?" Carmen said.

"Yes, I think so. But it's an abstraction; no ethical choice is ever theoretical. That's why I would prefer altruism, because it implies an enduring personal resolve."

Chris welcomed the challenge whenever Carmen dissected his reasoning. He wasn't offended by this, for she had become a kindred spirit for him.

He came to respect, admire, even cherish her and realized that her presence ignited in his being an uncommon spark of vitality.

"It's become a lot warmer now; we won't need to put on all those winter clothes. Would you help me carry all this stuff out to my car?" Carmen asked.

"Sure." Chris got his arms around all of it.

Chris remarked, "One of these days I will have to take you out to a place where the tab will be lots higher." It was a sly way for Chris to suggest that they might actually go out as a couple on a date.

"That's a wonderful idea. I know just the place to go."

Chris said, "Okay, you make the choice."

"Does this mean that you are even going to get dressed up, or is that too much to ask?" She said with an impish smile.

Diana overheard, "You can just pay twenty-five apiece right here; no need to go elsewhere. But remember the twenty percent gratuity."

Chris waved off her remark and dashed off to his pickup, feeling happier than he'd been in years. His mood had already been brightened by the brisk air, but it was now greatly enhanced by the awareness of his attraction to Carmen.

When he came to a stop near his shack, it seemed unbearably shabby. For him this was an unexpected epiphany. He questioned how he could have lived in such a place and how he could have done so for so long.

He spied Ernesto at the garden plots preparing the ground for winter plantings. He had sprouted lettuce and spinach set in seed tapes and was setting them out in rows. He lifted the mulch and set it aside to make room for the rows of plants. With a small hand implement, he made a half-inch furrow into which the new sprouts were placed. Ernesto saw him coming but did not interrupt his work. Chris stood to the side and watched his progress.

Finally Ernesto edged the mulch back so that the entire surface was again covered, except for an inch or so where the seedlings, while mostly hidden, had an opening to emerge.

Ernesto arose slowly from his stooped position, so that his back muscles had time to adjust. "This should be a time of celebration. What kind of ceremony marks the beginning of the growing season? You Americans have no customs for this, and I have lost most of what I brought from Mexico. My mother would be able to tell me what we should be doing for the plants if she were still among the living. Would it be the same if I invented some new ritual, or would that have no real meaning?"

"I'm not sure, Ernesto. Don't we give meaning to anything we do just because we do it?" Chris abruptly changed the subject, "What would it take for me to put up an adobe house?"

The question startled Ernesto. "You mean you really are tired of your shack? What brings this sudden change? I always thought you took pride in your ability to live simply."

Ernesto's surprise made Chris aware that he had suddenly changed his attitude. He also surmised that his attraction to Carmen was the cause and that he had hidden this even from himself. "I don't know, really. I was just thinking that maybe I should have a nicer place, if people came to visit me."

"That's for sure. You don't even have room for anyone to sit down comfortably. I can give you some advice on how to do adobe, but I can't do any of the work myself because I've got my hands full with the garden. I know a couple of fellows who are working at Verde Gardens, and they have friends who know how to do adobe. It's a sure bet that they would be looking for work, but they would want to be paid in cash. You know, it's usual for day laborers."

Chris said no more about it and let the subject drop.

Ernesto sensed that Chris was about to head back to his shack. He added simply, "Let me know what you want to do."

Meanwhile Ernesto pulled mature lettuce and trimmed and washed it for drive-up customers. Water for this was supplied with a line from his shallow well.

43

MILES STANTON ARRANGED A public meeting at the Cottonwood to inform the community about the proposed land swap, which would put a portion of the Arena Rim into private hands. He alerted Bill and Tony about the meeting and assumed that they would be present.

After the village town hall, concerns about the village's water supply were on everyone's mind. The land swap was still pending, so Bill was not ready to reveal his plans, and he didn't wish to be present at Stanton's public presentation, lest he be identified and be pressured to reveal his plans. Fortunately the Mulcton firm had agreed to take his place, without identifying him or revealing his plans. Bill and Tony did not attend.

At the meeting, opposition to any change on the rim emerged, even though the Mulcton attorney insisted that the only thing at issue was the land swap and nothing else. He insisted that the only item on the agenda was whether the Verde Forest should approve it.

Nevertheless the discussion could not be kept in check. It became clear that no change to the Kallisto would be tolerated and that the area of the land swap should not approach it. Protecting the Kallisto was repeated again and again. The Mulcton representative insisted that it was up to the new owner to reveal any plans he might have at some time in the future.

44

WHEN A BROWN ENVELOPE arrived from the Verde National Forest, Bill nearly mistook it as an advertising blurb because its plain appearance did not suggest the importance of its content. When he ripped it open, he was disappointed because it made no mention of the land swap; it only invited him to appear at the Verde Forest headquarters in Gila Center at 9:30 the following Thursday. Bill was irritated. Couldn't they at least give him some idea of their decision about the land swap?

Bill called Tony. "I got a letter from the Verde Forest, but it makes no mention of their decision. There's just a summons for a meeting on Thursday in Gila Center. Why couldn't he have told us what his decision is?"

"Patience, my friend. For him it's just part of a day's work. It's better that way, for if he knew our plans in detail, he probably would have said no long ago. I suggest we keep it low-key and routine. I'm sure the meeting will be about the land swap."

"You always seem to know how to put a positive spin on things. I admire you for that. But there's trouble afoot that your sunny attitude can't dismiss. Did you attend the town hall a couple of weeks ago?"

"No, I usually avoid public meetings. It's usually a politician trying to convince me to pay more in taxes."

"This was different. It was an open discussion about the village's shortage of water, and it's the result of the state clamping down on excess water usage—something they call 'safe yield.' I listened to people gathered around Stella Mantilla after the meeting—she said that the village wasn't getting as much water from the Kallisto as it used to. Do you understand what that means?"

"It means we've got a problem," Tony said. "There's going to be lots of scrutiny about our water plans now that it's on everyone's mind. We've got to get our plans underway as soon as we can."

"Wait, there's still more. At the meeting they went into the water laws. I always assumed that groundwater rights were clear-cut: if you own the surface, you own what's below; simple as that. But the way they explained it got me all confused.

"I think we need to ask Mulcton to look into the law, because someone suggested that any well up there would diminish the flow of Kallisto Wells. If that's true we may as well pack it in. I'd like to call Killian and have him check into whether we really can go ahead."

"Are you sure you aren't asking for trouble you don't have?" Tony was alarmed that Bill was rethinking his plans and that his ranch's water shortage might not be solved after all. But he had to help Bill overcome his doubts. "I suppose it's best to be sure. Go ahead and give Killian a call. He can't charge us because he agreed to ten percent. We may as well make use of him."

When Bill called, Killian was annoyed. "We've already had Hydro Resources look into this."

Bill's worry wasn't allayed. "I know that, but some people in the village seem to think that if I expand my well, it will decrease the Kallisto. I've got to have an answer by Thursday, because that's when I'm meeting with the Verde head forester to finalize the land swap. If we can't get water, we have to call it off."

Killian knew that Bill's worries were not amiss, yet he was reluctant to give up on a project that he believed could be a real winner for the firm.

He tried to calm Bill. "Nothing's ever entirely certain, but we've already got a report. Besides we don't have time to do another investigation by Thursday."

Bill protested, "My question is really a simple one. Can I enlarge my existing well? That shouldn't be complicated."

He could detect Killian's sigh over the phone. "Okay, I'll try to get another firm out there for a second opinion."

Bill insisted, "Can you get it done right away? I've got to know by Thursday." Finally Bill added, "Remember, I'm going to commit lots of money on Thursday, if the swap goes through."

45

SAM LAYTON DROVE HIS truck tentatively around the streets of San Lean-dro. It was his first visit to the valley, and he was looking for someone who could give him directions. He had done some consulting for the Mulcton law firm in the past, but usually he had plenty of time to do an investigation at his office before heading to the site. This time he was given the shortest of deadlines, only a day.

He received a short list of questions from Killian. His job was to get answers to them and not go any further with his sleuthing. The investigation centered on the nature of the water source called Kallisto Wells: whether it could be considered groundwater or not. He would need to do a site visit to get the answers he needed. His problem was that he had no idea where the Kallisto was located.

Sam was in luck. He saw a pickup with the San Leandro village logo on the door. He made a quick turn and flagged down the driver. "I'm new here and need some directions. Can you show me the way to Kallisto Wells?"

The question aroused Anton Wehrli's suspicions. He took note of the company name on the questioner's pickup door. "Sure, can you give me a minute? I've got to jot down this address before it slips my mind."

Instead, Anton flipped the pages of his pocket notebook and wrote down the stranger's company name and phone number. "Okay, you're in luck, because I'm the mayor. Wehrli's the name. And you?"

"Sam Layton from Geo Sciences in Gila Center. You've got a nice town here. The scenery is outstanding."

"We like it. Can you tell me what brings you here? The Kallisto is out-side of town and I can take you there, but I'd like to know what interest you have in it."

"I don't know exactly. I've just been asked to investigate the site and get answers to a few questions. I've been hired by a law firm, and they put me on a short timeline."

"Pardon me for asking, whom are you working for?"

Sam was getting a bit skittish about all the questions. Yet, he decided that the mayor could obtain the information anyway. "I'm working for the Mulcton firm in Phoenix."

Anton wanted more answers, but he did not want to raise suspicions. "Follow me. I see you have a truck that can handle the road."

Anton led him up Switchback Trail, then along the top of the rim to the Kallisto. He waited while Sam walked the site, examined the headgates, made calculations, made notes and measured the rate of flow in a number of places. Finally he bagged a few samples of rock. Anton pretended to be busy with paperwork, but he was actually observing Sam carefully.

Before long, Sam returned to his truck and was busy making sketches. Anton walked over nonchalantly. "Did you find out what you were looking for? If you have any questions, I might be able to help you." At this point Anton got a good look at Sam's clipboard. He noticed the heading, "Project Mulcton: Starret."

"Just one. Those headgates, where does that water go?"

Anton would have preferred not to answer the question, but he realized that, as the mayor, he could hardly pretend not to know. "Three different places: Verde Gardens just below, the Masterson Ranch, and the village."

"Thanks, I appreciate your help. I believe that's all I need to know." With these words he started the truck and gave a wave of the hand as he departed. Anton still had some questions, but he wouldn't get his answers from Sam.

46

Sam reported to Killian on Tuesday afternoon. The meetings of the partners took place on Wednesday mornings and Killian knew that Bill needed his answer by that same night. Killian fretted that everything complicated had to have an impossible deadline.

The agenda of the partners' meeting had to be finalized by Tuesday noon, so he needed to get a place on the schedule. His presentation would be worked out later.

At the Wednesday meeting, Killian was getting more and more nervous because his turn came last on the agenda and the huge wall clock was slowly creeping toward lunch time. If he were put off until next week, he wouldn't know what to say to Bill.

Finally it was Killian's turn. Mulcton glanced at the clock and was about to propose that they quit for lunch, but Killian caught his eye and pressed upon him the urgency of the Kallisto issue.

Killian quickly reviewed the background of the case: Bill's development plans, the critical need of water, the land swap with the Verde Forest, the purchase agreements made on behalf of Star Holdings, and Mulcton's agreement to accept an equity interest in it.

He then summarized recent complications in the plan: the village's determination to solve its water shortage and their interest in enlarging their share of the Kallisto; the complexities of water laws relating to surface and underground sources; Bill's decision that he would not proceed if Star Holdings' water rights would not hold up in court; finally the urgency on the part of Bill to reach a decision because of his meeting with the Verde Forest the next day. Killian caught his breath and apologized for the short timetable.

Mulcton came right to the point. "What are our chances to prevail in a legal proceeding about water rights? Give me a percentage."

169

Killian felt put on the spot. "My guess is less than one out of four. We would be using our own legal team, but we would be suffering serious disadvantages. First we would need to establish that Star Holdings has the right to enlarge a well above the Kallisto in order to obtain additional groundwater. It is quite likely that this is the same water that now emerges from the ground and forms a pond. Therefore it becomes surface water which has been put to beneficial use for generations by three different parties. One of these parties is the village of San Leandro, and the village is under pressure to increase its supply.

"Secondly the law treats an underground flow as surface water if it is considered to be underground incidentally. That's different than an aquifer, which has no directional flow. A good attorney will establish that the Kallisto is surface water and only incidentally underground. If this argument prevails, the judge will throw us out of court.

"Finally, there is the legal doctrine defined as prior appropriation. This means that when someone puts water to beneficial use, they acquire a permanent right to it. A good attorney will argue that our position, based on it being groundwater, can't prevail against the obvious intent of the law of prior appropriation."

Mulcton said, "It seems to me that one out of four is optimistic. Why are we even thinking about this?"

Killian responded, "Remember the terms of our partnership with Star Holdings. If it succeeds, we get ten percent of the value of the enterprise. If the venture comes to a halt now, we get nothing. Since we would be using in-house resources to represent Star Holdings, we would not have any out-of-pocket costs. We still have an outside chance of winning in court. I know it's a gamble with long odds, but there is a chance that it could pay off. Of course Bill Starret, our client, will be putting more than a million at risk. If he really understood the odds, he would be stupid to go on."

Mulcton was reluctant. "We do have attorneys that are well-versed in water rights, so we wouldn't be at a disadvantage on that score." He addressed Killian, "Can you find time to head up our legal team? As for Starret, we have no obligation to advise him against his gamble, if he decides to make it."

Killian nodded. "If it is our decision to proceed, I will tell Starret to go ahead with the land swap."

Mulcton had one more problem. "I don't like to take on a lawsuit that we are in danger of losing. It hurts our reputation. When the case gets written up, try to influence the plaintiff not to use our name. Make it Star Holdings vs. whomever."

47

BILL AND TONY WENT to the Verde National Forest offices at 9:15. Bill signed the entry log for his 9:30 appointment with Miles Stanton. They sat down on two of the grungy, plastic, back-to-back chairs. Tony found a tattered shopper that featured ads for secondhand heavy equipment and paged through it without purpose or interest.

Bill sighed, "What irks me is that we don't even know if they are going to agree to the deal or turn us down."

Tony replied, "At least we got some encouragement from Killian."

"He didn't seem all that positive to me. He talked a lot about the uncertainties of a lawsuit if our drilling plans were challenged. For a while I thought he was going to tell us to give it up."

"Lawyers are like that," Tony said. "They build up the downside so you'll be suitably impressed when they win.

"Bill, I have to give you credit for the idea of offering him a ten percent interest because it has turned out well for us. If we were facing the likelihood of lawsuits that we had to pay for on our own we probably wouldn't be here today. We'd have decided to cut and run."

A woman in forest green called Bill's name. "Follow me, Mr. Stanton will see you."

Stanton was perched on a stool peering at a Forest map on which he had outlined the Arena Rim property that Bill had requested in the swap. "I just want to be sure that we are in agreement about everything. I've got your blowup of the Arena Rim above San Leandro.

"The property you wanted is shaped sort of like a bowling pin. Come look at it. Are these the boundaries that you wanted? I see that on the wider end it extends a little beyond the top of the rim. On the lower side it goes downhill to the bottom of the slope. We have made a small adjustment on the upper boundaries because there were concerns about keeping Kallisto Wells totally within the Forest boundaries."

Startled, Bill scrutinized the chart and recognized that the new boundaries placed Forest land next to his family holdings. "I'm not happy with those changes. It puts a barrier between my two parcels—the one I already have and the one I want to get."

"Sorry, things don't always work out the way we first envision them. We received a number of concerns that the swap would endanger access to Kallisto Wells, and we took these concerns into account."

"I urge you to reconsider the change you made. It's important to me that my two parcels form one piece."

"No, this has to be the boundary. You can refuse the swap, if that's how you feel, or you can make another proposal. Suppose you take a few minutes to think it over. I'll be in the office next door. Call me when you've decided."

Bill leaned on his elbows and peered at the map dejectedly as Tony looked on sullenly. "With these boundaries it will be difficult for me to enlarge that old well. We'd have to cross Forest land to get to it."

"He said we could propose another swap," Tony said. "Let's offer only the Upland Energy property and leave out the old church camp."

Bill sank onto a stool still squinting at the chart and muttered resignedly, "I guess we really don't have a choice."

Tony called Miles over. "We feel that the swap is not nearly as attractive now, so we will offer only the Upland Energy property. If that it agreeable, we can move on."

Miles, who had always thought that the swap was overly generous, agreed.

Bill asked, "Will the Forest allow access to my property across Forest land, so that I can enlarge my old well?"

Miles replied carefully. "Variances like that are always given consideration. I would urge you to make the application right away."

Bill was reassured. "In that case, I believe we are in agreement."

Miles nodded. "Let's go to the land management office. They'll have everything ready for your signatures."

48

MARTHA SIMONDS OF SAMSON Industries, a road building firm, met with
Bill Starret at the Cottonwood. He had already laid out a topographical chart
of the Arena Valley, and, when Martha arrived, he outlined the Switchback
Trail project. "I would like to have a cost estimate for improving Switchback
Trail along with three side streets. I want to get this done as soon as possible."

"You've got all the permits, I assume?"

"Don't need any. It's all on my property."

Martha focused intently on the topographical map. "I noticed the
steep slope when I drove up. This map shows how steep it really is. It's about
at the maximum incline consistent with slope stability. I'm sure you're aware
of this, and that you know that it is a factor in how much this will cost."

"I know," Bill replied evenly.

Martha pressed Bill for an explicit reply. "Let's take a look at this chart,
which gives us elevations. As you can tell they are extreme."

"I'm aware of the incline," Bill repeated insistently.

"You've certainly chosen a very challenging site." She made one additional comment about the slope. "You realize, I'm sure, that a level site
would be a lot less complicated and much cheaper."

"Of course I do," Bill insisted. "Everybody seems to want to remind
me of this."

"For good reason. You want to upgrade the road to handle construction equipment—really big rigs like earth movers, cement pumpers, well
drillers. You can't cut corners with that kind of traffic. Any mishap would
really be costly."

"Yes, yes." Bill became irritated.

"All right. I'll get our engineers to go over this and we'll give you an
estimate."

"Soon," Bill added insistently.

"We won't be sitting on it," Martha said in defense. "But we do have a couple of projects in the hopper right now."

Bill raised his hand to show his insistence. "Right away! I have reason to be in a hurry. Put your other projects on hold and get to this immediately. I'll make it worthwhile."

Martha was taken aback. "Is there some reason for . . ." She thought better of it and replied submissively, "I'll tell them to put it at the top of the list."

"Good." Bill kept up the pressure. "I'd like to know by the end of next week."

"We'll do our best," she added, recognizing that there would be no reason to keep the estimate low. Nevertheless, she decided to mention that they had taken steps to decrease the cost. "We were given a heads up about this and we have already determined that a good supply of rock and gravel is available locally. This will cost substantially less than it would if we had to use the rock from our usual quarry. All I have to do is accept the local quarry's cost estimate.

"We need to totally reroute the old trail in order to make it suitable for the traffic you're anticipating, so we're talking about hundreds of yards of rock."

"I realize that. You also need to factor in three intersecting streets to provide access to individual housing units."

Finally Bill gave Martha a ride up Switchback Trail to the top of the Arena Rim. He pointed out to her the location of the old well and where a turn-around was needed. In addition he fixed the location of the side streets and the retaining walls on their upslope sides.

Martha sketched the topography, the locations of the streets, and the distances. "Like I said, our engineering unit will start right away. I know that they will find the job interesting and challenging," she added needlessly.

49

THE SAN LEANDRO VILLAGE council arrived at the Cottonwood at 7:00 to start fleshing out a village water policy. Anton and Stella arrived shortly thereafter, equipped with an armful of records. Anton sighed heavily as he parked his frame into an overstuffed chair. "This is going to be a slog, gentlemen. The best way to make sure that we get it done is to set a deadline for two weeks. Let's schedule the next town hall two weeks from now and have our proposals ready by then.

"There is another reason for swift action, especially if we are to have any hope of obtaining additional water from the Kallisto. The other day a fellow from Geo Science, a consulting firm from Gila Center, came to do some research on the Kallisto. I took him up there mainly to find out what he was up to and for whom he was working. He was retained by a law firm, Mulcton, Killian, and Smart. This means that there is someone else interested in that water."

"Is there any way to find out who it was?" Benevides asked.

Bill Starret shifted uneasily in his chair, but remained silent.

Wehrli decided not to challenge him. "No legal firm would ever give us that information. I didn't explicitly ask him because I knew he wouldn't tell me anyway."

Starret was busily shuffling papers and tried to show no interest in the conversation.

Benevides persisted, "Isn't there some way to find out who's interested in the Kallisto?"

Anton shrugged and then made a sidelong glance at Starret. "We'll simply go on with our plans, unless either of you has a good reason not to."

Benevides turned to Starret. "I guess not. What do you think, Bill?"

Bill was intently staring at the papers in front of him. He answered with a disinterested shrug.

The councilors came to agreement about the general outlines of their plan. The linchpin was conservation that relied upon Stella's spade work. A threefold plan emerged: prohibitions of excess usage, subsidies to encourage lower usage, increases in water rates to fund the subsidies. Working out the details was left to Stella and Anton.

50

ERNESTO AND CLAUDIA MADE another trip into the desert to replace the three jugs of water. Claudia was nervous this time because she now knew that it was Unruh who had set up the camera, so she deliberately omitted any t-shirt message. She could not dismiss the possibility that they could run into him. But it was a different surprise that greeted them. The jug was turned over and emptied.

Ernesto was delighted. "Someone made use of the water we left."

Instead the sand was wet, which indicated that the jug had been dumped out. A message was traced on the wet ground with a stick. It read: "Criminals." Claudia kept her back to the camera and quickly wiped out the message with her shoe before Ernesto had a chance to see it.

Claudia pulled on Ernesto's sleeve with urgency, "Don't go any nearer. It's time to give this up. You told me that a couple of migrants stopped at your garden for water. That's a better way for you to help them than out here."

"Why? Why would someone mess with our simple water jug?" Ernesto complained.

"Who knows," she replied. "In any case our jug was emptied on the ground. See the wet spot here."

As they were leaving, Claudia suddenly stopped. "We should also do something about that camera. Let's just change its aim so that whoever planted it there will know that his secret is known. I expect whoever left it there will get rid of it when he realizes that it's been discovered."

Claudia wanted to be sure that Ernesto would never know who had been spying on them. She circled around behind the little tree where the camera was mounted and simply broke the branch that supported it. It was now aimed straight down onto the ground. "I see no reason for us to come back here." Claudia said this in the hope that Ernesto would come to the same conclusion.

WHEN STANLEY UNRUH VENTURED once again into the desert, he made his way to the site he had visited so often and anticipated that another message awaited him, recorded once again on the t-shirt of a mysterious visitor. He had walked toward the site so often that a footpath was now vaguely distinguishable. The jug of water he expected to see wasn't there.

He wondered why the people who left the water suddenly stopped doing so. The camera was messed up too, but it wasn't damaged, or taken away; only the juniper branch was broken. He hoped the clip would provide an answer.

Unruh was in for another surprise. The people who messed with the water jug were clearly visible on his chip. There were three of them. They were young guys, not migrants. One of them carried a rifle. Then he saw the couple whom he had captured on his chip before. He concluded that they had disabled the camera.

51

ANTON WEHRLI MADE A return visit to Brett Masterson at the ranch that bore his family name. The drive followed the bank of the Arena, which carried a small surface flow. When he rumbled over the cattle guard onto the Masterson spread, he slowed to maneuver his way around a small herd of Herefords who had no fear of four-wheeled vehicles.

At the ranch's corral, Brett was separating brood stock from heifers who were destined for finishing. Brett heard his approach and ducked between the fence rails to meet him.

"How do you like the looks of these? They're close to a thousand pounds on grass alone and only need a few weeks in the lot to finish them off for market. They won't take much grain to fetch a good price, especially because leaner beef has come into favor."

Anton looked on admiringly. "I'll take a steak from any one of them right now. You certainly raise some outstanding beef."

"I guess you're not here to pay me compliments on my livestock. What brings me the pleasure of this visit?"

"You remember that I was here a while ago and talked to you about the water you get from the Kallisto. Have you noticed anybody up there nosing around?"

"I appreciate that you are up front with me about this. I have noticed some strangers up by the headgates. They showed lots of interest but have never stopped by to tell me what they're up to. I am suspicious of all that activity up there."

"Brett, you're not the only one who's got questions. Just a few days ago someone from the big city came here asking how to get to the Kallisto. I took him up there and kept my eyes open. He took a look at everything, made some measurements, and even removed some rock samples.

"When he got back to his truck he made a bunch of drawings. I was able to find out that he was on retainer by a law firm in Phoenix. I couldn't get any more information because I didn't want to make him suspicious. So your concern is not amiss. There is something going on. In fact, that's why I'm here today, and why I am asking you to let me know if there's anything that concerns you. The village gets water from the Kallisto too."

"I can promise this, you'll be the first to know."

"Good man. That's all I'm asking. Now I know you have things to do, so I won't keep you any longer." With a wave of the hand, Anton got in his truck and drove back to the village. He felt reassured that even if it was really Bill Starret who had his eyes on the Kallisto, the village would still be first to know for sure.

52

"WHAT'S GOING ON?" CHRIS was amazed by the activity at Carmen's rock quarry.

"They're replenishing my supply of crushed rock. I can't afford my own crusher, so I have these guys bring their portable unit. They chew away at the mountain, use dynamite when they have to, stoke the machine with my loader, and crush it to size. It only takes them a half day and I'll have enough for at least a year."

"I didn't know that you could rent this stuff," Chris said.

"Around here, you can; it's one advantage to being around mountains."

"That's got to cost a bundle."

"I'll make out okay next week thanks to the Samson road builders. They bought a huge supply of rock; that's why I needed to crush some more. This machine also sorts the rock into different sizes."

Chris stood by, captivated by the action and the noise of the crusher, while Carmen hurried over to the crew to direct where she wanted the separate mounds of rock to be piled.

Chris hadn't come to watch the action in the quarry but to ask Carmen when she would like to go out to dinner. When she returned to his side, he shifted his feet and uttered, "You said you knew just the place to go for dinner . . . ? When would you like . . ."

"Oh, you're talking about our night out. How about a week from now . . . next Wednesday? Can you pick me up at my home about five?"

CHRIS ARRIVED AT EXACTLY five o'clock, and Carmen was waiting.

She wore an ankle-length blue skirt with a deep red blouse topped by a matching flowery cape that partially covered a necklace of varicolored stones.

Chris arrived at the door of her single-wide and was about to knock when she opened the door.

"Well, you clean up very nice," she said with delight. "I didn't know that such wonderful threads could be found in your shack."

Chris's cheeks reddened a bit. "I had to make a trip to Gila Center."

"You made a shopping trip just for me?" Carmen exaggerated her delight only a little.

THE ENTRANCE TO LA Carbonara Ristorante was lit with colored displays that suggested the charcoal campfires of the nineteenth-century belligerents who fought for Italy's national unity. The reds and yellows and oranges were dazzling as they flickered to suggest the partisan campfires.

"These lights are a patriotic display for Italians."

"I like it," Chris said. "It's not as ostentatious as fireworks."

Carmen took his hand and beamed. "I always like to come here and indulge my Italian roots . . . and I'm so glad that you're here with me."

WHEN THEY APPROACHED THE receptionist, Carmen announced that she had reserved a window booth, where the colored lights from the outside produced a lustrous glow of alternating colors.

Once they were settled, a waiter in black tails handed them a wine list and described their featured vintages. Chris watched in fascination as Carmen considered the choice. "A red Frascati is my preference." She asked Chris, "Is that okay with you?"

Chris had no idea. "Fine with me. You're the expert."

The waiter reappeared, poured the wine, and departed.

Chris raised his glass. "A toast is called for. What shall I say that's worthy of our time together? To my wise breakfast partner who is lovely even in Dickies."

Her eyes sparkled. "And to my disheveled, village scold whose wisdom I cherish."

They each had a sip.

Another waiter appeared with an antipasto tray.

Carmen said, "Thank you, and a little later bring each of us a garden salad with olive oil and wine vinegar on the side."

Carmen sampled a morsel of prosciutto. "Do you think that Desert Gardens will be enough to keep you occupied?" She was probing about Chris's future plans.

"When Ernesto entered my life, he made a big difference. I used to focus on the past and its disappointments; now I'm looking toward the future a little more. It's hard to explain the difference."

"I can tell the difference. You're not the same person you were when I sold you that patch of desert a few years ago." She caught his eyes and said ardently, "And I really love the change."

Chris realized that Carmen understood the change within him—a change that he had not yet sorted out himself. Fortunately at that very moment the salads arrived.

The waiter suggested that they should place their orders now. He pointed out some house specialties: Arista de Maiale, a Florentine boneless pork roast; Osso buco alla Milanese, a roasted veal shank; and finally the various pasta dishes for which the restaurant was well known. Carmen chose penne served with a sauce of olive oil accented with a touch of tomato and garlic. Chris decided to splurge with the Osso buco. Before departing, the waiter replenished the wine.

The entrees arrived under cloches, which the waiter removed with a flourish. They heard the sound of music and singing in the distance, most recently a rendering of "O sole mio." A duo of musicians, with a violin and a guitar, took the serving of the meals as their invitation to entertain. Eventually they arrived and asked Carmen whether she had a favorite song.

Carmen sat back and relished the moment. "Could you do 'Che sarà, sarà'?"

"Of course, Signora."

Carmen closed her eyes and swayed with the music.

Chris offered the duo a tip; Carmen was still humming the tune.

He broke the spell, "You're certainly not rich, so you must be pretty; I wish you rainbows, day after day."

Carmen gazed into his eyes and took his hand into both of hers. "I couldn't ask for more."

Their waiter offered a choice of dolce or a cheese and fruit tray. Again Chris was at a loss. Carmen opted for the tray. They prolonged the evening munching on a variety of cheeses and wedges of fruit.

Finally cups of espresso came as well as the check. Chris grabbed it gallantly.

"Let's split the tab," Carmen said.

Chris would have none of it. "This dinner with you has been priceless."

They walked hand-in-hand in the cactus garden, which was interspersed with the lights of make-believe campfires.

"I want to ask you something," she said, while turning to face him and wrapping her fingers on the lapels of his jacket.

"What?" He replied cautiously.

"Never come here without me. Promise?"

"Never."

53

THE TRUCKS, DOZERS, AND graders of Samson Industries rolled into San Leandro unexpectantly on a chilly February afternoon. It was not long before their purpose was evident. The Switchback Trail that wound up from the valley floor to the rim rocks above was being transformed into a usable road.

Everyone wondered what was happening. "What's Bill up to? It's got to be something big because that road building is costing a lot of money!"

Bill kept mostly out of sight and kept his plans under wraps. Anton Wehrli, who was suspicious about what Bill was up to, made it his business to ask him what he was doing. Bill answered cryptically, "I decided that the trail up the hillside just needed some work."

"You must be planning on moving some heavy stuff up the hill. You mind telling me what you have in mind?"

Bill answered truthfully, but dismissed the size of his project. "I've got a client who is interested in constructing a summer home up near the rim rocks. In order to do it, I need to upgrade the road." Bill wouldn't elaborate.

Anton remained unconvinced. "That's lots of roadwork for just a single residence. You must have found someone who's got deep pockets."

"He's not a pauper," Bill replied simply with a tone of voice that suggested that he wouldn't say anything more.

The project proceeded swiftly with a large commitment of men and equipment. Within two days the job was done, and Bill took pleasure in a drive up to his grandfather's well. He surveyed the second growth ponderosa forest and made plans that would transform the entire area.

THE FOLLOWING WEEK BILL made another trip out to Two Gun Ranch. "We had better not waste any more time," he declared decisively. "We need to get

184

that well dug so we have enough water for about twenty kivas; that's what I'm going to call the homes on the side of the cliff. With all the concern about water, getting the well drilled is urgent. We've got to put the facts in our favor.

"Let's get up there with a big rig and get it done before there's any chance for opposition to emerge. Larson Drilling can handle a six-inch casing. My guess is that the new well won't be much deeper than the old one. If we get up there real early and start at dawn, we could have it done before anyone knows what's happening."

"Good idea, Bill," said Tony. "Can you get Larson out there right away? There's no time to waste."

"Okay, I'll run over to Gila Center this afternoon."

ERNESTO NOTICED A PROBLEM before the road builders had pulled up stakes and left. Suddenly Vasquez Creek was no longer flowing. During prolonged dry spells in the past, it had never gone totally dry. He walked upstream to investigate and found out that the road builders had blocked the Vasquez at its source.

Ernesto was alarmed. He told Chris about his discovery. "If the creek stays dry my plans are going to be worthless."

"This is Bill's doing."

Before the day was done, Ernesto met with Alma Fortner and explained to her that the new road had obstructed the flow of Vasquez Creek. Alma sent a registered letter notifying Bill that his obstruction was illegal and that he was granted one week to undo the damage or face legal action.

IX

MARCH 2017

54

CHRIS COULD NOT RECALL when the village first became aware of activity above the Arena Rim. There were a number of early reports before 7:00 a.m. It could have been the campers who returned to the village early in the morning with reports of the noise of motors and the unmistakable clanking sounds of a bulldozer's drive wheels. Ernesto was cutting salad greens early and he heard the intermittent laboring of a heavy motor; he mentioned it to Stella when she stopped by for spinach. A forester was undertaking a survey of timber resources some miles distant, and she also heard the sounds and reported them to the Verde Forest headquarters, who inquired, in turn, of Anton Wehrli whether he had any information about mysterious activity above the rim. Brett Masterson also reported the noise of a motor before daybreak. These reports had become a topic of urgent conversation throughout the village.

Benevides and Wehrli listened to the engine noises and agreed that they came from above the rim near the Kallisto. Brett Masterson called the Forest Service, because he believed that the activity originated from within its boundaries. By 9:00 a.m. the news turned into an insistent concern about the water supply at Kallisto Wells.

At the Pancake House someone had posted a notice in black marker saying, "Hurry up the Switchback. Stop the water theft!"

This alerted Carmen, who gave Chris a call and urged him to go with her to the Arena Rim. Chris quickly alerted Claudia, who spread the word even further.

By eight o'clock a procession of protestors was snaking up to the Arena Rim. Sheriff Unruh noticed this line and took a cruiser up the newly rebuilt Switchback Trail to see what was going on. The Forest Service alerted a deputized officer, but he would not be arriving from Gila Center before noon.

BILL HAD SET HIS alarm for six in the morning. He dressed quickly and immediately headed to the rim. He did not turn on his headlights so that his F-350 would not attract attention. When he arrived the Larson crew had everything in place and was ready to start.

"We have to move the drilling rig over that way." Larson motioned toward the right. "Those ponderosas are in the way. Is that Forest Service land?"

The problem hit Bill with a jolt. After the boundaries for the property swap were changed by the Verde forester, Bill needed to apply for a variance to cross Forest land, but it had slipped his mind. He turned around, stamped his foot in dismay. "I forgot about the variance. Dammit!"

Del insisted, "I have to get the rig over there now, with or without a variance. You'll have to deal with the Forest people afterwards."

Bill grimaced. "You're right. Go ahead. This can't wait."

Del's workers stood waiting for instructions. "We've got to clear a way past those trees so we can move the drilling rig over where that old well is," Del said.

One of the laborers lugged a heavy chain saw. But Del made a dismissive gesture.

"Forget the saw. Use the dozer, topple them over and push them out of the way." It was quick work. By eight o'clock the site was cleared of ponderosas, and only a little more leveling needed to be done in order to set up the drilling rig.

A crowd of villagers had gathered and began to interfere with the crew.

One of the laborers mounted the dozer to cut down an outcropping of rock and to fill in holes where the ponderosas had stood. A community college student took a stand in front of the dozer's blade. He waved his arms and yelled.

The dozer operator stopped the machine when he came within six feet of the protester. A celebration broke out. The student became a hero. A boisterous crowd surrounded the dozer, and the laborer retreated in defeat.

Bill was alarmed by this delay and spotted the sheriff. "Unruh, these people are trespassers. They've got to be stopped. I've got a crew here, and I need to get the job done."

It became unmistakable to Benevides what Bill was up to and he ran up to Unruh. "Don't you see what Bill is doing? He wants to enlarge that old well. That's going to draw water from the Kallisto! You've got to stop him."

Unruh was caught in the middle. He did not want to face the ire of the crowd or confront Bill: He settled on a middle course of indecision.

Wehrli overheard their exchange and his suspicions about Bill were confirmed. When Masterson arrived from his ranch, he told him, "There are plenty of us here already; find someone to go with you and get Alma Fortner to write a restraining order against Bill. It should state the cause as interfering with the water rights of the village as well as your ranch and the Verde Gardens. It will take time to get a judge to serve the order, but it's probably the best thing you can do now."

Larson ordered the operator to mount the dozer again. "Don't stop this time, they'll back away."

He throttled the idling dozer to a roar, set the blade, and pushed forward. Immediately a crowd took positions in front, waving and shouting. Others crowded around the machine and threatened the operator. Once again he stopped the dozer, fearing the passion of the crowd.

Dozens of onlookers leapt for joy at their success and encircled the idling dozer. They whooped and hollered to celebrate that they had prevailed and had saved the Kallisto.

Bill was angry but even more determined. He called Larson aside. "Let's pretend that we're packing it in. Load up the tools, turn the flatbed around, move the drilling rig to the circle . . . but do it all slowly. Act like we're defeated so they get the imnpression that they've won the day and we're giving it up. When they leave, we can start up again."

Bill's scheme was working. The protestors, ebullient in their success, began to return to San Leandro, many for lunch at the Pancake House. The laborers took their time in stowing everything on the stake bed; they turned the drilling rig around and readied it to run back down the Switchback. Soon they were sitting in the cab waiting for the signal to leave.

Bill and Larson eyed the few villagers who were still there. "When are they finally going to go?" Bill complained.

Meanwhile, Wehrli noticed that the crew had stopped their activity and were just sitting there. He told Benevides, "We'd better stay here until that crew actually leaves."

Chris had never been so exhilarated by a citizen action. As he and Carmen surveyed the stalled dozer, he said, "It's like being a teenager again. It's wonderful to see people get excited about standing up for what's right."

Bill shouted for the sheriff. "Come over here. Stan, I'm going to get this job done; I have every right to do so.

"Del, you run the dozer yourself. Shift to the slowest gear and run it at idle speed, so it just inches along; there'll be no reason for anybody not to get out of the way. If someone gets hurt it's his own fault. Whatever you do, don't stop."

Carmen and Chris had wandered over to the Kallisto pool, where their joy was rudely interrupted by the sound of revving motors. "They must be starting up again. We've got to stop them." She grabbed Chris's hand and ran toward the sound of the dozer.

When they arrived, nearly the entire morning crowd had vanished. There were only two protestors in front of the dozer now.

Del Larson took over the controls as Bill had directed. He shouted at the two protesters who had taken their stance in front of the dozer. "I'm going to go real slow, but I'm not going to stop. You hear me! It's not going to stop. You've got to get out of the way. It's up to you."

Bill stepped up on a rock and yelled, "Get out of the way! The dozer won't stop!" He cupped his hands, "Stay back! You hear me? It's not stopping."

Carmen ran up to Bill and pleaded with him. "Bill, you can't do this! You are stealing water from the village! It doesn't belong to you! Stop that dozer, please!"

Bill turned his back and gave a circling signal with his finger for Larson to keep going. The dozer inched forward. He kept the blade at ground level, so that it would not bite into the earth and overwhelm the engine running at idling speed.

Carmen tugged on Bill's jacket and screamed at him. "Stop it! You can't do this!"

Bill continued his signal to keep going, while the two remaining protesters joined hands and stayed unmoved in the path of the dozer. Carmen ran to the side of the dozer. "Stop it!" she screamed. Chris ran up to join her.

Convinced that she couldn't stop Bill or Larson, she ran to join the two who had taken their stance in front of the dozer. Chris joined her. Four protesters now stood resolutely, arms waving, shouting, and confronting the machine.

Unruh yelled out to them, "It's not going to stop, get out of the way, before you get hurt!"

Wehrli ran to the rear of the dozer and tried to mount it from the back. Larson turned to confront him with a socket wrench.

Larson's laborers remained in the stake bed, transfixed by the drama before their eyes.

Bill shouted to Larson, "Don't stop! They'll get out of the way!"

The blade of the dozer moved level with the surface of the ground. It was rolling some rocks that were too large to escape under the blade. The foursome, with Chris at one side and Carmen toward the middle, were only a few feet from the moving blade and the rocks which were tumbling in front of it. Until the very last instant, Carmen remained convinced that the dozer would finally stop.

The blade was only three feet away when she flinched. She moved abruptly backwards and to the side, but it was too late. One of the tumbling rocks tripped her. She was sent sprawling flat on her face with arms outstretched.

Chris, who was also moving away, caught sight of her fall with the corner of his eye. He reached down towards her, but the rock was now on top of her and her left arm was already caught under the blade of the dozer.

Chris screamed as he balanced himself on top of the blade, with one hand holding on to its supports. He tried desperately to reach Carmen with the other. The rock rolled off her, Chris caught sight of the horror on her face as she was tumbling along in front of the blade. Then her severed arm disappeared under the machine.

Chris grabbed at the dozer's frame while balancing precariously on top of the blade. He tried to reach down to her. Carmen rolled over again in front of the blade. The look of terror was now gone from her face as the light fled from her eyes, and the memory of Chris's hand extended toward her faded into oblivion.

Unruh ran to the dozer. "Stop! Stop!"

Bill, now in panic, jumped up to the operator's seat and shouted, "Stop! Carmen's run over. Raise the blade! Back up!"

Chris barely escaped from his perch as the blade rose. He dove clear toward the side. As the dozer backed up, he leapt to Carmen's side and felt—he sensed—the caress on his cheek of her final exhalation of breath.

Larson rammed the gear shift of the dozer into neutral and hopped forward onto the tracks to peer ahead. Now he saw the mangled form of Carmen's body in front of him. In horror, he leaped back to the controls, shouted at his roughnecks to start the stake bed and the drilling rig.

He revved the dozer's motor to a roar, shifted to reverse, made a sharp left turn, and hollered to his workers, "Get going! We're outta here!"

But he didn't get far. Unruh remembered his duties and rounded up everyone who had witnessed the tragedy. Larson's machines were impounded and left in place and their operators detained. They were escorted by the deputy down to the sheriff's offices for questioning along with the two students, Chris, Wehrli, and Bill Starret.

Bill was stricken with conflicting emotions of anger, sorrow, and despair; he covered his face with his hands and moaned, "I warned her . . . didn't want this . . . an accident."

The sheriff's office became the site of intense activity. Statements were taken from each of the principals and witnesses. Unruh did the questioning of both Larson and Starret himself and, since he was also a witness, was able to obtain unvarnished statements. By late afternoon, Unruh had completed a report of the tragedy and had forwarded it to the county prosecutor.

A deputy remained at the crime scene, which was cordoned off to preserve it.

Clara Studer, the medical examiner, arrived to verify that Carmen was dead and to establish the cause as multiple trauma. She retrieved the severed arm that now folded in three and placed it at the body's side. The body was then removed to Gila Center for an official autopsy, more detailed because the cause of death was a homicide. It would not be returned to San Leandro until four days later.

THE EARLY LUNCH CROWD at the Pancake House was especially large, which kept Diana hustling to keep up. It was also a happy crowd, for everyone was rejoicing about the success of the protesters in stopping the dozer on the Arena Rim. Protecting the Kallisto was on everyone's mind, and now, it seemed, the village's water supply had been secured.

At about two o'clock Diana noticed that the crowd suddenly became quiet. Word spread from table to table that someone had fallen under the blade of a bulldozer. No one seemed to know who it was.

Diana usually got off work at about 3:30 once lunch business was over. She was worried about what had happened to Chris, for she knew that he had gone up to the rim early in the morning.

Someone had brought the news that all the machinery had been left up on the rim and that everyone who had witnessed the accident had been detained at the sheriff's office. That's where Diana went to find out what had happened to Chris.

"Is Chris O'Brien here?" She asked the sherrif's dispatcher.

"He was here earlier; but his statement has been taken and he left about an hour ago. I hear there's going to be a memorial service for Carmen. Maybe that's where he's headed."

Diana drove to his shack and found that his pickup was backed up to the front door and Chris was loading it.

"What on earth are you doing?' She demanded.

Chris dropped an armload of clothes into a cardboard box, turned around, and headed back inside for another load.

Diana jumped onto the steps and grabbed him from behind around his shoulders. "What's going on?"

Chris looked down at his feet and muttered. "I'm going back north."

"Why?"

He mumbled, "Whenever I went somewhere else, somebody died."

"Sit down, you fool!"

She grabbed him around his chest and pushed him onto a chair. She knelt down in front of him and clasped his hands. "Listen to me. You're not going anywhere."

She regretted having shouted at him. He was passive. Neither had any words to say for a while.

"When you said 'back north,' where were you thinking of going?"

Chris finally looked at her directly and said in a plaintive voice, "I don't know. It doesn't make any difference."

"You can't just leave without any place to go. Lots of people here care about you."

"Who?"

"Dammit, Chris. I do." She made little fists to pound on his chest, and began to weep.

She finally penetrated Chris's melancholy. "Carmen and I . . . the two of us . . . we were . . ." Chris melted into her arms, and she held him close.

Diana looked around the room and surveyed the chaos scattered about the floor. "Let's straighten up a bit; unload the pickup. I'll help you. If you're really going to leave us, you need to do it right."

It took longer than either of them expected. Chris became comfortable working with her and it took his mind off Carmen. When they were done, his shack was in better shape than it had ever been. She sat down with him and invited him to relax with her.

"There's going to be a memorial service tonight. I want to go with you."

"No, no. I don't think I can do that."

"Why not?"

"They'll expect me to say something."

"You don't have to. I'll be sitting with you. Nobody will bother you. I'll take you there and bring you back here tonight."

The memorial service for Carmen took place in the San Leandro church that evening. Carmen was well known in the community and a crowd of nearly two hundred had gathered.

Fred Martinez, the pastor, struggled to craft some opening remarks. "At times like these I'm supposed to say something that makes some sense of what has happened. I don't have any words like that. What's happened to Carmen makes no sense. All I can say is this. Life teaches us that when we live for what's beyond ourselves, we achieve our ultimate purpose. Usually that doesn't call for a sacrifice like Carmen made today. Sometimes, it does."

After more than a dozen had spoken, Chris finally rose and moved toward the microphone to offer his own words of remembrance. He halted to suppress the sobs that rose within him and he could do nothing more. Diana rushed to his side. "Let me mourn with you; we both loved her."

DIANA TOOK CHRIS BACK to his shack. "Can I make you a bowl of soup? When is the last time you had something to eat?"

Chris only shrugged and showed no interest in food. "I'm not hungry, just exhausted." He plopped down on his bed.

She bent down to whisper to him, "Will you promise me to come to the Pancake House tomorrow morning?"

Chris made no reply.

She helped him out of his jacket, shirt, and trousers and put him to bed. "You have to promise me to come tomorrow morning for breakfast. Will you promise me to do that?" He nodded.

Diana left his bedroom and pretended to open and close the outside door. Instead she waited silently until she felt that Chris was asleep. She was soon rewarded by the gentle, rhythmic sound of breathing issuing from behind the wall.

Diana opened the outside door soundlessly. She fished out a credit card to hold the movement against the door's edge while closing it. She entered her car and sat for a moment, started the engine, hoping that its sound would not penetrate Chris's consciousness, backed away, and returned to her apartment.

DIANA WAITED IN VAIN for Chris to show up for breakfast the next morning. Every time customers entered, she expected to see Chris and every time she was disappointed. After nine o'clock, her worry about him could no longer be put off. She called Claudia, who immediately alerted Ernesto.

Ernesto was already out at the Gardens preparing a bed for new seedlings. At Claudia's request, he walked over to check on Chris.

The pickup was gone. He knew where Chris's spare key was hidden and let himself in. There was no sign of him and it was clear he hadn't had anything to eat. The bed was unmade, but that was not unusual. He noticed that Chris's vintage rifle was missing. Ernesto called Claudia with the news. After a return call from Claudia, Diana's worry increased even more.

Ernesto drove to work at Verde Gardens, but he couldn't dismiss his uneasiness about Chris. He decided that he had better enlist the assistance of the sheriff, just in case. He found a picture of Chris and was at the sherrif's office within ten minutes.

"I'd like you to keep your eyes open for Chris O'Brien. We couldn't find him this morning and we're worried about him because he was a good friend of the woman who was killed up on the rim."

The dispatcher took a special interest in Ernesto's request. "You're talking about Carmen Montez aren't you?"

"Yeah, she's the one who was killed. Chris O'Brien took her death very hard, and now he's disappeared, and I'm worried about him."

"Just a minute. The sheriff is free and he will take the report himself. I'll let him know that you are waiting for him."

Ernesto did not expect to speak to the sheriff in person. He had just taken a seat when Unruh appeared at his office door and beckoned him to come in. "I don't think we have met. I'm Sheriff Unruh. And you?"

Ernesto introduced himself. He explained that Chris O'Brien was missing and that he might be suffering from shock at the death of Carmen Montez.

"That was a horrible accident. I tried my best to prevent it. Sometimes our best efforts just aren't good enough. We have filed a report with the prosecutor. Were you a witness too?"

"No, I wasn't there," Ernesto said. "But I'm worried about Chris O'Brien."

"You say he's missing? If he doesn't show up after twenty-four hours, we will issue a missing person alert. Meanwhile, may I get some information about him?"

Unruh flipped through the folders on his desk top and then looked into a couple of desk drawers. "I seldom use those missing person forms. I can't remember the last time we had one in San Leandro. Where did I put those forms?"

He swiveled his chair around to face the credenza that lined the wall behind his desk and opened its sliding doors. He moved the contents from side to side and then began to take items out, so that he could get to the bottom of the shelves.

He grabbed a camera and placed it on top of the desk behind him.

Ernesto recognized the strap on the camera immediately, blind stamped with alternating stars and moons. It was the hidden camera which he had seen taped to a juniper in the desert.

He was stunned and momentarily frozen in place by the sight of the camera that had so often captured his image.

Fortunately, Unruh was still facing the wall and did not see his jaw drop in disbelief. Ernesto had to make an excuse to leave the office and find time to think. With a flash of awareness, he recognized that Chris could be in real danger; his mind began to race through the possible outcomes.

"Excuse me, officer, while you're looking, I need to use your facilities."

Unruh didn't turn around but just made a motion with his arm indicating the direction. "It's in the hall to your left."

Ernesto made his escape, while Unruh continued his search for the elusive forms. He rushed to the men's room, entered a stall, and sat down to ponder his options. He recalled that Chris had told him that he knew who had left him for dead. Now he, too, knew who it was, the sheriff himself.

He turned over in his mind the possible outcomes, should Chris encounter Unruh. If the two came upon each other, would Chris interpret the sheriff's approach as a threat? Since both Chris and the sheriff were at the scene when Carmen was killed, was Chris holding him responsible for her death?

Chris had taken his old rifle with him; in his disturbed state of mind, would Chris be gunning for the sheriff?

Ernesto now regretted that he had come to the sheriff's office in the first place, but it was too late to call off his search request. Then a solution came to him; he would tell the sheriff to look where he was certain Chris would not be found.

"Sorry for the interruption," Ernesto began as he reentered the sheriff's office while fighting mightily to suppress any trace of emotion from his voice.

"No problem. It took me almost this much time to find the forms. Please fill in the personal information at the top: name, address, phone number, vehicle license plate, etc. Then I will ask you some questions to help in the search."

Ernesto hesitated to give even his name and address, but there was no avoiding it. He was grateful for the precautions he and Claudia had taken so that their faces were never clearly in view of the sheriff's camera. Even so he was worried that he might be recognized. He handed the form back to Unruh.

"Do you have any idea where Chris might have gone? Some place that he liked to visit? It could be a place where you went together with him?" Unruh asked.

For an instant he pondered what sort of reaction he would get if he mentioned the desert site with a juniper tree holding a camera.

Ernesto knew he had to lie, and had to make the lie convincing. He hesitated in order to give the impression of giving careful consideration to his answer.

"I'm really not sure. He goes off by himself sometimes, and I never pay much attention. We don't go hiking together."

He faked another period of hesitation. "I do recall that he has an interest in identifying birds. And I know that he once took a long hike in the National Forest about ten miles on the way to Gila Center. Of course, I can't be sure he would go there again."

"Would that be on the River Road past the Two Gun Ranch?"

"Yeah, somewhere out there."

Unruh had some additional questions, which Ernesto negotiated successfully. He was immensely relieved when he left Unruh's office without being recognized. He drove on to his job at Verde Gardens with the realization that he had a daunting task before him, because finding Chris would have to be his job and his alone.

When he met Mr. Uribe at Verde Gardens, he asked for some time off. The search couldn't wait.

55

WHEN CHRIS AWOKE ON the morning after the memorial service, the winter night was far from spent. Normally he would have rolled over to find a comfortable position to resume his sleep. Not this time. Yesterday's tragic loss displaced everything else from his mind and enforced a reluctant wakefulness.

The taste for life was forsaking him just as it had when Angela perished beside him years ago.

Like a zombie he performed his morning routines—a quick bathroom visit, early morning public radio, which sounded in his ears but did not register in his mind. He recalled his promise to go to the Pancake House, but he didn't want to talk to anyone, even Diana. Instead he shuffled to the door and noticed the faint light of dawn in the east beyond the rim rocks above.

He returned to his bed, closed his eyes, but could not quiet his distress. Reluctantly he sat up again and pondered why the simple choice of just resigning from life wasn't possible.

Chris wandered off alone, as he had done so often in the past when the loss of Angela overcame him. He caught sight of his old Winchester and decided to take it with him. After having stowed it behind the seat, he remembered ammunition and found a half-empty box. After donning a warm jacket and grabbing a walking stick, he went over to Ernesto's supply shed to help himself to a few daffodil bulbs.

It was still dark when he started up the newly rebuilt Switchback Trail. He circled around Larson's impounded drilling rig and found the place where he and Carmen had confronted the dozer. He found the fatal spot in the half light and planted a dozen daffodils where the rock that crushed her had come to rest. When this little ritual was finished, he returned to his pickup and drove slowly down to the valley below.

His drive took him past the Pancake House, where he knew Diana would be sympathetic and attentive. However, he craved solitude rather than company. This led him to reverse direction toward the desolation of the Nudoso Hills and the parched valleys which opened beyond them. He found a little-known trail head where he could leave his pickup undetected. From there he trudged into the wild without purpose or destination.

By mid-morning he had scaled the top of a hogback ridge and dropped down precipitously into a hidden canyon, where surprising stands of ponderosa grew to towering heights. The sun's heat penetrated the depths and baked the sandy bottom, where tempering winds could not find access. He slipped off his jacket and his shirt and lay back with his head sandwiched between parallel rocks in the warmth of the morning sun.

His mind retraced the events of the previous days. He rehearsed those critical moments when he was balanced on the blade of the dozer reaching down in vain toward her. He recalled with revulsion the abject horror he read on her face and the cry that issued from her lips, just before another rock rolled down upon her chest.

He sobbed and doubled over in grief. No tears were there to lubricate his aching hurt. Finally the emotion wore itself out, so that his body stilled itself and only fiery anger remained.

He shouted up the reverberating canyon walls, "No! God!" But God made no reply. "You hate me so? Why did you do this?" Again there was no answer as he curled his body in a fetal position.

After a time, he stood tall, picked up a rock and hurled it with all his might. It cracked and splintered on a boulder. Again and again, he heaved stones until his arm ached and his energy was sapped. "I loved her. Why is she gone? Why, why, why?" His voice tailed off as his anger ebbed into defeat.

He sat down upon a fallen log, long since dead and decomposing. Here he stared down blankly at the sand about his feet.

Time passed unmeasured—possibly he had dozed off for a time. He rose and shuffled along the arroyo at the canyon bottom. He kicked the rocks in his way and gave wide berth to a white thorn acacia. He encountered a trace of darkened sand that suggested a hidden spring of water issuing from above and tried to trace its source amongst a jumble of rocks; then he looked up to the cloudless sky and held it to blame for the arid ground.

After startling a pair of mule deer, who scooted off into a copse of creosote bushes, he was challenged by a fierce javelina that was protecting its young. He bowed elaborately to give it right of way.

When a hawk dove suddenly to find its prey, he voiced his regrets.

Chris attempted to scale the canyon walls directly, in order to reach the top of the ridge, but was defeated by the sheer cliff. He returned to the canyon floor after some precarious steps and handholds, remembering finally that descents are always more difficult than their corresponding ascents. So he accepted this defeat as a sign of his fate and began slowly to retrace the way from which he had come.

There was no short cut for his return and no alternative but to backtrack. When he reached the crest after a grueling hike, traversed the ridge, and descended to his truck, he regained a small measure of decisiveness. He reached the roadway and took a turn in the direction opposite to San Leandro following the River Road toward Gila Center. Along the way a row of secluded roadside cabins with an attached bar and grill greeted him with its flashing neon sign. Here he resolved to spend the night.

He rented a cabin and walked to the bar. In spite of multiple TV sets tuned to various basketball games and the casual camaraderie of the regulars, he created an island of seclusion for himself and nursed beers without notice or interruption. The evening slipped away as his heart unpeeled the hurt of his wounds. Chris stayed late, allowing all of the noisome ambience of the bar to wash over him.

A woman, who had been visiting with the bartender and was clearly a regular, approached him with an inviting smile. "You all by yourself, handsome? You care for some company, a good time?"

She leaned suggestively against the walls of his booth. Chris held his gaze firmly into the void which existed somewhere between the bar and the neon beer signs. She continued, "I could use a beer, then we can talk." Chris now looked at her, and with a low voice that registered exhaustion and resignation, told her, "Don't take this personally. I want you to leave me . . . alone."

Chris was not the last one to leave, but nearly so. The bartender eyed him repeatedly, especially after his would-be companion fled in haste and confusion. He finally settled his tab, returned to his shabby room, and descended into a deep sleep.

56

ERNESTO LEFT DESERT GARDENS and set out immediately to search for Chris. He took binoculars and a local map that included all of the remote two tracks and hiking trails. He was worried about what could happen if Chris and Unruh encountered each other. Would they come to blows, or even gunshots?

He went first to where Chris had rescued him in the desert. Next he took the rebuilt Switchback Trail up to the Arena Rim. Believing that there was a good chance that Chris would be visiting the site of Carmen's death, he searched the dozer site and then walked the edge of the Kallisto pond. Then he hurried down an old logging road but gave up after a mile. When he returned to his Jeep, he slumped into the seat and wondered where to go next. When no other options came to mind, he dejectedly returned down the Switchback Trail to the village.

Ernesto stopped to ask Wehrli for advice but received no useful leads. The afternoon was spent, so he returned to Desert Gardens.

In the evening he searched Chris's shack again; maybe something amidst his belongings would give him a clue. Nothing. Ernesto abandoned his quest for the day and stopped at the clinic to share his disappointment with Claudia.

"Where have you been?" She asked while scrutinizing his bedraggled look. "You look like you've been in the desert for a week!"

Ernesto rattled off his distress. "I've been looking for Chris all day. He's gone and I don't know where he went. He took his rifle; I'm worried that he could run into Unruh; he knows that Unruh left me for dead and he probably blames him for Carmen too."

Claudia understood the dilemma. "It's too late now; you'll have to wait until morning. Where have you looked?"

Ernesto told her about his search. "I don't know where else to go."

"Remember the time we went to the Arena Gorge to watch the waterfall? Chris said that he had gone there whenever he felt depressed. Try that tomorrow morning."

"That's the best lead I've had." Ernesto found some reason for hope.

"Now let's pray for his safe return."

Ernesto's look revealed his doubt. "How can our prayers change what's already happened?"

"I remember a science course years ago, when I was getting my nursing degree. The prof surveyed quantum theory and cosmology. I remember being astonished when he explained that an electron could be a long distance from the nucleus and other electrons yet retain a constant substantive link with them. It could be as a substance or a wave, but it would always remain attached. When I pray I think of myself as that wayward electron still in contact with my nucleus."

Together they prayed for Chris's safe return—for Unruh as well, and for the village of San Leandro.

"Here's a mild sedative. Take it tonight and continue your search tomorrow.

57

BRIGHT SUNSHINE STREAMED THROUGH a curtainless window and awakened Chris from a deep sleep. He glanced at his watch and was surprised by the late hour. He dressed hurriedly and found that his appetite had returned. He ordered the breakfast special with a side of chorizo. In addition, he asked for a ham and cheese sandwich to go.

Upon returning to his pickup he had, as yet, no destination in mind but made a left turn instinctively, which led back San Leandro. He splashed over the River at the low-water crossing, bypassed the turnoff to Yolanda Alonso's compound, and came to the foot of the Arena Gorge. He parked at the trail head, which had recently been flooded by the November storm. He left his sandwich, water, and rifle and scrambled resolutely up the canyon.

The beginning of the ascent was easy. He circled around the scattered boulders that had tumbled down from the heights. Chris felt invigorated by the exertion. The way forward steepened rapidly, at times causing a tiny waterfall. The flow was now reduced to a trickle that brought a spray of tiny water droplets upon his face whenever he surveyed the way forward.

Chris had reached the side of the cliff opposite the viewing area that he, Ernesto, and Claudia had visited weeks earlier, when the gorge was flowing full force. He squeezed by where a large boulder constricted the way, and hugged a fifty-foot wall of sheer granite.

He found a small rock ledge that jutted out from the cliff's side and sat down, resting his head and shoulders against the cliff behind him. Droplets of water from above rushed toward him like so many tiny missiles, which only missed him by inches as they splattered on the protruding rock at his feet. The platform on the opposite bank with its sheltering overhang appeared to be so near that it seemed to invite him to leap toward it. Below him the water flow disappeared and reappeared intermittently as a white ribbon.

Christ found comfort in this watery enclosure. He sat motionless and serene, allowing the sound of the splattering droplets to take possession of his consciousness.

Here he recalled the occurrences of the previous days, not as events or happenings, but as saga and parable. In his reverie the dozer's blade recalled the depth of his present loss, as well as those of the past. Images of the car crash in Montana and the dozer's relentless approach replayed in his consciousness. Yet the dark cloud of past calamities receded to reveal the promise of a beckoning horizon. He sensed the presence of Carmen, soulfulness neither substantial nor imaginary, real even though formless and impalpable.

My love for you is forever now and this can't change. Her voice seemed inmost to his identity. *Your destiny will come into view, just as through the mist of this waterfall you can see the opposing bank. It will bring renewed life to your soul just as the spray of water brings coolness upon your face.*

The moment captured Chris in its magic. His eyes closed as his spirit was encompassed in a restorative embrace. He sat calm and motionless, beginning to feel comfort and solace.

It may have been only minutes before Chris emerged from his spell. He felt strangely invigorated and began to venture further up the Arena Gorge. The way forward was challenging even for an accomplished climber because the rocks were slippery with lichen and moss and were invariably huge, since smaller ones were more easily dislodged by intermittent torrents. Now his attention was absorbed by the constant challenges of the climb, and he felt refreshed and renewed by his exertions.

Chris set his mind to conquer the gorge all the way to the top. He planned to emerge at the summit, walk along the Arena Rim, descend to Desert Gardens, and ask Ernesto or Claudia to take him back to retrieve his pickup. He continued upward undaunted, always reconnoitering in his mind the path that would allow him to emerge beyond the next barrier. His progress had taken him far beyond the point where return to the bottom would be less challenging than continuing on to the top.

Nearing the summit he reached an impasse where an immense boulder totally blocked his side of the canyon. Crossing over to the opposite bank was the only option, but this maneuver was not an easy one. He needed to find purchase on a flat slab of rock, which was resting on the stream bed and which was supporting another larger rock in a hidden and precarious balance. A leap of four feet was required.

After calculating the distance, he leaned forward poised on his right leg. He swung his arms and leapt forward. His momentum took him just beyond the slab's center of gravity; it tilted down and away; the boulder upon it rolled backward and came to rest against another rock with his foot caught in between.

He could not move. The larger boulder's height came up to his waist; he had no hope of budging it. Even after he managed to untie his shoelaces, the pressure still held him fast.

Desperately he pulled up on one leg while exerting downward pressure on the other. The pain became more intense the more he struggled, yet he couldn't loosen the grip that held him fast.

He collapsed forward and laid his torso upon the offending rock in defeat. Then the stark outcome of his predicament became devastatingly clear. He realized that giving up meant slow death, and the longer he was caught the weaker he would become. He had to get free now or he never would.

Chris found a handhold on the top of the rock so that he could keep himself upright. Then he drew his midsection away from the rock in order to lift his free leg and plant it against the boulder. He used the power of his free leg to force himself backward while using his handhold to anchor his upper body. Every ounce of his energy was now concentrated on his trapped leg. He strained even more than he thought was possible. Yet there was no movement. He tried at the same time to wiggle his leg from side to side within the boot, but he was held so tight that there was no movement. The pain became unbearable and he couldn't tolerate it any longer.

He leaned over the offending boulder and lay down upon it to lessen the torment. The pain began to pulse in time with his elevated heart rate. He raised his head and looked around disconsolately, and muttered to himself.

Sorry, Chris, this is it. This is where you will die. Will I lose consciousness soon? When? I tried my best. This is what God has planned for me. I wonder if anyone will ever find my body.

Resigned to his fate he sensed that there was a voice calling for him.

58

ERNESTO'S ALARM SOUNDED AT first light. He took the rebuilt Switchback Trail up onto the Arena Rim. He believed that there was a good chance that Chris would be visiting the site of Carmen's death, but there was no one in sight.

Next he followed up on Claudia's advice and went to the observation platform at the Arena Gorge. He entered the chasm and peered up and down, but found no sign of activity. Seeing nothing, he shouted Chris's name and there seemed to be a reply from far above.

Ernesto scrambled further into the gorge and blinked into the descending spray. He could see nothing, for boulders obstructed his line of sight, and the constant spray blurred his vision.

He shouted again as loud as he could. Once again he heard a reply. He picked his way up laboriously, gaining vision ahead by degrees only to be blocked by the next boulder. He gained elevation and the replies seemed nearer. "Is that you, Chris?"

"Yeah."

When Ernesto climbed past another boulder, he caught sight of Chris ahead.

"I'm caught in the rocks. I can't move," Chris shouted.

He raised his arm to stop Ernesto from coming any further. "You can't help me here! You can't move this rock. Call for help!"

Ernesto unclipped his cell phone and realized that it would not be wise to call the sherrif. Instead he called Wehrli and explained the situation. Wehrli immediately contacted the Forest Service and requested the assistance of their mountain rescue squad. Meanwhile, Ernesto continued his ascent and finally was able to stand side by side with his friend.

Ernesto first wrapped his arms around Chris. "You've got to tell me where you're going," he admonished him in a grateful voice. "I've been looking for you for two days."

Chris did not have the energy to reply.

"I called Wehrli. He's contacted the Forest Service rescue unit. We'll get you out of here."

Chris sank down upon the top of the rock, puffed for breath, and moaned to vainly address his pain. The minutes passed interminably. Ernesto had a little water. That was all he could do to help, except for reciting the Lord's Prayer as he kept Chris company.

Whoap, whoap, whoap. Ernesto craned his neck to spot the chopper, but it was hidden by the cliff above. "They're here!" He shouted. "We'll get you out!"

Soon a rescuer rappelled down, opened his first aid kit, and gave Chris a shot to deaden the pain. He called up to his companion to come down with a pry bar.

With this tool they established a fulcrum near the base of the boulder and moved it the fraction of an inch needed to free Chris's foot. The rescue crew lowered a basket to bring him to the top. Ernesto made his way out of the gorge with the assistance of climbing gear provided by the rescue crew.

Willis Carr piloted the chopper. When Chris was safely inside, he saw Ernesto. "There's room for you too."

Ernesto found a place next to the EMT who was already fixing an intravenous saline laced with a painkiller. Chris was barely conscious.

Willis summoned an ambulance to meet them at the Ysidro Country airstrip. Chris was in the care of an orthopedic surgeon within fifteen minutes after his rescue.

An x-ray revealed that there was no fracture, but severe bruising. Ice was applied to lessen his swelling, with intermittent applications of heat to enhance his circulation. Fortunately his rescue had come shortly after the accident; otherwise the pressure trauma would have required an amputation. As it was Chris faced weeks in a boot, the use of crutches, a regimen of painkillers, and applications of ice packs and heat pads.

X

APRIL 2017

59

WHEN CHRIS WAS RELEASED and had returned to his shack, Claudia arranged for the daily visit of a nurse to assist him in his recovery.

Ernesto dropped by to see him and said, "I stopped at the sherriff's office to ask them to look for you when you went missing. When I talked to Unruh, he grabbed the very camera that he had planted on that desert juniper. He put it in plain view on his desk.

"I had to think quickly. I knew that you had taken your rifle along and that you had every reason to blame him for Carmen's death. I was afraid that you would end up in a gun fight with Unruh, so I misdirected his search to a place where I knew you would not be found.

"Remember, months ago I asked you not to tell me who had left me for dead. Now I found out who it was on my own."

Claudia said, "I found out it was Unruh when when he stopped at the food bank and made ugly remarks about leaving water in the desert."

Ernesto told them what he planned to do. "I'm going to tell him who I am."

"Why?" Chris said. "Now you know who it was that left you in the desert and he doesn't know that you know. Isn't that the perfect outcome?"

"I want an acknowledgment, maybe even an apology, from him. As an assurance against any reprisal against me, I plan to let him know that at least four other people know the story. So if any harm came to me, he would be a prime suspect."

Chris responded skeptically, "Why bother? It won't do you any good and it might even bring you trouble that you don't need."

"If I get an apology, it will be easier for me to forgive. If I forgive him I'm freed from any resentment about what he did."

These words startled Chris and forced him to recognize his own dilemma. "I guess you're suggesting that I should forgive Bill? I don't think I can do that. Maybe he didn't mean it, but it was his greed that took Carmen from me."

"I've got something to tell you. When I was dying in the desert, I had a vision. It was not an event—at that time I was no longer aware of things happening in order as events do—it was an experience. It must have been just after Unruh left me, and I had given up any hope of rescue. I felt myself floating onward up a path and was letting go, one by one, of the grasps of an endless line of outstretched hands representing my present life—not just people, but possessions, places, attachments. They all had outstretched hands. I took leave of them all, one after another. Their line extended backwards toward infinity, all of them extending their hands to me, as much in leave-taking as in a kind of salute. The line finally included Marcelino, or rather what he represented to me. I had no regrets or reluctance; it seemed to be a pleasant journey to leave them all behind.

"But it turned out I wasn't leaving them at all. I found that all these people, attachments, and experiences appeared again in front of me, somehow transformed. They were changed and seemed enlivened and were beckoning me to join them. I sensed that I too was to take on a new life.

"But the experience wasn't all positive. I also saw myself facing people who had wronged me. Some were from Sinaloa long ago who had made life difficult there, also the coyote whom I had never met but who had been too cowardly to leave us any water, and finally the helicopter pair who spotted us in the desert.

"Our roles were reversed. I stood before them and they cringed as if I were holding them in shackles. One by one, as I saw their misery, I was moved to forgive, and their shackles melted way. Released, they joined the others who sent me on my way.

"When your arms embraced me and my lips tasted the water you gave me, my journey stopped abruptly. I must tell you that I didn't want it to stop at all, but wanted to keep going. You called me back, and in a moment's flash I held once again all of the hands that I had unclasped before. It all happened in an instant. I came back with a jolt, when my eyes opened and I saw you for the first time."

Chris was puzzled by the story and had no comment beyond the question, "Why are you telling me this?"

"Because I think I finally figured out what the vision meant. It had always been a puzzle and I had even put it out of mind. The memory of it came back to me after you were caught by the rock in the canyon. I finally asked Claudia what it might mean."

"So what did she say?" Chris asked.

"At first, she said she couldn't explain it. When she saw that I was disappointed, she said that she could put forth a theory, but that I was the only one who could understand it, since it was my experience, not hers.

"But that didn't help me solve anything, and I was about to leave when she asked me, 'When you had that vision, you said that it was Marcelino whom you saw last. If you had that same vision today, who would be the last one?'

"I was dumbfounded and replied dubiously, 'Unruh?'

"Claudia was surprised too. 'Wasn't it Marcelino who saved your life? And wasn't it Unruh who left you to die?'

"'Yes, it was.'

"'Marcelino represented love for you,' Claudia said. 'In the case of Unruh, it's hatred. And what is the instinctive reaction to hatred? Wouldn't it be anger?'

"I struggled with where she was going. 'Whose anger? Mine?'

"'That seems to be what you're saying,' Claudia said. 'Your anger was holding you, not his. You've figured out the meaning of your wonderful experience. When you let go of your anger, you were freed. I suppose Unruh is also held captive by his own anger, and he left you to die because of it, but that's not part of your vision. It's been about three years since Unruh left you,' Claudia said. 'The passage of time does heal anger gradually so that one can recall its cause without renewing its emotion. But forgiveness is the only way to finally put it to rest. Anger is displaced by someone's love—real human love, not disembodied spiritual fervor which works only for saints, and maybe not even for them. In the end all of us must come to forgiveness.'

"I asked, 'What about an apology and an offer of forgiveness. Isn't that the ideal way?'

"'Of course, it is. But it doesn't happen nearly as often as it should, because for most of us it's extremely difficult. There's fear, and pride, and simple stubbornness. If we could just get rid of anger and fear, we'd have a world transformed.'

"When I was preparing to leave, Claudia held my hand a while longer. I told her, 'Thank you. I mean that sincerely. Your experience has been enlightenment for me.'"

Chris listened to Ernesto's story and his conversation with Claudia and said, "You're telling me that I need to let go of my anger toward Bill, aren't you?"

"Only because it hurts you. I can only say what the experience has come to mean for me. What you decide is up to you."

"Maybe it's right for you, but not for me. When I think of Carmen crushed by that rock, I can't help but be angry. Claudia said that the passage of time will help you let the anger go, but you can make it happen sooner."

"Let me just add this, then I'll keep quiet," Ernesto said. "Letting go is not giving in. You've heard the saying, 'What you possess possesses you.' That's how it is, whether it is things, attachments, people too, even anger. Love frees, possessiveness enslaves. When I was on that journey, leaving all those outstretched hands behind me, it was a friendly force that beckoned me onward. I have come to think of it as a sort of rebirth.

"It is a hard saying, but you must do the same with Bill. Love displaces anger, Claudia said. Carmen can lead you on, if you allow her to do so, by enlarging your love for her to include even Bill."

60

Ernesto stopped at the sheriff's office the following day, immediately after he had completed his work at Verde Gardens. He handed the dispatcher a note in a sealed envelope. "Please hand this to the sheriff. I will wait here until he reads it. I believe he will want to see me after he does."

Unruh read the note. "I am the person whose picture you took with your desert camera. If you would like, I will fill you in on the details. I'm waiting outside your office now."

Unruh was thunderstruck. He thought he had finally put this torment behind him. He had removed the camera from the juniper tree, but now the one person he feared, and had dismissed from his worries, has come back in person.

Unruh opened the door with trepidation only to find the hispanic fellow who had reported a missing person some days before. Unruh was speechless. Ernesto did not wait for a signal from Unruh, but brushed by him and took a seat across from his desk while motioning Unruh to take his seat as well. It was as if it were his office and not the sheriff's.

Ernesto began. "I want to thank you for doing the search for Mr. O'Brien. I went out to search for him myself and I found him. He was injured and would not have made it on his own, but he's okay now."

Unruh couldn't imagine what the connection was between O'Brien and the person on the camera, but he was too confused to make any reply or pose any question. Ernesto faced a blank, vacant stare as he continued. "You would be interested in knowing that O'Brien was out in the desert some years ago and came upon an individual who was dying of heat and thirst. He rescued him—that's me."

Unruh began to connect the dots. *He knows! Why is he here, telling me this? What does he want?*

Ernesto saw his confusion and also noticed his eyepatch. Touching his eye he commiserated, "You've lost an eye. How did that happen?"

Sympathy from Ernesto was the last thing that Unruh expected. "I got hurt fighting with some smugglers. They got away."

"I'm sorry to hear that. I bet you must be angry about what they did to you."

Unruh's world of black and white was coming undone. He stammered, "Not your fault."

"Remember when I came in here to tell you about a missing person? That person was Chris O'Brien. He is the one who rescued me and who saw you leave me for dead. When you fished out your camera from your credenza, I knew it was the same camera I saw in the desert where we left jugs of water.

"When I saw your camera I knew it was you whom Chris saw leaving me to die, and I was afraid that the two of you might come to blows, so I went out to find him myself. I knew that Chris had a gun and I wanted to prevent the two of you from meeting. So I told you to look where I knew Chris would never be found. I found him myself. In fact, I saved his life."

Unruh took it all in and was deflated. In a weak voice, he mumbled, "What do you want from me?"

"Just tell me you're sorry."

Unruh was incredulous. "Is that all?"

"Yes, that's all."

Unruh's confusion moved Ernesto to elaborate. "I need to forgive, and if you say you're sorry, forgiving is much easier. Until I forgive, the past can't really be over and done for; it will still have a hold on me."

Unruh found the reasoning unreal and returned a vacant look.

Ernesto elaborated, "You're still mad at your loss of an eye. You need to put it behind you. As long as you harbor hatred, it possesses you and you can't move on."

Unruh finally ventured a response. "There was a time when I would have arrested you and sent you back where you came from. I guess you're legal now. Did you leave messages for me on your shirt?"

"Yes, we did."

"When you left the passage from Luke, was that a promise of forgiveness?"

"It was."

"I wanted to contact you, but I was afraid."

"The offer still holds."

"Actually, I did leave you there in the desert, but I thought that there was no hope for you in any case. I didn't think I could have saved you no matter what I did and I was going to come out the next morning to pick you up. It was a big surprise when a call came in that very afternoon. When I didn't find you there, I was amazed, and then it became clear that you had survived after all. I should never have left you. I know that now."

It was not quite what Ernesto wanted, but he realized that there would not be more. "Thanks for listening to me. I do forgive you."

61

WHEN THE COUNTY PROSECUTOR, Will Gutierrez, received the report of Carmen's death from the medical examiner, he interviewed witnesses of the incident and read the sheriff's report in order to determine whether the death was accidental or whether it might be cause for manslaughter. His interview of Larson came first, who admitted to operating the dozer but insisted that he had no idea that anyone had fallen under its blade. Chris and the other two protesters all agreed that the dozer was being driven at very slow speed and that they nevertheless believed it would eventually stop, just as had been the case earlier that morning.

Anton Wehrli confirmed that Bill Starret had instructed Larson to take the dozer's controls and that he had made it clear to everyone that the dozer would creep along at very slow speed, but would not stop. Sheriff Unruh did not recall making any statement about the dozer to anyone. He insisted that his first inkling that anyone was in any danger was when he heard shouts from the protestors.

Gutierrez indicted both Del Larson and Bill Starret for manslaughter.

STAR HOLDINGS FACED BANKRUPTCY as a result of the multiple claims lodged against it. The Forest Service did not enter a criminal complaint against Bill Starret but preferred to launch a civil suit for damages, amounting to $30,000. A Verde forester surveyed the site and estimated that the damage to the flow of Kallisto Wells would have resulted in a permanent loss to the village, Verde Gardens, and the Masterson Ranch.

Meanwhile the Mulcton firm reacted to the media coverage by filing a notice of intent to terminate its association with Star Holdings upon the receipt of ten percent interest in its residual value. Finally a suit filed by Ernesto Ramirez sought damages resulting from the obstruction to Vasquez Creek.

BILL ENTERED TONY'S BUNKHOUSE and lowered himself into a chair at the rough-sawn table, this time with nothing in his hands. Tony eyed him guardedly and neglected to call the ranch house for refreshments.

"I guess I won't get to restore the ranch to its original size," his voice quavered.

It caught Bill off guard. Tony's motivation was never really that important for Bill, and now it seemed trivial. Bill squirmed and finally forced himself to look at Tony directly. "I'm facing a charge of manslaughter!" he snapped. "And I've lost over a million."

"And what do you suppose I've lost!" Tony blazed up in reply, while getting to his feet, turning to the side, and jamming his fists into his pockets.

Bill sank into submission. "What do we do now?" he uttered in a tiny voice.

Tony turned. "Those forest properties are gone! And our million with them! What we've got is a slice of worthless, barren hillside."

"I know, Tony." Bill gazed at the plank flooring at his feet. "I've got to get an attorney, or I'm going to jail."

"We should have used Alma Fortner to begin with," Tony hissed.

62

ALMA FORTNER HAD HANDLED Bill's legal work in the past, but this appointment with her was awkward, for she had not had any part in the creation of Star Holdings. Alma snatched a legal pad and suggested that Bill fill her in on all that had transpired. The briefing took the greater part of an hour. Alma had intended to ask Bill why he had taken his legal work to Phoenix, but after she had filled four pages of notes, the reason was clear.

Alma commented sternly, "If you had come to me at the beginning, I would never have let you get into this." Bill could only hang his head. Alma tapped her pencil on her legal pad rhythmically as she tried to devise a way forward. She made some notes on a fifth page, while Bill sat by in silence. Finally she outlined what needed to be done.

"First of all, you've got a manslaughter case facing you. I don't handle felony cases. Get yourself a good criminal attorney.

"Next is the matter of the land you acquired. I think the only logical buyer would be the Verde Forest. I would try to recoup something by offering to sell it back to them. Maybe they would forgive the lien they have placed against the property. Whatever happens, you are going to be a lot poorer.

"Finally let me know what Mulcton is up to. Don't make any deals with them without consulting me first. You can let them know that you have retained legal counsel, but you don't need to let them know who it is. They haven't treated you very well and don't deserve any courtesies. There are ways that we can counter any demands they make."

STANLEY UNRUH WAS SHAKEN by his confrontation with Ernesto. His worst fears had finally come to pass. His misdeed in the desert was now exposed, and what it would mean in the future was beyond his control. His desert victim knew who he was, and he could not depend on the secret being kept.

Furthermore his inaction up at the Kallisto when Carmen Montez died could still be called into question. He had not been indicted, but he had been less than candid about his own actions, or lack thereof, and he was not sure what the other witnesses may have said about him. Unruh decided that it was time to move away from San Leandro.

A law enforcement newsletter listed openings in the field. A position in Gila Center caught his attention. He would no longer be in charge of his own jurisdiction, but it was a decent position as part of a large metropolitan force. He applied for the position of coordinator for special events, a job roughly equal in status to the one he presently held. The search was closing shortly, so he had hopes of making the move without much delay.

63

Aaron Raines drove a Verde Forest crew-cab to the Kallisto site. He had with him a crew of three as well as a small dozer loaded on a trailer. They came equipped with chain saws and an assortment of logging and landscaping tools. Aaron had been one of the protesters when the progress of the dozer was halted by a solitary student from San Ysidro. He had participated in the celebration before returning to the village. He heard later on about Carmen's death, and it moved him to contribute modestly for a memorial for her.

Aaron found the site exactly as the Larson crew had left it. While his men were unloading the small dozer and tools, he hiked over to the clearing to examine the tracks left by the fateful dozer. The details of Carmen's death were familiar to him from Unruh's account. He followed the dozer tracks to see if he could locate the spot where Carmen died. A line of rocks which had obviously been pushed by the dozer marked the end of its forward progress. He noted the undisturbed dozer tracks and where they came to a stop. At this point he found the unmistakable signs of a sharp left turn.

In addition, seepage of water had filled in the final few feet of the machine's tracks. Evidently this flow of water resulted from the disturbance of the rock formation which Larson had been clearing away. Aaron knew that he had located the spot of Carmen's death.

Aaron called his crew over to join him. "This is where it happened. Look here. The tracks of the crawler stop here and the rocks it was pushing are still in place. One of these rocks crushed her. Let's stack them up as a cairn so that the spot where she died won't be lost. In my report to the Verde I'm going to inform them of this spot and ask them to respect it. I'm sure they will."

64

THE CUSTOM PERSISTS IN some communities to observe the thirtieth day after the passing of an individual with prayers and remembrances. In Carmen's case, this observance took on special significance.

The simple memorial erected by Aaron Raines and his crew had become the site of spontaneous tributes to Carmen. The appearance of emerging daffodils at the cairn caused some to take this as a special sign. Her picture was mounted on top of the cairn; messages and personal tributes were stuffed between the rocks. Her memorial became a destination for hikers and admirers of her life and the courage of her death.

Thirty days after her death, a group gathered on Water Street to make the trek up to the rim. The crowd grew spontaneously. Even without explicit planning, individuals from the village came together at the head of the enlarged Switchback Trail. Chris joined the procession on an ATV, for he was still using crutches. He remarked about the irony of the trek. "She crushed the rocks upon which we are walking."

When the procession arrived, it formed a circle around the cairn. At intervals, words of commitment were expressed about the causes which Carmen had come to represent.

It was at this time that Chris came to understand the truth of Ernesto's advice to him. He stepped forward and began to speak as if he were addressing Carmen herself. Everyone strained to catch his remarks.

"I will always love you, Carmen. You are forever in my heart. Now you belong to this village and to these people, for they have adopted you as their inspiration and model. You will live on, not just in my heart, but in the hearts and minds of this entire village. This is not a goodbye, for you are with us all."

CHRIS RECEIVED A REGISTERED letter from Alma Fortner, which invited him to appear at her office.

Chris couldn't imagine why he was summoned so formally.

Alma addressed Chris. "Last year Carmen Montez asked me to be her executor and drafted her will. I have asked Ernesto Ramirez and Chris O'Brien to act as witnesses."

Carmen had named Chris as her sole heir.

Ernesto hugged Chris. "I am happy to have you as my new landscaping company.

CHRIS PUSHED THROUGH THE entrance at the Pancake House.

Diana saw him coming and was delighted to see him. "Don't expect to get anything special today."

"So nothing's changed. The same old lousy food and worse insults."

"Only if you behave yourself and don't wander off and get yourself caught in rocks."

She poured coffee and placed her hand upon his shoulder. "You really had me worried when you didn't show up for breakfast after Carmen's memorial service. Don't ever do that again."

Chris didn't meet her gaze but cast his eyes down in remorse. "I just wanted to know if I'd be missed . . ." He regretted this stupid quip immediately. "I'm sorry . . ." and sank back into silence.

Diane had made her point. "How's the rock quarry doing?"

"It's a lot of fun playing with the heavy equipment. I can't imagine how Carmen managed to make it pay. It keeps me off the streets."

"Will I be seeing you on Tuesday mornings?" Diane asked.

"Sure."

She gave him a friendly pinch on the cheek. "I might even round up someone to eat with you."

"If you vouch for her, I couldn't ask for more."

Epilogue

In the week that followed the collapse of Star Holdings, the San Leandro village council presented their water management proposals. At the outset Wehrli reported that the village's share of Kallisto had been preserved and acknowledged the critical role of the citizen protestors in bringing this about. He made special mention of the heroic and tragic action of Carmen Montez. The core of their water management proposals dealt with conservation measures.

"Each household of two is allocated two thousand gallons a month with an additional five hundred gallons for each additional member. The water rate charged for this level of usage is frozen at present levels, while usage above this level is subject to a surcharge based on the percentage of excess. Most users will exceed their allocation and will be subjected to some rate increase, and this will allow for subsidies for the installation of low-use fixtures.

"The village will open a car wash which will be available to village water customers at a nominal fee, just enough to prevent overuse. When this facility becomes available, all outside use of water, except for captured rain water, will no longer be permitted.

"Each household is permitted a kitchen garden of four hundred square feet which may only be watered using drip irrigation approved by the village.

"The following conservation measures are encouraged and will be eligible for village subsidies based on the availability of funding from surcharges: low-use fixtures and appliances, rainwater harvesting, even the replacement of grass with desert landscaping will receive a ten percent reimbursement.

"Permits for new construction within village limits will be honored but the construction code will be amended to encourage low water use."

Alma Fortner assisted Bill in the dissolution of Star Holdings and its property on the Arena Rim. The Verde National Forest indicated interest in repossessing the property when funds became available, at a price agreeable to both parties.

The Mulcton firm laid claim to a ten percent interest in the Arena Rim property. Fortner countered that all files relating to the law firm's work for Star Holdings would be requested should Mulcton pursue this claim. The fact that Killian estimated the legality of Star's claim for the Kallisto's waters at twenty-five percent dissuaded Mulcton from pursuing the matter any further.

The criminal case against Bill for manslaughter ground slowly onward. Chris's presence at the scene, his account of the incident, and his relationship with Carmen were central to the case for the prosecution. Chris, to the amazement of the prosecutor, stated that he had forgiven Bill and also requested that all charges against him be dropped.

The judge was not so lenient; Bill was put on probation for five years and enjoined from seeking or acquiring any water rights within the Santa Cruz AMA.

BILL HAD SERVED AS the chair of the finance committee at the San Leandro church, a position he had held for the past year at the recommendation of his wife. At its next scheduled meeting, no one came. He stopped by the parish receptionist to ask whether the meeting had been rescheduled. Instead she handed him a note, signed by all the committee members requesting that he resign.

The following day he returned and asked to see Fr. Fred. "Go right in. He's expecting you."

He found the pastor reading at his desk. Without a word of explanation he sheepishly handed over a satchel which held the finance committee records, then added in a subdued voice, "I can't continue on the finance committee. Here are the files." He hesitated, awaiting a word from Fred before leaving.

Instead Fred pointed to a chair. "I heard that the committee preferred a new chair. I suppose you probably know why."

Bill fidgeted with car keys, averted his eyes, and mumbled, "Yeah."

Fred spread his hands in an inviting gesture and continued in a soothing voice. "Well, all of us make a mess sometimes. It's what you do afterwards that counts."

Bill didn't say a word. "I understand it was quite a moment at the court when Chris asked that charges against you should be dropped. Did you expect that to happen?"

"No."

"When Chris did that, he acted in a way that a real Christian should. "It's forgiveness. That's what we're all about here. Without it, I've got no reason to do what I'm doing."

Bill wasn't following, so Fred forged onward. "We usually see forgiveness as one-sided, but it isn't. Forgiving is actually the easy part; accepting forgiveness is the hard part." Fred left the statement hanging.

Bill made no reply. Fred shifted in his chair and looked squarely at Bill. "What do you suppose it means to accept forgiveness?"

Challenged, Bill became uncomfortable and shuffled his feet.

"I know that was a tough question," Fred said sympathetically. "Very few know the answer to that one. I've got a few years' experience in this business and I can tell you, when you get forgiveness the answer is that you have to have a change of heart. Whatever you were forgiven for, that's what's got to change. Otherwise none of it makes any difference. You may be forgiven, but it doesn't really do you any good. Like I said, Chris did the easy part; you've got the hard part."

Fred's manner had a calming effect on Bill, and he said, "I always believed that if I worked hard for the best outcome and if everyone else did the same, the result would average out and be the best for everyone."

"That might work—theoretically—if everything else, and I mean everything else, is equal. There's a well-read novelist who even insists that altruism is a trap. That sort of thinking doesn't square with what we believe here."

Bill replied, "The community doesn't want to see me around here."

Fred rose and extended his hand to Bill. "Here's a couple of books I would like you to read. Take your time. Remember, what your job is: a change of heart."

He placed his hand on Bill's shoulder as he walked him to the door. "I know you'll make it. It'll take some time. When you're ready, you won't need to ask to join this community again. They'll invite you."

List of Principal Characters

Ernesto Ramirez—migrant rescued by Chris, founder of Desert Gardens
Stanley Unruh—policeman, then sheriff, finally special events officer
Chris O'Brien—rescuer of Ernesto, friend of Carmen Montez
Claudia Gomez—nutritionist, manager of San Leandro clinic
Frederic Martinez—pastor at San Leandro
Carmen Montez—realtor, friend of Chris O'Brien
Bill Starret—San Leandro developer, village councilor
Diana Flores—waitress at Pancake House
Leon Weiser—insurance agent
Artemus Killian—Partner in Mulcton, Killian, and Smart law firm
Alma Fortner—San Leandro attorney
Tony Friedson—owner of Two Gun Ranch, business partner of Bill
Colin Foster—agricultural extension agent
Yolanda Alonso—San Leandro village matriarch
Brett Masterson—rancher, neighbor of Friedson
Edgar Moon—realtor under contract to Mulcton law firm
Anton Wehrli—mayor of San Leandro
Stella Mantilla—Wehrli's assistant
Angel Benevides—San Leandro councilor
Arch Minter and Robert Manson—advisors to Wehrli
Martha Symonds—estimator for Samson Industries
Carson Fowler and Sam Layton—advisors to Mulcton law firm
Del Larson—well driller employed by Bill
Arturo Uribe—manager of Verde Gardens
Miles Stanton—head forester

CPSIA information can be obtained
at www.ICGtesting.com
Printed in the USA
LVHW021622191121
703844LV00016B/1337

9 781725 289109